Also available from K[

Love on the Hudson
A Christmas Cabin for Two
A Little Rebellion

The Secret Ingredient deals with topics some readers might find difficult, including family alienation, mentions of homophobia, and religious trauma.

THE SECRET INGREDIENT

KD FISHER

carina
press

carina press®

Recycling programs
for this product may
not exist in your area.

ISBN-13: 978-1-335-95714-6

The Secret Ingredient

Carina Press
22 Adelaide St. West, 40th Floor
Toronto, Ontario M5H 4E3, Canada
www.CarinaPress.com

Printed in U.S.A.

For Cooper, the only man I'll ever need

THE SECRET INGREDIENT

Chapter One

Adah

All my life I've been running. Running through the woods so fast I thought I could leave myself clean behind. Running from the reverend anytime he got that mean look in his eyes. Running to get free.

Now I'm setting down roots. Roots that will grow stronger and deeper with time. Roots that no storm can wash away.

I glanced around the apartment. Our new home. Sunlight bouncing off the yellow walls and settling down on the black and white checked floors. Sloped, slightly uneven ceiling in the living room. Exposed brick wall behind the couch. Windows thrown wide open, filmy white curtains drifting in the warm breeze. A heavy door with a heavier lock I checked three times before I signed the lease.

"Mom!" Peter poked his little blond head through the bedroom door. "This whole room is really mine?"

"Yep." I shook the suds off my hands and grinned. "All yours. But you better keep it clean. Understood?" A shudder rocked though me at how much I sounded like my mama.

"I will. It's so cool to have my own room." With that, he disappeared back into the tiny bedroom, door closing softly behind him. I loved the sound of my son's voice, still high and sweet and colored with the nasal Midwest accent so different from my Ozark tongue.

It was time he had a room of his own. Living in an efficiency studio in Chicago had been fine when he was a toddler, and tolerable when he was too little to be bothered by the lack of personal space. But next year Peter would be ten. He needed room to breathe. We both did.

And we'd found it in Maine. In this second-floor walk-up so close to the ocean I could smell the salt air. The place wasn't exactly big, but it was affordable and clean and only a ten-minute walk from the restaurant. I didn't mind that I'd be sleeping on the pull-out couch and waking up at all hours to the chattering of gulls and drunken sounds of men arguing in the bar next door. Drawing in a long, slow breath, I plunged my hands back into the soapy water and resumed scrubbing the kitchen floor.

Tomorrow I would start my new job. Head chef at Bella Vista, a fine-dining Mediterranean venture opened by the restaurant group I'd spent the last five years in Chicago busting my tail for. Riccardo was taking a big chance on me, and I was determined to do him proud. Smiling softly to myself, I lifted my eyes to my freshly pressed chef's whites hanging on the bathroom door. I'd seen the pictures of the kitchen. My kitchen. I'd scrolled through them hundreds of times trying to picture myself running the operation. Brand-new and bigger than any space I'd worked in before. Gleaming pots and pans, top-of-the-line range, everything open to the tastefully decorated dining room. I wanted to squeal with excitement but bit my lip and started in on scrubbing the baseboards.

I lost myself in the methodical work of cleaning and nearly jumped out of my skin at the sound of two loud raps on the glass pane of my front door. My eyes squeezed shut and my whole body stilled.

Squaring my shoulders, I stood tall and let my gaze shudder over to the door. All my breath rushed out of my body and a smile tugged at my mouth. A middle-aged lady with black rimmed glasses and shoulder length brown hair beamed at me and lifted a hand in greeting.

"Hi there." I tried not to sound too breathless as I yanked the door open. It stuck a little bit but that was just fine with me.

"You must be Adah. So nice to meet you in person. I'm Vanessa." The woman thrust a bouquet of sunflowers into my hands and let herself right on in.

It took my whirring brain a moment to catch up. Right. Vanessa Tyler. My landlady. The sweet woman who'd spent the last month filling my email inbox with helpful tips about my new city in Maine. The fairy godmother who, upon discovering my single-mother status, dropped the rent by four hundred dollars a month. I wanted to hug her but that really wasn't my style.

"Nice to meet you, ma'am." I rubbed the back of my

neck nervously and a few drops of soapy water slithered under my T-shirt.

"Ma'am nonsense. I do love that accent though. Where'd you get that? I thought you moved from Chicago."

"Sure did." I bit my lip to hold back the instinctive *ma'am* I'd been raised to keep in my mouth. "But I grew up in Missouri." I tried for a smile. "You've got quite the accent yourself."

Vanessa laughed, a hearty chuckle, and batted the air with her hands. "Well, that's because I'm from so far north I practically grew up in Canada. You're lucky I'm not speaking goddamn French." She winked and glanced around the apartment. "You getting settled in okay? Place looks great. Nice to know you're clean. The last guy was a real disaster. Pizza boxes stacked as high as my shoulder." This word was pronounced without the final *r*. "Where's your young man?"

Peter, never one to pass up a grand entrance, burst out of the bedroom and waved at Vanessa. "I'm here." My boy wasn't shy, I had to give him that.

"You certainly are. And what a handsome young man! What's your name, sir?"

"Peter. Peter Campbell. Nice to meet you."

"And you're polite! I'm Vanessa." She extended her hand and Peter shook it without hesitation. "I live right downstairs. You liking South Bay so far, kiddo?"

Peter nodded and I took a moment to admire my son's earnest politeness. I'd been busy when he was little, swamped with culinary school and work, but he still turned out sweeter than any of my siblings despite all the manners forced on us. "It's really pretty. I think I might miss Chicago, though. It seems a little boring here."

"Well how about tomorrow I take you to the beach while your mom here gets cooking?"

Peter's blue eyes flashed wide and I could practically hear the *please, Moms* radiating off him.

I pressed my lips together. As nice as Vanessa seemed, I didn't know the woman from Adam. I'd hired a nice woman with state background checks from a reputable nanny service to take care of Peter for the two months until he started school. "Oh, you don't have to do that. I've got a sitter. You've been too kind already."

She nodded seriously. "Look, I get it, Adah. You don't know me. I'm just your landlady. I could be a total weirdo. But I was the principal at Water Street Elementary for almost two decades. I can give you references, and I won't charge you." Her expression was soft, the sort of open kindness I'd always looked for in my own mother's eyes.

"Really, you don't have to do that. You've done so much as it is."

"Mom," Peter whined, "I wanna go with Ms. Vanessa. *The beach.*" He cast a wistful look out the window.

Guilt twisted in my stomach. After two full days of driving, retrieving the keys from underneath the flowerpot Vanessa described in great detail in one of her emails, and collapsing onto the couch for a fitful few hours of sleep, I hadn't exactly prioritized fun excursions for Peter in our new hometown. When we'd discussed moving up to Maine, we'd spent hours looking at slideshows of hiking trails, lighthouses, and wildlife in the frozen north. So far all we'd done was clean, eat pizza, and walk around the corner to buy light bulbs. Not exactly thrilling stuff for a nine-year-old. Or for a thirty-one-year-old, for that matter.

Vanessa tapped away on a giant smartphone. "Okay. I just sent you a list of five references you can call. Teachers I worked with, admins in the district, and my best friend Sally. Oh, and the pastor at my church for good measure."

I kept my face neutral even as her final phrase lit up every one of my nerves like fire tearing through dry brush. *Deep breath in, hold it, push all the air out.*

Finally, after Peter crossed the small kitchen to tug on the hem of my T-shirt, I relented. "Alright. Well if you really don't mind, I can check in on your references. I'll text you the number for the restaurant and my friend Jay's number in case you can't get a hold of me. I have to get over there first thing tomorrow to meet with management. Is around seven thirty okay for you?"

It would be a godsend not to have to pay the sitter the agreed upon fifteen dollars an hour. Money was stretched tight as it was. But guilt reared its very familiar head at the thought of not paying Vanessa anything to watch Peter. Maybe I could at least arrange some kind of barter, free dinner once a week or something. Then fear climbed on top of guilt, just as familiar and just as unwelcome. What if despite the references and sweet veneer, Vanessa turned out to be a bad egg? What kind of person just agreed to help someone like this? I needed to move my body, burn off some of this frantic energy buzzing through me. I bit my lip hard. This would be fine. Everything was fine.

"Sweetheart." It took me a long moment to realize Vanessa was speaking to me, not to my son. "I know this is a lot. New job. New place. I understand how hard it can be to start over. Let me help. Please."

I wanted to argue. I didn't need help. Not from her. Not from anyone. Instead, I forced my tight muscles to relax just a little. Relief seeped into my limbs and the sensation was strange. I usually only felt this way for a few minutes after a particularly punishing run or when I lost myself to the rhythm of work in the kitchen.

I nodded. "Thank you."

You could have knocked me over with a feather as I stepped into my new kitchen the next morning. My kitchen. Mine.

No pixels on a tablet screen could have prepared me for the gleaming expanse of stainless steel and clean white tile. A giant copper hood fan arced over the space and a wide, polished concrete pass separated the kitchen from the front of house. Everything smelled new, like a hardware store. Like possibility. My ears heated and my eyes fizzed. I squeezed them shut, hoping this wouldn't all disappear.

Next to me, Riccardo, the owner of Zest Restaurant Group, and Sean, the general manager of Bella Vista, were talking a mile a minute about…something. I should have been listening and chiming in. This mattered to me as much as it mattered to them. More, maybe. For Riccardo, Bella Vista's failure would mean a huge financial loss and a disastrous business gamble in a new market. For Sean, who had a fancy-pants track record managing Zest's fine-dining spots in Manhattan, failure would mean personal and professional disgrace. For me, Bella Vista had to succeed. I'd uprooted my family, left the only city—heck, the only kitchen—that had really felt like home. And when I did something, I did it right.

Opening a high-end, high-concept Mediterranean seafood restaurant in a city known best for chowder and lobster rolls was a risky proposition. I was still reeling from Riccardo's decision to hire me for this of all jobs.

Of course, in a lot of ways it made sense. I'd spent the last three years as the sous-chef at Café Eloise, his chic French small plates restaurant. I'd worked my tail off for him. And when the head chef disappeared in a cloud of cigarette smoke and expletives, I'd taken over for a few months, pushing the restaurant out of traditional chicken liver pate territory into serving creative takes on Provençal classics. I revamped the menu and we ended up winning a few small, city-magazine awards. Our food was artistic without sacrificing flavor. We had a solid group of regulars and tourists alike. And I knew how to run a kitchen.

When Riccardo found out I'd grown up fishing on the streams in Missouri and knew how to debone a trout with my eyes closed, he called me into his office for a chat about my future. And when he discovered I was looking for a change of scenery, he offered me the job in Maine on the spot. Executive chef. I wouldn't admit it to anyone, barely to myself, but I was nervous. The stakes were high. Besides, at the end of the day I was still more at home frying up catfish than I was whipping up lobster gnocchi. But I was determined to create a delicious, innovative menu that would do us all proud. Bella Vista would be a success.

"Adah, does that sound agreeable?" Sean asked. His voice carried the impatient edge of someone who was aware he was being tuned out.

"Oh yeah. Absolutely." I nodded curtly and met his eyes. Jay, my best friend and the pastry chef at Café Eloise, had warned me that Sean could be difficult and that he didn't always respect women in the kitchen.

Riccardo chuckled warmly. "You were spaced out, darling. Sean and I thought the three of us should take today to personally assess some of the other fine-dining spots in the area."

I perked up. I'd done thorough research on the local competition. There was a lot. The city had been named a culinary destination to watch by a number of food publications in the past few years. Although we would be on the higher end of the offerings, there were a few I wanted to see in person. One in particular.

"We'll start with The River Street Café. Then I want to take a look at Commonwealth Provisions. And what do you think, Ric, should we bother with Osteria Mina or have they gone too far downhill?" Sean shifted his body just enough to make it a two-man conversation.

I took a step toward him.

Riccardo looked to me. "What do you think, chef?"

I bit my lip to hide my smile. "I'd like to check them out. See the space and maybe talk to a few people in the front of house if they'd be willing. I think it will be good to start off on the right foot with folks." I paused, looking from Sean, who had crossed his arms, to Riccardo, who was nodding along vigorously. "And what about The Yellow House? I really want to see what they're doing over there."

I didn't mention that my interest in the local-coffee-shop-turned-award-winning-culinary-destination had a whole lot to do with a profile I'd read a few months earlier of Beth Summers, the laid-back owner. Waiting in line at the grocery store, I'd picked up an issue of a splashy food magazine specifically because the cover image had caught my eye—a gorgeous woman laughing with her head thrown back, a tumble of auburn curls, a decidedly non-cheffy lavender dress, a hodgepodge of crystal necklaces.

Then I'd flipped to her interview. I'd been fascinated with her business philosophy even if it didn't make a lick of sense to me. In theory, using only local ingredients, ensuring a competitive salary and full health benefits for all staff, and cooking almost everything in a wood burning oven sounded amazing. In the cold reality of the restaurant world, though, those things were almost impossible to do. Still, when she breezily mentioned her dedication to visibility for queer female chefs in a male-dominated industry, I'd actually bought a copy of the dang magazine so I could read the full interview. Several times.

Riccardo made one of his dramatic affirmative noises, whereas Sean's brows crashed together. "That tiny place in the middle of nowhere?" Sean practically scoffed. "I don't think we need to worry about them. Overhead like that they'll close next month."

I tried to rein in my prickly, only-sister-among-six-brothers instincts and kept my voice as even as possible. "Last year alone they were named the best restaurant in Maine and won a Martin Williams Award. I think they might be worth checking out."

"Yes." Riccardo clapped his hands and the sound echoed through the cavernous kitchen. "We will go there first."

Chapter Two

Beth

The flames wandered over the kindling, sparking golden as the rich scent of wood smoke filled the kitchen. It was early still, the sunlight weak and soft. Outside, the clear crack of Andrew chopping wood mingled with the cries of chickadees and jays. Inside, I was alone. I drew in a deep, steady breath to greet the dawn.

I was exhausted. The night before had been long, with a private event yawning long past midnight. The morning came too early and too busy. My to-do list snaked through my mind unrelenting: update the menus online, proof the boules, fill the tart shells, pick up the blueberries from my dad, answer at least fifty emails, follow up with vendors... Realistically I needed to hire someone else. But the last two guys I'd brought on didn't have the right energy. They cut corners and didn't connect with our mission. The recent onslaught of guests and publicity meant, however, that Andrew, Nina, and I were constantly exhausted. It wasn't sustainable.

Okay, so priority number one: create a new job listing to post on Craigslist that might attract someone more attuned. Really, what I needed was another me. Or the ability to work endless hours with no sleep and no personal time. Or to pack up and leave this whole operation behind in favor of a beach in Tulum. I couldn't even remember the last time I'd been to yoga or taken Hamlet on a hike. The last time I'd dreamed of anything but invoices and health inspections.

"Coffee... Must have coffee." Nina's scratchy voice preceded her round, flushed face.

I inclined my head to the blue and white speckled percolator keeping warm next to the hearth. "Just made another pot."

"You're a goddess." Nina was still dressed in her running clothes, a pair of tiny spandex shorts and a hot pink tank top. Her golden hair was pulled back in a sloppy ponytail. We'd been inseparable since childhood and drunkenly slept together a few times before settling back into a cozy, supportive friendship. She was a gifted cook, responsible for the vegetable-forward dishes that helped put our tiny kitchen on the culinary map. Nina poured us each a mug, adding a healthy splash of milk and two spoonfuls of sugar to mine. "What time did you get here, anyway?"

"Five." I tried not to let any exhaustion creep into my voice.

"Beth!" Nina looked as though she might slap me. "You need to sleep, honey! Want me to do the job posting stuff?"

Guilt swelled in my stomach. This wasn't just about me. Being short-staffed and busier than ever also meant Nina and Andrew suffered. "No," I sighed. "You can get started on your prep. I can't stop thinking we're never going to find the right person. Roy was such a disappointment."

Nina scoffed. "Yeah, in more ways than one."

A laugh bubbled up from my belly as I turned back to the oven to ensure all of the wood had caught. The temperature needed to regulate by eight thirty so I could get the first of the breads and pastries in.

The door clattered open and Andrew walked in, a stormy expression eclipsing my brother's normal goofy half smile. "Beth. Some people outside to see you."

Since The Yellow House had been awarded Best New Restaurant in the Northeast by the Martin Williams Foundation, a prestigious culinary organization I'd never heard of prior to receiving the letter in the mail, we'd been bombarded with reporters, bloggers, and more diners than we could possibly keep up with. Usually, though, they didn't show up a full four hours before we opened for the day.

Peeking through the window at the small gravel parking lot, I spotted a gleaming black Mercedes and three people sitting at one of the picnic tables in the garden. I wiped my hands on my apron and patted my hair, hoping that my curls hadn't dried in a frizzy mess. Dressing in the dark, I'd hardly had a moment to make sure my socks matched before dashing out of the house. A few too many times these visitors were enthusiastic with the photos and

I appeared in Instagram posts and blog entries looking like a wild and unruly thing.

"Good morning!" I called as I bounded down the stairs. The morning air brushed cool against my clammy skin. Before the fire settled down, the kitchen tended to get unbearably hot. The sunlight had gathered itself into soft rays that glistened off the dew in the vegetable and herb patches. A monarch butterfly fluttered across my path and I paused, letting it take its time. Medusa, the barn-cat-turned-restaurant-mascot, snoozed on one of the picnic tables, blissfully oblivious of the visitors.

At the sound of my voice all three of them stood: a tall, slim man in a beautifully tailored suit, a shorter man with a ruddy, irritable face, and another person with their back to me. She turned. Immediately my cheeks heated, and an awkward laugh bubbled up from my throat.

She was like something plucked from my adolescent queer fantasies. Bad boy and tough woman rolled into one. She wore dark jeans, a thick leather belt, and a white T-shirt with the sleeves cuffed a few times up to reveal sinewy biceps. Her dark blond hair was pushed back from her flawless, angular face in a messy not-quite-pompadour. Straight eyebrows a few shades darker than her hair. A long, delicate nose. Lips that probably would have been ample were they not pressed together in a tense frown.

"How can I help you folks?" I bit back the comment that we didn't open until eleven and offered a sweet smile instead.

The woman stepped forward without missing a beat, extending her hand. I closed the gap between us, shivering as her long fingers brushed my palm. Her skin was warm and a little work-rough. A heavy quiet settled over me as we shook hands. I had the strange thought that I could have held her hand all day. Up close I realized her narrow, wary eyes were a soft shade of green. They widened for a fraction of a second before she stepped back, shoving her hands into her pockets.

"I'm Adah Campbell, the new executive chef at Bella Vista. This is Sean Jacobs, our GM, and Riccardo Visconti, the head of our restaurant group." Beneath the formal veneer of her words, her voice thrummed with life. Her accent wasn't quite Southern, more country than anything else. It was the sound of humid thunderstorms and steaming biscuits slathered in home-churned butter. I never wanted her to stop talking.

I exchanged far briefer handshakes with the two men.

"Well, lovely to meet you." I fiddled with a stray curl that kept bouncing in and out of my peripheral vision. "I'm Beth Summers, the madwoman behind this whole operation." I jabbed my thumb back at the house.

I had no earthly idea what Bella Vista was. To be fair, though, I hadn't eaten at another restaurant in ages. Most of my meals consisted of late-night affairs conjured up after the final guests left for the night. I'd developed the bad habit of burrowing into my own life so deep I sometimes forgot a world outside of The Yellow House existed.

The angry-looking man, whose name I'd promptly forgotten, glared at the cottage behind me like it had single-handedly murdered his entire family. "So, the Williams Award, huh? Pretty big deal. How are you guys handling the attention? I bet you're getting a lot more customers than you're used to."

He was talking to me like I was a child running a lemonade stand with her parents' money.

I shrugged and smoothed my apron, letting the pleasant texture of the coarse linen distract me from the unpleasantness of this man's voice. "It's been a wild few months, that's for sure. Lots of folks from away coming to eat here. But it's amazing to build a community of people who really care about good food." The sun inched higher in the sky. I needed to get back inside, put the first loaves of sourdough in the oven, and start prepping the berries for the tarts.

A long, tense silence stretched between us. Normally, I would have invited them in for coffee and a few fat slices of peach cake left over from last night's dessert service. But something about the three of them unsettled me. The fancy suit, the rough demeanor, the…well, I didn't have time to think about why Adah had me all out of alignment.

"I read your interview in *Bread & Wine*. Sounds like you take the whole 'farm-to-table' thing pretty seriously." Mr. Jerkface said *farm-to-table* like a particularly foul swearword.

"Sure do." I plastered a smile on my face. I felt like a politician when all I wanted to do was stop talking and start working. "My dad's a lobsterman and my mom ran this place as a coffee shop my whole life. This is my home. I want the food to reflect that. To taste both familiar and exciting." As much as I meant it, it was a canned response. One I'd given a dozen or so times since people started asking me silly questions about my culinary philosophy. Whatever in the world that meant.

"What's your staff situation look like?" I half expected this guy to pull out his phone and start recording. Adah and the fancy suit dude exchanged a meaningful look.

"Well…" I trailed off for a long moment, letting the irritation creep up my throat just a little more. I didn't owe these people anything. And they still hadn't told me what they wanted. Was this a thing big shot restaurant people did? Drive out to small-town eateries and pester the owners with weird questions? I sighed. "It's just me, my best friend Nina, and my brother, Andrew, in the kitchen. Plus Ahmed, our front of house superstar, and our two servers." I left out the fact that one of said servers spent most of his time on shift getting stoned and that I was desperately in need of about five more people I could not possibly afford to pay a decent wage, which meant I was a living, breathing poster child for overwork. I rolled my neck and inhaled deeply.

"That's a pretty lean operation." Adah shot me an unreadable expression.

Usually, I could get a sense of a person's energy within the first few minutes of meeting them, understand who they were and what they were looking for. My mom called it empathy. My brother called me a psychic. Really, people just made sense to me. But not this woman.

Adah squinted back at the cottage, shielding her eyes with her elegant hand. Smoke poured from the stone chimney. Fuck. I'd forgotten to adjust the flue before rushing outside and the fire had gotten too hot. In all likelihood the kitchen temperature had climbed from hot as hell to face-meltingly sweltering, meaning my dough would be trash. This little conversation had cost me a good thirty minutes of work. Now instead of slipping the breads into the oven, I'd have to tamp the flames, start over on my choux pastry, and recalibrate my entire morning. No way in hell was I getting around to the job posting today.

"Looks like your oven's burning too hot." Adah nodded, a sharp definitive motion.

Suddenly, rage engulfed me, whole and scalding. Maybe it was the exhaustion. Maybe it was the ache in my lower back. Maybe it was the fact that after years spent running away from my hometown I was still reeling from my decision to come back. When I spoke, my voice was brittle and too loud. Unfamiliar. "Thanks. I know that. You all have been taking up my morning and I have to say, I'm not quite sure why. So, if you need something, please enlighten me. Otherwise, I have to get back to work." Probably by most standards I wasn't being that rude. The few disastrous months I'd spent at culinary school had taught me that most chefs and bakers carried explosive tempers beneath their neatly starched whites. But that wasn't me. At least not usually.

At my words Adah visibly stiffened and took a step away from me, her face going from unreadable to stormy. Mr. Jerkface muttered something under his breath. The guy in the slick suit stepped forward, the perfect picture of hospitality polish.

"Of course." His voice was heavily accented and butter smooth. "We've been terribly rude. Allow me to apologize. And to explain. My restaurant group is opening a new fine-dining spot in town. Bella Vista, as Chef Campbell mentioned. None of us are from the area and we wanted to get to know some of the other local talent. Your restaurant has made quite the impression and we wanted to see it for ourselves. But of course, I understand how busy you must be." He shot me a winning smile and handed me a business card. "Please come by anytime. Our soft opening is in two weeks. We would love to see you there."

I wanted to be gracious, but my words remained bitter and harsh, like tea brewed too strong. "Well thanks for stopping by. Like I said, I have to get back to work." I should have turned on my heel then, marched back into the cottage, and poured myself a fresh cup of coffee. Instead, my mouth kept moving, a good fifty paces ahead of my brain. "Besides, I don't think that we'll have a big overlap in business, so you shouldn't worry. The cruise ship crowd doesn't make it out to Port Catherine all that much. If you're looking to get a better sense of your competition, I recommend you stop by Caruso's on the waterfront." Okay, now I was definitely being rude, both to these folks and the poor Caruso family, who ran a perfectly respectable, if old-school, seafood place. Sure, I was frustrated by the influx of people from Boston and Manhattan coming up to Maine to buy up property, drive up rents, and replace family-run businesses with soulless corporate operations. But I had no idea what this Bella Vista restaurant was even going to be. And really, I thought it was nice that they were reaching out personally to other businesses.

An apology was on the tip of my tongue when the kitchen window clattered open and Nina's blond head popped out. "Beth, sorry to bother you, babe, but what's-his-face at Moonbeam Farm just called. I guess the storm the other night wiped out his spinach. Andrew says we have a little bit left in our beds but either way we need to totally rethink tonight's menu. I could do the tomato and green garlic orecchiette again but..." She trailed off, prob-

ably aware that she was shouting her stream of conscious-
ness thoughts across the courtyard.

After holding up a finger and shooting my best friend
an amused eye roll, I turned back to the group. Fancy
suit guy was once again extending his manicured hand,
politely thanking me for my time. I tried for my kindest
smile and stammered an approximation of an apology for
my earlier rudeness and busy morning. But Adah, the one
I oddly wanted to hear my words, had stalked away. She
leaned against the car, arms crossed over her chest, infu-
riating blank expression on her face. I was too damn busy
for this kind of thinking, but for a brief moment I thought
she looked like the tough greasers I'd fantasized about after
devouring *The Outsiders* when it was assigned as summer
reading in seventh grade. I imagined the rough feel of her
hands on my face, tangling into my hair, the soft brush of
her lips against mine. She would smell like soap and citrus
with a slight spicy base note. And she would taste...

No. Nope. No way. Not going there. I needed to focus.
I had a restaurant to run.

Chapter Three

Adah

It turned out starting your own kitchen from scratch was nothing like being promoted up from sous-chef. The past two weeks had been a blur of writing and scrapping menu idea after menu idea, interviewing staff, trying and mostly succeeding to block out my general manager's blatant sexism, and consuming genuinely unholy quantities of caffeine.

But this morning as I speed-walked the six blocks to work, large iced coffee in hand, the warm sea breeze caressing my cheeks, the usual hordes of tourists clogging the brick sidewalks didn't even phase me. I took in the details of my new town that I usually tuned out during my short commute: the mix of kitschy tourist shops selling T-shirts printed with bad lobster puns, the old man tossing bread crusts to a teeming mass of pigeons and seagulls in the town square, the way the clear morning light made the cobbled streets and brick buildings look like something out of one of Peter's old storybooks. Confidence and something like hope swelled big and bright inside my chest.

I'd done it. I had a great menu, with simple takes on mostly Spanish and Italian coastal classics, and a fantastic team. Well mostly fantastic. I was particularly thrilled with Mac, the quiet storm of a woman I'd hired as my sous-chef. She'd started out as an oyster shucker at what she described as "a shithole tourist joint" in a town in Massachusetts I'd never heard of and worked her way up to an assistant chef position at one of Boston's finest restaurants. She was fast, serious, and tough.

My only concern lay with the pastry chef Sean had insisted on hiring. I'd wanted to hire Grace, a peppy young woman, who, yes, was relatively inexperienced but had also made a perfectly textured olive oil cake with fresh peaches and a delightfully silky sabayon sauce. Instead we'd gone with the culinary school grad with a mile-long resume and blasé, entitled personality. Not only had our new hire shown up for the interview ten minutes late, it appeared he never stayed more than a few months at a given establishment, seeming to bounce around all of the buzzier spots in town. I wanted someone committed. Serious. Sturdy. Worst of all, I'd been underwhelmed by his blood orange panna cotta. Pastry wasn't even my strong suit and I could have whipped up something better. I'd been downright vexed when the guy didn't bother to show up at our first staff family meal. But my mama's words slid down their well-worn groove in my mind: *kindness, forbearance, and patience, Adah.* Best to put my head down and see what came of the situation.

I stopped in front of the restaurant, drawing in a deep breath. The summer air here was clean and pleasantly briny, a far cry from the exhaust-choked humidity of Chicago and muddy river smell of home. I shook my head. No. This was home now. This red brick building by the sea. The cedar-shingled apartment with its squeaky floorboards and tiny, always-dripping shower. This unfamiliar state where no one knew me, and I was just fine keeping it that way.

Well, two people knew me. I pulled my phone out of my back pocket and sent a quick text to Vanessa and Peter.

Heading into work now. Call the restaurant if you need me. Hope you two have fun today.

Immediately my landlady-turned-guardian-angel responded with a slightly out of focus selfie of her and Peter in flour-dusted aprons. A moment later another message came through.

We're cooking this morning in your honor. Making blueberry muffins to bring on our hike! Don't worry we'll eat something healthy too. Go get em girlie!

I laughed softly to myself then started at the sound of someone coming up fast behind me. My heart hammered hard in my chest and my throat clenched tight. I willed myself to breathe.

"So, you do smile, huh?" My sous-chef's low voice was a welcome sound.

"Sometimes." I shrugged, hastily trying to compose my

features. Neutral expression. I couldn't afford to start today off on the wrong foot.

Mac took a long sip from a jar of…something green and murky. She was dressed in loose jeans and a wash-worn Prince concert T-shirt. Her arms were muscular and heavily tattooed in a vintage style. She pushed back her mess of dark curls and smirked at me. "It's a nice day and all, boss, but what do you say we head inside and get to it."

Today was our soft opening and there was no room for error. And for the most part everything went off without a hitch. My staff communicated well, moved quickly, and everyone showed up on time. Everyone, that was, but our dang pastry chef. He didn't bother to show up at all. Five hours into the day, after I'd frantically reprinted the menus to replace his planned assortment of petit fours and chocolate cherry torte with the blueberry puddings one of the assistant chefs pulled right out of thin air, the stupid jerk left a message informing us he'd accepted a gig in Boston instead. Great.

I knew what I should do. I should check in on everyone's *mise* and follow up with a few suppliers whose deliveries hadn't been quite up to my standards. I should sift through the other applications and make a few calls to find someone else. Instead I stalked down the dimly lit hall to Sean's tiny office. Technically it was my office too, but I wasn't exactly eager to share seventy-five square feet of space with the guy. He sat behind his computer, one of the stupid acoustic covers of punk songs he loved playing a little too loud.

"He quit, Sean." My voice was calm.

Sean smoothed the front of his black dress shirt. "Who?" His voice simmered with barely restrained boredom. I didn't miss the subtle eye roll and soft sigh, like he was bracing himself for a pointless discussion. I knew he thought I was difficult. And that was just fine with me. I could be plenty difficult when I needed to be.

"Your dang pastry guy." I explained about the message and the job in Boston.

Sean raised his eyebrows. "Okay then. That's a disappointment. I'll make a few calls, maybe I can shuffle things around and get one of our people from New York."

"No," I snapped, a plan crystalizing in my mind like perfectly spun sugar. "I'm calling Grace. She's who I wanted and she's who we're hiring." I tried not to visibly bristle at Sean's dismissive laugh.

"Adah." My name dripped with artificial sweet. "Call her if you want but you and I both know a girl like that isn't the right fit for what we're trying to do here. She won't be able to keep up with the pace or handle the pressure. We need confidence. Energy. Creativity."

I bit down on my tongue. He was talking about me. I knew he thought I couldn't do this job. Knew he wished Riccardo had hired some flashy chef with a big social media following instead of a nobody who had to look up what Snapchat was. He thought I wasn't good enough. He was wrong. Plastering the same stony, unobtrusive expression on my face I'd perfected over decades, I reached for the phone on his desk. Our desk. I reminded myself yet again that this was my office too.

Grace answered on the first ring, shouting over a rumble of background noise. Kitchen noise. My stomach flipped.

"Hi, Ms. Park. This is Adah Campbell from Bella Vista. Do you have a moment?"

"Oh my god! Yes hi!" Her voice carried a nervous edge.

I willfully trained my gaze on the wall calendar, a bland photo of mossy woods, instead of Sean's face. I knew his smug expression too well already.

"Great. Well I'd like to hire you on as our new pastry chef. Are you available to start," I swallowed hard, "today?"

"Shit. I mean, crap. I'm so sorry and thank you so much for the opportunity but I actually accepted another job. When I didn't hear from you guys I kinda figured it was a no. So, I took this job at The Yellow House. Have you been? It's a really cool little spot... Wow two job offers. I feel like a rock star. Ugh, sorry I'm rambling. But thank you so so much. Seriously. I can't believe you even considered me."

The Yellow House. Of course she'd gone there. For what felt like the thousandth time since our visit two weeks earlier, I tried and failed to banish the memory of Beth Summers and her stupid vibrant hair and dumb luminous skin. The dang beautiful restaurant she'd built: fragrant wood smoke, tangles of herbs, and spills of summer blooms. The embarrassing late-night hours I'd spent scrolling through her restaurant's breezy, surprisingly funny social media feeds. The way her big brown eyes had flashed fierce and angry in response to Sean's patronizing tone. *No, Adah. Focus.*

"Right. I understand. Best of luck in your new endeavor." I ended the call.

"Sounds like that went well." Sean laughed.

The tiny ember of desire I'd felt for Beth Summers transmuted then into a searing rage that boiled up my spine. I wanted to stomp my feet, break a pencil, do something to let out the panic and fear that threatened, seemingly out of nowhere, to consume me.

Of course. Of course, Beth, with her effortless restaurant and easy manner, would snap up my staff. Outlandish, unfair thoughts stacked on top of each other in my mind like layers of puff pastry coming together to form a solid mass of animosity. She didn't deserve her success. She was nothing but a pretty face. She probably didn't even know how to bake. The logical part of my brain tried to remind me that Beth Summers and The Yellow House were not, in fact, the problems at hand. Sean's reluctance to let me staff my own kitchen was the problem. My abject terror in the face of failure was the problem. The fact that I didn't know if I could do this… Tears threatened. I closed my eyes. It was so much easier to hate Beth Summers.

Even down a pastry chef, the soft opening turned out to be a moderate success. My hunch had been right and Mac was amazing in the kitchen, picking up slack the few times the other cooks fell behind. The front of house staff was great, too, good-natured and attentive. The blueberry puddings hadn't been a very exciting dessert and one of the bartenders had apparently quit halfway through her shift. Sure, the few times I'd gone out into the dining room to greet guests or discuss a dietary restriction, my stomach had dropped as I searched the room for Beth. Not that I'd expected her to show up. Goodness knew she was probably too busy giving interviews and posting photos on Instagram to show up to the soft opening of a restaurant she'd been so quick to write off.

Regardless, as I nursed a lukewarm seltzer, feet aching from a solid sixteen hours of standing, eyes crossing as I reviewed order numbers for tomorrow, I couldn't help but feel proud. I'd done it. I'd actually run my own kitchen.

Our food had been beautifully plated, flavorful, and people had loved it. The zuppa di pesce with grilled focaccia had been such a hit we sold out by the nine o'clock reservations.

My phone buzzed on the counter next to me and I answered without looking at the screen, assuming it would be Vanessa wondering when on earth I might actually come home. Peter would be long asleep, but I looked forward to running my fingers through my son's soft hair, listening to the steady rise and fall of his breath.

"How was it?" Jay's voice bloomed in the air around me and I grinned. I missed Jay, who'd started as Café Eloise's spitfire pastry chef and had become my best friend in the universe, with a desperation I hadn't expected. I pictured them curled up on their tiny, garish pink couch, reality TV playing in the background. A pang of homesickness echoed through me. "Have you seen a moose yet?"

I shook my head and smiled. Jay had asked the same ridiculous question every time we'd talked. "No. I told you, South Bay is a city. Well, kind of. Still no moose here. Not that I know of anyway."

"Okay, okay. Whatever you say, genius Executive Chef Campbell." I could hear the twist of pride and mirth in their voice. "How the hell was it? Was Sean a total fuckface? God, I hated working with him at Osteria Verde. But actually, he's a waste of time to discuss. Tell me about the food. I bet people went berserk over the cod croquettes, right?"

I glanced around the empty kitchen. I'd seen the last of Sean and Riccardo a few hours earlier, after we'd cleaned up and given the requisite pep talks to staff. "Yes, to all of that, but I'm still in the kitchen." I scrubbed a hand over my face. "But yeah it was good, I think. I don't really know. We sold out of the zuppa a few hours into service. Oh, and the dang pastry guy quit. Then when I tried to get the woman I'd liked all along she'd gone to work at that stupid Yellow House place." No way, no how was I allowing the disappointment I'd felt when Beth didn't show up to the soft opening to creep back in. Why the heck would she come? She thought Bella Vista was a tourist-trap joke. Besides, she had her own fancy-pants vanity bakery to run.

Jay scoffed. "Stupid Yellow House place, huh? The place owned by that cute redhead you mentioned about a dozen times? That particular establishment?" At my stubborn silence they forged ahead. "But yeah, of course that dude quit. I could have told you he'd be a no-show. And actually..." They trailed off. It was so unlike Jay to lapse into silence that my nerves pricked.

"What?" I asked, my voice tight. "Everything okay? Shoot, sorry I haven't even asked you about your life. I'm an awful friend."

"Nah. Everything kind of sucks, though, to be honest. Oh, let's see..." I could picture them ticking the strokes of bad luck on their fingers. "Café Eloise has turned into a complete and utter shitshow since you left. The new chef is, I don't know, like either totally fucked up when he gets to work every day, in which case, like, dude, let's get you some help, or he's totally bad at his job and spacey as hell. Half the front of house quit to go work at that stupid gourmet burger place that opened down the street. And, well, Amy moved out. So yeah, my life is basically a miserable hellscape at the moment." All of this was delivered with Jay's customary audible grin.

"Jay!" My voice reverberated through the kitchen, pinging off of stainless steel and freshly scrubbed tile. "Oh my word. I am so sorry." My heart broke for them. Jay was not only the hardest worker I'd ever known, but they were the kindest, most generous person on the planet.

"Eh, shit happens." Jay's voice broke and my heart shattered with it. They'd been with Amy for more than three years. The two of them had been talking marriage, buying a condo together. They'd adopted a dog, for goodness' sake!

"Do you want to talk about it?" I hated when people pushed me to discuss hard stuff, so I kept my voice as level and calm as possible, even if I did want to find Amy and guilt-trip her to Timbuktu and back.

"I do not. I mean I do, but not right now. But what I really want is to join you up in the land of lobstah and mooses. Mice? What the fuck is the plural for *moose*? Anyway, may I interest you in a recently single, classically trained pastry chef to grace your lovely new kitchen?"

Even after all of the stress and joy the day had delivered, this was by far my favorite moment. I let every ounce of my enthusiasm flood into my words. "You're hired."

Chapter Four

Beth

I shaded my eyes against the sun glistening off the sea and breathed in deep. Seaweed and sunscreen and salt. It was early still, just after sunrise, the sky a pale blue dotted with soft rose gold clouds. Seagulls dove and bobbed, crying out into the morning air. The beach was empty save for a few joggers and diligent tourist families setting up their umbrellas and armadas of folding chairs. As soon as his paws hit the sand, Hamlet shrugged off his collar and bounded toward a group of sandpipers running in the surf. I called feebly after him but he was too focused on the ocean to care.

It was my first day off in months. Maybe my first day off since I'd taken over The Yellow House. Grace Park and Eitan Blumenthal answering my rambling mess of a job posting had been a stroke of positive fate. Grace brought boundless energy, gleaming positivity, and a baking intuition that was almost certainly better than my own. And Eitan was her exact opposite. Quiet, steady, organized. Excellent at breaking down large cuts of meat from the local farmers and blisteringly efficient in the kitchen. In the weeks since they'd both started, guests had been happy, the menu had blossomed, and I'd gotten more than four hours of sleep each night.

Gazing out at the piney islands dotting the horizon, I welcomed the day. This was the version of myself I liked best. Calm, light, connected. I'd been terrified of what I'd turned into the last few weeks. I'd become a monster fueled by adrenaline and caffeine alone. When I'd agreed to take over the coffee shop and decided to turn it into a bakery-slash-restaurant, I'd set intentions. If I was going to be stuck in my hometown instead of backpacking through Italy with Maya, I'd at least have a few things to hold on to: reasonable hours, honest food, good energy. The last few weeks those intentions had incinerated in front of my very eyes. Now I could get back on track. Start practicing yoga again. See my friends. Maybe even revisit the paintings lying abandoned in the shed out back.

"Hey!" A sharp voice yanked me from my thoughts. "Can you get your dog under control?"

Cold panic sluiced through me. I scanned the beach for the voice, for Hamlet. I found him rolling in the sand, tongue lolling out, at the feet of a young boy. The boy was laughing and bending down to scratch my dog's enormous exposed belly. Two women looked on. One, older with silver-streaked brown hair, snapped pictures and laughed.

The other woman…was none other than Adah Campbell. Her angular face was, surprise surprise, completely impassive as she waved me over. Her blond hair was wind tousled and she wore a pair of loose, light-wash jeans cuffed a few times at the ankles and a plain gray tank top. Blank expression aside, she looked more relaxed than the first time I'd seen her. I hazarded a guess that this Monday was her first day off in a long while, too.

Heaving a sigh, I jogged over, tugging up the hem of my long skirt so I didn't trip and fall face-first into the sand.

"The signs say no dogs." Adah's voice was a harsh rasp. She eyed Hamlet like he was a rabid wolverine, not a dopey docile mutt.

"Aw, honey, it's no big deal. It's barely seven in the morning. Lots of people around here bring their dogs before it gets crowded. Lord knows I used to." The other woman tossed an indulgent laugh into the breeze. She had a heavy Maine accent and I immediately liked her. I glanced between her and Adah, sensing a maternal warmth. But they didn't seem to be related.

"Sorry," I mumbled, face flushing hot as I clipped Hamlet's leash back onto his harness.

The little boy looked disappointed, big blue eyes flicking from me to Hamlet like I might whisk away his new best friend. "He's huge. What kind of dog is he?"

"I'm not quite sure. I know he's part Great Dane but the people at the shelter weren't sure what the other part is. Do you know a lot about dogs? What do you think?"

The boy sighed, world-weary, and cast a meaningful look in Adah's direction. "I don't know anything about dogs because my mom says we can't get one. She's a chef so she's too busy."

I glanced between the two of them, awareness pricked. Upon closer inspection, they really did look like mother and son: same shade of wheat-colored hair, same long, straight nose. But where Adah was reserved, even cold, he was all bright bouncing energy. In all of my pointless speculation about Adah since I'd met her and all but chased her away from my restaurant, it hadn't occurred to me that she might be a mother. I'd envisioned her shooting pool and swigging beers in the local dives with the line cooks, not reading bedtime stories and joining the PTA. I brushed my hand over my face to hide my grin. I liked this new, softer vision of Adah.

I wasn't quite sure if I should be polite, stick around and chat, or leave them to their family morning. Was that older woman her partner? Mother? Friend? I tried to banish any assumptions and focus on the particulars of having a conversation like a normal fucking human being. But why had I even assumed Adah was queer? She wouldn't be the first or last woman to cut her hair short and dress with practicality in mind for the kitchen. Wishful thinking, I supposed. "How's everything going?" I asked before I could stop myself. "At the restaurant, I mean." Something about Adah threw me off-kilter, that was for certain. My thoughts were a jumbled mess.

Adah shrugged, crossing her arms over her chest. I'd never met someone with more closed-off posture in my life. "Fine. Well mostly fine. Aside from you stealing our pastry chef, that is."

I cocked my head. Stealing their pastry chef? "You mean

Grace? I didn't know she worked for you." I meant the words genuinely, but they came out sarcastic, a challenge.

"Well I'd wanted her to." Adah sighed, sounding exhausted. "My GM insisted on some bozo who never showed up. Anyway, it's all fine now, I found someone perfect for the job." A small smile tugged at her full lips. I wanted to see more of it.

"I'm glad to hear that." Again, I sounded far sassier than I'd meant to. What was it about this woman that inflamed my typically easygoing disposition?

"You two know each other?" the other woman asked, grinning at Adah and waggling her eyebrows. Okay, so unless they had a very open, very encouraging relationship, they probably weren't together.

"Adah and some folks from her restaurant stopped by my place a few weeks ago and I was busy and ridiculously rude." I gave Adah my best contrite expression, hoping it came across as genuine. "Sleep deprivation apparently makes me into an as—um, jerk."

Adah said nothing, her face as placid as ever, eyes now fixed on the horizon where a cruise ship chugged toward port. Okay, then, so that apology attempt went up in smoke. *Note to self: this woman is cold as ice and decidedly not worth the fantasies of her showing up at the restaurant, pressing you against a wall, and kissing you until you can't think. Probably.*

"You're a chef too?" The other woman's voice pulled me from indulging, yet again, in said ridiculous fantasy.

"Oh, um." I made a seesaw motion with the free hand not holding Hamlet's leash. "I'm a baker mostly. I own The Yellow House over in Port Catherine."

The woman's face lit up. "No way! You're little Elizabeth

Summers? I thought you looked familiar. My husband and I used to come in a million years ago when your mother was still running the show. I heard you're making a big splash over there, kiddo. How's your family?" I half expected her to pull me into her arms for a not unwelcome hug.

I beamed. "My mom finally retired a few years ago. And by retired, I mean works four days a week at Wordsworth Greenhouse and basically turned her yard and mine into a farm. My brother, Andrew, works with me at the restaurant and he's hoping to start an actual farm of his own as well." I rifled around through my memories, trying to match a name to vague impressions of the woman's face twenty years younger.

As if she'd read my mind, she batted the air between us. "You probably don't remember me, huh? I'm Vanessa Tyler. I'll bet you remember my Charlie though. Big red beard? He used to bring you and your brother all kinds of stuff he whittled."

I did remember him. He'd been larger than life with a booming laugh. I also remembered my father mentioning his funeral some years back.

"How come I've never met your husband yet?" the boy asked, pausing his dedicated scratching behind Hamlet's floppy ears.

"Peter." Adah's voice was clipped. "Don't ask those kinds of questions, it ain't polite." Apparently when she was irritated that accent of hers got thicker. It sort of made me want to rile her up some more.

Vanessa smiled at Peter and shook her head. "It's okay. He passed away. But I'm lucky to have you and your mom looking out for me." She winked.

The boy, Peter, snorted and looked at me. "She looks out for us. Ms. Vanessa watches me most days because my mom works a ton. It's okay though because she takes me to a lot of awesome places. Last week we went on the ferry and ate ice cream on two different islands." His expression shifted from wistful over what I could only assume were happy memories of giant quantities of ice cream, to shrewd as he narrowed his eyes at me. I wanted to laugh at the intensity of his expression but then he spoke again. "You're pretty." He turned to Adah. "Mom, she's really pretty, isn't she? You should date her."

While Vanessa and I dissolved into laughter, hers likely genuine, mine to stop myself from vigorously nodding in agreement, Adah stood stock-still. The only indication she'd even heard Peter's words was the blush staining her high cheekbones and the daggers she was glaring at her son.

Vanessa patted Adah on the shoulder then turned to me. "Your father still going out on the water?" She had perfected the art of small-town small talk.

As much as I wanted to continue along the conversational path Peter had led us down, I followed Vanessa's lead instead. "No. Thankfully, my brother and I finally convinced him to call it quits. But he's growing blueberries and writing mystery novels and basically driving everyone in town up the wall. He keeps trying to help out at the restaurant too, but other than handyman stuff I have to keep him away. I swear the man can actually burn water."

As Vanessa and I chatted I stole a glance at Adah. It was impossible to tell if she was listening or not, her eyes once again fixed on the ocean. But one thing was crystal clear. She looked suddenly and unspeakably sad.

★ ★ ★

The rest of the day stretched out in front of me, shapeless hours I had no idea what to do with. After getting home from the beach, I'd spent a little time pulling weeds in the garden, inhaling the green earthy scents of sage and rosemary, and reveling in warm morning sun on my neck. But my mother had stopped by earlier in the week to "tidy up" my herb and flower beds, which meant they looked the best they ever had. Idly I wondered if Adah liked to garden. What her family had been like growing up. I pictured a big yard bursting with produce and frantic with chickens pecking all around. Then I started thinking about her tall lean body and the way her hands might feel on mine. Groaning, I shook my head to dispel the thoughts.

Taking a new tack, I sat on the porch with a cup of chamomile and the book I hadn't been able to keep my eyes open to read. But my vision blurred as I stared at the page, my mind unable to focus on the story. Instead, my thoughts drifted, once again, to Adah. I wondered what her favorite book was, if she liked to read at all. I imagined her snuggled on the couch with her son, reading books out loud and doing different voices for the characters. Enough was enough. I snapped the book shut, downed the rest of my tea, and stalked inside. Finally, I changed into my painting clothes, a pair of tattered linen pants and an old shirt of my dad's, and retreated to my neglected studio.

My stomach flipped as my eyes raked over the painting I'd been working on before I took over The Yellow House. I hadn't picked up a brush in months. The composition, a dreamy tumble of flowers rendered in shades of purple, was completely alien to me. I ran my fingers over the dry paint hoping to connect to the piece but felt nothing.

No matter. I dusted my hands briskly on my shirt like I did when baking and pulled a fresh canvas from the stack in the corner. Paintbrush in hand, I allowed my eyes to flutter shut. Colors filled my mind's eye. Soft green like new leaves. Like sea glass. Like…goddammit. Adah's eyes. No. I set the paintbrush down and heaved a heavy sigh.

The only thing that would get this excess energy out of my system was baking. Kneading dough and sifting flour until my mind reached meditative quiet. It looked like I was going to be working on my day off after all.

Chapter Five

Adah

"I need two bouillabaisse for table sixteen *now*!" I roared over the din of kitchen noise. Service was going as smoothly as any packed Saturday night could go. The last three weekends had been absurdly busy, but I wasn't about to complain. Jay had settled right in and created a unique but still approachable pastry program. We'd added a Sunday brunch that a local food blog had touted as the best in the city. And most importantly, Sean had stopped trying to meddle in my kitchen.

As if conjured by my thoughts, his ruddy face appeared on the other side of the pass. I nodded curtly at him before returning to checking that the plating on the branzino was up to my standards. It was, mostly. One plate looked a little sloppy and I called Mac over to fix it.

"Adah, I need to talk to you." Sean's face was unreadable, which made me break out in a cold sweat.

It also bothered me that he refused to address me as chef. I wasn't one of those arrogant jerkwads who insisted on some kind of rigid code of discipline. As long as everybody did their job and cooked good food, I didn't care what we called ourselves. I worked hard to ensure my kitchen was a safe, equitable space. Everyone was to be treated with dignity and kindness on my watch. Still, I was pretty sure if I were a guy Sean would call me chef. And I was absolutely positive that he wouldn't interrupt me in the middle of a busy weekend dinner service.

"Yeah, Sean, what's up?" I wanted to let my exasperation shine through, but instead I took a deep breath and turned to face my manager. Letting him know how much he got to me would only reward him. I knew that better than anyone.

"Can you come to my office for a second?"

My stomach dropped and blood roared loud in my ears. On the inside, I felt like a kid in Sunday school getting called in front of the class for talking out of turn. But I squared my shoulders and brushed a stray fleck of parsley off the cuff of my whites. Things were going well. As far as I knew Riccardo was thrilled with our business so far. What in the name of all things holy could I be in trouble for? I also wanted to remind Sean for the thousandth time that *his office* was technically *our office*, even if I avoided being in there with him like I did restaurants that dumped truffle oil on top of everything. Instead I simply nodded and ducked out of the kitchen, praying this would be short and sweet.

"So, how do you think things are going?" he asked, closing the office door behind me. Without thinking, my hand drifted to the knob, wanting to tug it open again.

"Good," I said evenly. "We're obviously busy tonight, so I don't have a ton of time to hang around and chat." I was letting the anger in. If too much rushed through the cracks I'd without a doubt say something I'd regret.

Sean smiled, a smarmy indulgent grin I wanted to wipe off his dumb face. "Absolutely. I wanted to loop you in, though—" He paused then like he wanted me to ask *on what?* I kept quiet. "I got in touch with Marcus Blanche. The restaurant critic. He's going to be coming in sometime this fall to check out the restaurant. This could be huge, so I want us to be our best. Best that you work out all the issues now, okay?"

"Of course." I plastered a grin on my face even as my hands clenched into fists at my sides. Was I out of my mind, or did the guy manage to be as belittling as possible during every gosh darn interaction? Of course I knew who Marcus dang Blanche was. He was one of the most famous restaurant critics in New York, a big deal food writer for *The New York Daily* before he'd struck out on his own to start *Gourmand Magazine*. And what issues was Sean even talking about? Service ran smoother than fresh-churned butter and I knew our food was excellent. Heck, I'd checked our Yelp reviews and the only complaints were the typical fine-dining gripes about small portions and high prices.

I remained stonily silent the rest of dinner service and through the end-of-night cleanup. I only managed to string more than a few words together when Jay tugged me into the muggy alley behind the restaurant and demanded to know what was wrong.

I leaned against the bricks, still warm from the sun, and scrubbed a hand over my face. "Nothin'." I sighed. "Just Sean being a moron as usual."

Jay nodded but narrowed their eyes at me. "Yeah but Sean's always a moron and you usually don't go all Silent Bob on us."

"Yeah," I admitted. "He just had to pull me out of the rush to tell me about Marcus Blanche coming in the fall. Acted like there was no way I knew who the guy was and basically warned me to get it together."

Jay scoffed. "Oh for fuck's sake. He's such a douche. But yeah I was actually gonna tell you about that. Remember my friend Lupe? She writes for *Gourmand* and told me yesterday that they're doing this huge profile of New England restaurants for their January issue. Putting together a top ten list and doing in-depth write-ups of the favorite five places. Big photo shoots, chef profiles, the whole nine. She said that Yellow House place is a top contender. I guess Marcus is pretty obsessed with your girlfriend over there."

I scoffed. Although Beth had been on my mind and in my dreams almost constantly since our run-in at the beach a few weeks ago, I had made a valiant effort to avoid any mention of the woman. Or her stupid, overrated restaurant. But it seemed everyone under the sun was determined to talk about that place and sing Beth's praises. So naturally Marcus was going to go there too. For all I knew he'd already decided on The Yellow House for the number one spot because he and Beth had gone to culinary school in

Paris together. Not that I knew the first thing about Beth's history. Or Marcus Blanche's for that matter. Probably best to look into that. Marcus's background, that was.

Jay waved their hand in front of my eyes. "Good lord you can space out. Did you hear anything I just said?"

I shot them an apologetic smile. "Yeah, yeah. The Yellow House. The article. And Beth is *not* my girlfriend. I'm not in the habit of dating...women like her."

Jay shrugged. "I think she seems pretty cool. In fact, Mac told me that her restaurant is hosting some kind of queer community dinner next weekend. We should go. I need to meet some other queers. Not that you aren't awesome. But you know, winter is coming and all that jazz. I need someone to keep me warm."

This comment sent my mind down a spiral of thoughts all starring the exact woman I didn't want to think about. Holding Beth's compact form in my arms. Her skin, smooth and soft. Her body underneath me. Running my fingers through her curls, tipping her lips up to meet mine... No.

I shook my head hard to clear the thoughts. Now more than ever Beth was my competition. No way was I having inappropriate daydreams about a woman who might steal the acclaim I worked so hard for. Especially because I had serious doubts that she worked very hard at all. How could everything look so dang casual and effortless at The Yellow House if she was busting her tail the way I had for the past decade? She'd just inherited a business and probably hadn't done a hard day's work in her dang life. Sure, the place looked great on paper but no way it was really that good. That effortless.

My irritation must have shown on my face, because Jay

laughed and patted my shoulder. "You need to relax, Adah, seriously. I get that this is a lot of pressure. I promise I do. But when was the last time you even took a day off?"

"A few Mondays ago. Remember I took Peter to the beach." As I said my son's name, guilt coursed through me. Other than the few early morning hours we spent reading books or walking to the coffee shop around the corner, I barely saw my own child.

"Girl, that was almost a month ago. You know Mac and I can pick up the slack if you want to take more time to, you know, be a human being. We're taking bets on how soon we'll find out you've been sleeping in the pantry. That new dishwasher chick, Hannah, swears up and down she saw a cot in there."

I knew Jay wouldn't judge me if I told them about my litany of fears. I worried Sean was searching high and low for a reason to send me packing back to Chicago. I worried if I loosened my grip on the kitchen even a bit, then I would lose control entirely. I worried that, despite the long hours and wrist burns and swollen feet at the end of each night, I wasn't doing enough.

Jay pulled their phone out of their back pocket and thumbed around on the screen for a moment before thrusting it in my face. Once my eyes adjusted to the brightness in contrast with the murky dim of the alley, I saw it was a Facebook event for "The Yellow House First Annual Big Queer Dinner, Dance, and Dream Extravaganza!" I scanned through the details: it was next Monday, tickets cost forty bucks, and the proceeds went to a local LGBTQ teen center.

"I can't." I looked up at the night sky, clear and scattered with more stars than I'd seen since I left Missouri. "You should go though. Maybe bring Mac."

Jay sighed heavily. "One, Mac has a partner. Two, I already invited both of them. And three, I want to go with my goddamn best friend. You know the one I moved all the way up here to hang out with…"

I barked out a laugh. "Not for the job, then?"

"Okay, fine, you and the job. Please, please, please. It will be fun. And you can, I don't know, gather intel on the competition to take her down. If you can't fucking relax think of it as work. You'll be like a culinary spy." Jay pointed finger guns at me.

In a total attempt to ignore the way my heart raced at the thought of spending hours in Beth's presence, eating her food, trying and failing not to stare at the sway of her hips, I rolled my eyes. "Fine. If I can get Vanessa to watch Peter, which heaven knows that poor woman is probably sick of my kid at this point, maybe I'll go." At Jay's whoop of excitement I repeated the word "maybe," already knowing I was going to show up.

When I pushed the door to my apartment shut behind me, I found Vanessa sitting at my tiny, secondhand kitchen table, mug in one hand, paperback in the other. "Oh sweetheart, you look exhausted. You want some tea? Maybe something stronger?"

Tears pricked at my eyes, sharp and unwelcome. I didn't deserve a scrap of her kindness. Why would this woman be so good to me? I hadn't done anything for her but take advantage of her generosity. No way was I asking her for anything extra. Besides, what kind of awful, selfish mother was I, wanting to take a night off from my own child, who I barely saw, to spend time with a woman I didn't even like?

Vanessa's gentle hand on my shoulder startled me from my thoughts and I had to keep myself from flinching away from her.

"Everything okay?" Her voice was soft as she gestured for me to sit down on my own dang couch.

I rubbed the back of my neck and nodded. "Yeah. Thanks. Sorry. I'm just tired is all."

She nodded but her eyes narrowed and she looked at me for a long moment. "You need a break."

What the heck? Had she and Jay somehow met and colluded on mission *Force Adah to Relax Against Her Will*? "Nah, just some sleep. Thank you so much for watching Peter again today. You sure you don't want me to find someone else? Or you could at least let me pay you?" We had this conversation almost every night.

"Adah, your kiddo is the light of my life. My grandkids all live in damn South Carolina. And between you and me I was getting pretty tired of book club and contra dance." Her shrewd gaze intensified. "You're not telling me something. I can spot deflection a mile off, honey."

Despite years of Sunday school and sermons that worked hard to convince me that such things did not exist, I was pretty dang sure that Vanessa was an honest to goodness mind reader. Collapsing on the couch, I pulled off my kitchen clogs and released a heavy sigh. "Well, I was going to see if maybe I could ask you if you'd be able to watch Peter next Monday night."

Vanessa made a rolling motion with her hand. She knew

I hardly ever took Mondays off despite the restaurant being closed.

"Yeah, I, uh, got invited to this dinner event. I just want to go to check out the competition...this other restaurant has been getting a lot of attention and—" I cut myself off to stop my rambling.

"Check out the competition, eh?" Vanessa beamed like I'd presented her with one of Jay's perfect slices of French butter cake.

My landlady—okay, I should probably start thinking of her as my friend even if the word felt funny in my brain— left a few minutes later in a haze of smug smiles and her now-familiar floral perfume. I collapsed back onto the couch and stared, unseeing, at the blank wall facing me. I knew it was high time to put up some decorations in this place. But I didn't exactly have fine art to grace the walls. No, all I had to my name were a few pieces of flimsy furniture from big box stores and spruced-up finds from the alley behind our Chicago apartment I'd been lucky enough to scoop up on trash day.

"Mommy..." Peter drifted out of his room, rubbing his eyes. I was grateful for the sound of my son's soft voice.

I opened my arms to him immediately, despite the buildup of kitchen grease coating every inch of me. But unlike my mama, who made all us kids scrub ourselves raw, I figured dirt never really hurt anybody. "Hey, pumpkin. Sorry to wake you." He settled in my arms, sleep-warm and smelling like his cherry-almond kids' shampoo.

"S'okay," he mumbled. "Will you sleep in bed with me?"

"Of course," I replied softly as I smoothed his hair away from his face. Peter was nine now and every parenting book under the sun would probably tell me I should stick to boundaries around co-sleeping. But I hardly saw my son as it was. And he was such a horrendous blanket hog I'd probably end up heading back to the couch after a few hours anyway. "Why don't you pick out a book—a short one—for us to read while I wash up for bed?"

As I stepped into the harsh bathroom light, I winced at the sight of my own reflection in the tiny mirror mounted above the sink. My hair was in desperate need of a trim, and even worse, I looked like a dang ghost. Although the last few weeks had been brilliantly sunny, I'd barely spent an hour outdoors during daylight hours. My face was fish belly white and dark circles deepened my eye sockets. Maybe Jay and Vanessa and just about everyone I came across were right. Maybe I did need a little rest.

Unfortunately for me, I highly doubted an evening spent in the presence of Beth Summers would be calming in the slightest.

Chapter Six

Beth

Sweeping my curls into a loose knot on the top of my head, I inhaled deeply. Tonight was going to be good. I could feel it in my bones. As much as I loved the wedding receptions and family reunions and business dinners people rented out The Yellow House for, I missed nights like this. People, my people, coming together, eating simple food, dancing under strands of fairy lights and a wide-open sky full of stars.

Nina sashayed into the kitchen, dressed to the nines in a black lace crop top and tiny cutoff shorts that emphasized her curves. I'd opted for a loose linen tank and a pair of well-worn jeans. It was nice to be able to wear my jewelry for once though, to hear the clatter of my bracelets and necklaces announcing my every movement. Besides, I wasn't here to impress anyone tonight. All I wanted was to make my guests happy, facilitate community, and rack up as many donations for the Melinda Coulter LGBTQ Center as possible.

"Ugh I hate you." Nina hip checked me out of the way to inspect her flawless makeup in the reflection of a particularly shiny pot. "You look like a fucking goddess. Meanwhile I watched three YouTube videos to figure out these new lash extensions."

I blew my friend a kiss. "You look amazing. Like the Instagram queen you are." Nina ran a body positivity fashion Instagram in addition to working magic on The Yellow House's social media.

"Okay so, we should probably pull the farro salad and the olive tapenade now to let them come to temperature. What do you think, slice the bread now or will it get too dry?" Nina yanked open our ancient refrigerator, yet another thing I'd been meaning to get around to replacing, and peered inside.

"I'll slice it in a few minutes and put cloths over it. Knives plus booze isn't a great combo."

We'd opted for a menu of fresh, simple dishes we could prepare ahead and arrange buffet style for folks to graze on throughout the night. I'd made an assortment of focaccias, rustic pizzas, and pastries, while Nina had put together platters of roasted seasonal vegetables, grain salads, and local cheeses. Then Eitan had surprised us all this morning with an announcement that he was going to grill chicken thighs and steam clams over the outdoor woodstove for anyone who wanted something a little heartier. We had good wine, cold beer, and three different kinds of infused water. Hopefully something for everyone. And if someone wasn't happy, we would make it right.

I glanced outside where my brother Andrew and our newish pastry assistant Grace appeared to be arguing over a floral arrangement. Nina followed my gaze. "Holy god have those two fucked yet? I walked in on the two of them bickering with Eitan about, like, saffron or something yesterday and I could have cut the tension with a knife. I really hoped Grace might be queer because that girl is cute as hell."

I shot Nina a reproachful look. "Be professional. She's our colleague. We don't need to start speculating about her identity or her sex life."

Nina stuck her tongue out at me but returned to arranging grilled peaches on a slate board. She was silent for all of fifty seconds before bringing up the one topic I was not interested in broaching. My sex life. Or complete and utter lack thereof.

"So speaking of..." She beamed at me. "I invited Kevin."

I turned to her, mouth agape, hoping she didn't mean what I thought she meant. "You what? Why?" Kevin Walsh was my fucking high school boyfriend. The guy I'd dated and thought I'd dutifully marry until I woke up to the reality that I liked girls a little more than guys and wanted a hell of a lot more than the life of a fisherman's wife. More than the life my mother had. More than this town.

The morning of graduation I'd swiftly ended things with Kevin and launched myself into a world of food, travel, and pleasure. A failed stint in culinary school and a failed fling with a high-powered corporate attorney who wanted me to tie her up in bed. A few months working on a vineyard in California and sun-drenched trysts with the vineyard owner's son. Almost three years spent working at the best bakery in New Orleans and falling into my only other real relationship to date. I tried not to think of Maya, the beautiful pianist I'd so easily left behind. Now I was back here. In Maine. Putting down roots I never knew I wanted. Roots I still wasn't so sure about letting grow down deep.

"Oh come on, Beth. It's not a big deal. I happened into him at Brew and Bean over in Fullerton…which he owns by the way. I figured you guys could catch up and talk about being business owners and shit. He looked good. Maybe I'll fuck him if you don't want to."

I didn't really spend a lot of time worrying about my sexuality the way I had in my twenties. A solid decade of experimenting with the way I looked and who I wanted to sleep with left me with the solid understanding that someone's energy did a lot more to attract me than their gender. Still, the idea of hooking up with Kevin held no appeal. I needed to focus on the future, not get bogged down in the past.

Nina pinned me with a knowing look and I rolled my eyes. "You're still hung up on that fancy chef chick, aren't you?"

My cheeks heated and I knew I was blushing. Stupid fair skin. "No." The word was as hollow as an unfilled pastry shell. "I don't have time for that stuff. Is everything ready? What are we doing for music?"

"Ugh yes. Ahmed made a playlist. Just chill, okay. This is supposed to be fun, remember?"

I drew in another deep breath and pushed the door open,

stepping out into the early evening sun. The breeze carried the sound of the little girl down the street haltingly practicing her violin and the distant brine of the ocean. The gardens were in full bloom now, big pink peonies and a riot of orange marigolds giving way to neat rows of vegetables and herbs. Even after nearly three years of running The Yellow House, sometimes it still took my breath away. All that we'd accomplished.

When I was growing up, The Yellow House had been Summers's Corner Café. My mom baked quickbreads and an assortment of whoopie pies that drew a sprinkling of tourists and a steady stream of people from town. The café was simple: open early for the fishermen and hunters, serving hot coffee and hearty breakfasts, always the place to sit and gossip or play a game of cribbage. It had been a cozy, if a little run-down, space. I'd spent most of my grade school afternoons at the counter daydreaming when I was supposed to be doing my homework.

Throughout high school my brother and I both helped out here and there, bussing tables and doing dishes as needed. As we got older, though, Andrew was usually too busy with sports. Then, because I come by my tendency to bounce around honestly, my mom's interests shifted from cooking to gardening and I slowly began to take on more and more of the work at the café. But once I'd set my sights on bigger and brighter things, I was out of Maine like a shot and hadn't looked back. At least for a long while.

It was only after I'd been living in New Orleans for a few years, panicking over the prospect of signing a lease with Maya, that my mom's announcement that she was thinking of selling Summers's Corner to a guy from Los Angeles drew me home as suddenly as I'd left. Just as impulsively as I'd ended things with Kevin and decided to leave home, I told Maya I couldn't stay and decided to go back. Three days of driving up back roads and singing along to Joni Mitchell to distract myself later, I was in Port Catherine again, preparing to take over the family business.

I tried not to dwell in the past. Tried not to feel guilty for abandoning Maya, a woman so joyful and bright I was almost blinded by her. Tried not to picture the easy life full of music and free of responsibility that could have so easily been mine. The life I'd run away from.

Instead, here and now in the present, I looked around and steeped myself in gratitude for what I had. Andrew, arms crossed over his chest, arguing with Eitan over how to arrange the makeshift outdoor bar. Ahmed sweeping from table to table, tweaking the vases full of wildflowers and herbs, eyeing the glassware he'd polished till it shone. Nina bustling back and forth from the kitchen to the buffet, platters of food in hand, shouting along with the music drifting from the speakers. They were all my family. We'd built this place together. It was our home.

The first guests arrived a few minutes before seven, a group of nervous-looking kids in their early twenties. After giving them a quick tour and checking their IDs, I situated them at one of the big farmhouse tables with a nice fruity rosé and an assortment of snacks. As always, Ahmed's music choice was perfect, a blend of lo-fi hip hop, '90s electronica, and mellow jazz. I knew as the night went on, the playlist would pick up and draw people onto the dance floor. I said a silent prayer to the universe that my perfect general manager never left me.

I was in the middle of an enthusiastic conversation with a sweet lesbian couple who'd moved to one of the islands along the coast when Nina poked me hard in the ribs.

"Hey!" I wheeled on her, only to find her shadowed by a towering, bearded man in a Red Sox T-shirt and khaki cargo shorts. Remove the beard and some laugh lines and there stood the boy I'd left behind. One of exactly two people I'd ever seriously dated. Although I wasn't even sure if a high school romance counted as serious. "Oh wow." My voice was probably only audible to Hamlet, who was begging for scraps next to the grill. "Kevin! Hi! Wow. It's been a while. How are you? Thanks for coming!"

Without warning he engulfed me in a coffee-scented bear hug. A laugh erupted from my lips as he nearly knocked the wind out of me. He hadn't changed a bit. This situation should have been awkward. After all, I had unceremoniously dumped the poor guy with a breezy *it's over* and left town without so much as a goodbye. But Kevin didn't have an awkward bone in his giant body.

"Little Beth Summers. Aren't you a sight for sore eyes." I'd forgotten how heavy his accent was. "I kept meaning to stop by and check the place out since you took over. Looks great. You did a hell of a job." He nodded, glancing around at the small clusters of people chatting and sipping drinks.

He kept an easy arm draped around my shoulders. I felt my face heat. Whether from embarrassment or some kind of weird touch-starved automatic response I couldn't quite tell. Maybe Nina was right and I really did need to get laid. But not by this dude. Unbidden, Adah's lithe frame appeared in my mind's eye. I shook my head. "Um, what can I get you to drink?" I asked, shifting a few inches away. Kevin didn't take the hint.

Behind me I heard a familiar voice and then my body really did flush hot. That soft country accent, a little irritated, a little amused. Then it stopped short. I wheeled around to meet the placid green gaze of Adah Campbell.

Chapter Seven

Adah

Beth's grin crumpled the moment our eyes met and she shrugged off the arm of the giant of a man next to her. As much as I wanted to turn on my heel and storm back to Jay's car, I couldn't help but admire how dang pretty she looked. As always, I worked to keep my expression as neutral as possible. I'd spent a ridiculously long time picking out what to wear only to settle for my customary uniform of Levi's and a plain white T-shirt. When Jay had shown up at my apartment in full dapper mode—gray slacks, crisp button-down, and freshly shined oxfords—I felt like a total wreck. So seeing Beth in a loose purple top and slightly tattered jeans set me at ease. Or it would have if she wasn't practically attached at the hip to some…guy.

Her eyes darted between me and Jay and an unreadable expression passed over her face. Then she snapped into what I immediately recognized as hospitality mode: a gracious smile that didn't quite meet her eyes, broad gestures, voice slightly higher than usual. "Thanks so much for coming. It's nice to see you again." Her silver beaded bracelets clattered together as she patted her hair. "Um, this is Nina Bernstein, our chef." She gestured to a perky blonde woman who looked like a modern-day version of a pin-up girl. "And this is my *friend* Kevin. We went to high school together." She stepped another few inches away from the man.

"Yup, this girl right here broke my heart. Ancient history though." The guy chuckled. He looked so at ease I wanted to throw him off kilter.

I lifted my hand in greeting. "Adah."

Thankfully, Jay, unlike me, had actual social skills and saved the situation from collapsing into stilted silence. "I'm Jay. I work at Bella Vista with Adah. Pastry chef extraordinaire. They/them pronouns, if you please." Jay flashed a charming smile, their gaze lingering on Nina for a long moment.

Quickly we all exchanged pronouns, with bearded Kevin looking distinctly confused by the process. I glanced around the outdoor dining area, purposefully keeping my attention anywhere but on Beth's flushed, dewy face. We'd arrived only a few minutes after the event start time, but already the tables and bar area were crowded. Strings of café lights stretched over a makeshift dance floor where a few brave souls bobbed along with the mellow music. A rustic wooden table groaned under the weight of beautifully plated salads, pizzas, and artful arrangements of roasted vegetables.

"This place is awesome," Jay enthused next to me. "It's sweet that you have so much garden space. I've been loving all the produce we've been getting. I've never really lived in a rural area before. I thought the whole 'Maine blueberries' thing was a gimmick or whatever, but those things are fucking delicious."

Jay and Nina lapsed quickly into an enthusiastic conversation about fruit, and stupid beard guy wandered off to get a beer. Leaving me and Beth. And silence. I shoved my hands in my pockets and fixed my gaze on my boots, way too aware of the sound of my own breathing.

After what was probably a minute but felt like an eternity, Beth started laughing. Her laugh was beautiful—bright and high and almost musical. I lifted my eyes to meet hers and felt the corners of my mouth quirk up. "What?" I asked, trying and failing to keep my voice even and low.

"You really don't like me, do you?" She didn't look offended, just mildly curious.

I shook my head, thrown off by her question. Her eyebrows arched and I had to resist the urge to step closer to her to brush my fingers over them. What was it about her skin that looked so soft? So impossibly smooth? Why did the golden evening light have to catch in the loose strands of her hair, making her look like she was glowing? "That's not true," I said belatedly, "I don't even know you."

"Fair enough." She grinned, then extended her hand to me. "Let's start over. I'm Elizabeth Anne Summers. Most people call me Beth. I'm a Taurus and I like long walks on the beach, strawberry ice cream, and my favorite color is…" She gestured to the yellow cottage behind us.

Try as I might, I couldn't stop myself from laughing. Hard. The kind of big full belly laugh I hadn't allowed myself in a while. "You're ridiculous." I raked a hand through my hair.

"You know it." Beth winked. She could, as my mamma liked to say, charm the pants off a snake. The expression didn't make much sense, but it was forever stuck in my brain right alongside hundreds of Bible verses. "Your turn." She made a go ahead motion with her hand. "Or do I need to ply you with liquid courage to get you to talk?"

"I talk," I muttered, sounding just as darn stubborn as I felt. "But yeah, a beer would be nice. What do you have?"

Beth slid her hand into mine and tugged me in the direction of the bar. I stared down at our fingers laced together for a bright moment, my heart flipping in my chest. Her hands were strong, a little rough. Baker's hands. Biting the inside of my cheek hard I focused on our destination. The outdoor bar. It was a heavy, antique-looking butcher block table covered in metal tubs of cold beer, wine, and a few big glass water jugs. Behind it a small guy with shoulder-length dreads seemed to be doing about fifteen jobs at once. Two seconds in his presence I could tell he was front of house and I could tell he was seriously good at his job.

"Ahmed, this is Adah." Beth made a gesture like she was presenting me to a crowd at the county fair. "Adah, this is Ahmed, our manager and my personal lord and savior."

"Nice to meet you." Ahmed grinned and shook my hand.

"Likewise." I returned his smile, my shoulders unclenching a little as I did so. Maybe I really did need to relax.

Ice clattered against cans as Beth dug around in the beer tub. "Okay, I bet you like lagers, right? You're one of those people that think IPAs overwhelm the palate and all that?" Beth arched an eyebrow at me and once again I had to laugh. She was right.

"Uh, yeah. I'll take a pilsner if you have that. I'm not too picky." She probably wouldn't take too kindly to my shameful admission that my favorite beer was usually just whatever was cheapest.

Beth pushed a tall, brightly colored can into my hands. "Nope, I'm going to ask you to at least try this. It's Billings Brothers' Puffin Pale Ale. Super clean and light and perfectly balanced." She cracked open another can. "And I want you to give this one a chance, too. Where are you from?"

The question threw me for a loop and I answered without thinking. "Missouri—" I took a long sip of beer. "Well, grew up in Missouri. Moved here from Chicago though."

"Okay, well no offense but I feel like most Midwestern IPAs are super hoppy... And kind of gross? I mean, they smell like weed half the time. This is pure juicy goodness. Tons of citrus." Again, easy as pie, Beth slipped her hand into mine and tugged me away from the bar. Away, I realized, from the whole party. After a quick detour to fill a plate with food, we were behind the cottage, surrounded by neat stacks of firewood and softly swaying forest shadows. It was quiet. Or maybe my ears were just buzzing with nerves.

Beth sat down on the back stoop, a narrow flight of three wooden stairs and gestured for me to sit next to her. Try as I might to leave space between us, it was in short supply and our arms brushed. Heat bloomed on my neck. It had been a long time since I'd been this close to anyone other than Peter or Jay. My body felt weird, sensitized and heavy all at once.

"Okay, so your turn." Beth turned to me, leaning in a little like we were sharing a secret. Freckles dusted her nose. She smelled like campfires and summertime with a hint of lavender. My gaze crashed down to the weathered wooden slats of the stairs.

"Um." I cleared my throat. "You already know my name—"

"I don't know your middle name. Or your sign. That shit is important." Beth's voice glimmered with mirth.

"Oh, well I don't really like it. And I, uh, don't know what sign I am."

"Why, were your parents, like, super hippies? Is it something like Storm, or Rainbow? Probably not since you don't know your sign. We'll get to that later…depending on how the night goes, I just might do your star chart."

I barked out a laugh and again my body relaxed just a little bit more. Taking a sip of my beer, which was, as promised, delicious and perfectly balanced, I shook my head. "No way. All of us kids have biblical names. My dad was a pastor."

"Ah, okay. So is it, like…Ezekiel? Elijah? Sorry, we never went to church."

"Gosh, no. It's Delilah. I'm just telling you so you stop guessing. Even I've never met anyone named Ezekiel."

"Aw that's pretty. I think it suits you. Adah Delilah Campbell."

I shrugged. "It's a mouthful."

"Do you have a lot of siblings then?" Beth asked, bending forward to grab a slice of bread from the plate resting on the ground. The purple crystal she wore around her neck glittered in the waning sunlight.

"Yeah." I didn't want to elaborate so I followed her lead and scooped up a piece of pizza. The perfectly baked crust had to be sourdough, with big air bubbles. It was topped with fresh corn, chiffonaded basil, and what smelled like sharp cheddar. I took a bite and couldn't suppress my groan. It was perfect. The crust was chewy with just enough crunch and the toppings just worked. Simple but really, really good, each flavor bringing out the best in the others. "Holy cow!" I said when I swallowed one more bite. "This is fantastic." The words were out of my mouth before I could even try to rein them in. Crap. This was Beth. The Yellow House. The dang competition.

As much as I wanted to find flaws, though, it seemed there were none. Even at this casual event, everything from the music to the food was perfect. Effortless, tasteful, and... I grudgingly admitted to myself, delicious.

"I love corn and basil together," Beth enthused. "What do you think of the crust though? I just started using a locally milled wheat. Does it overwhelm the toppings?"

"Wait, you actually made this?" My voice broadcasted my disbelief.

Beth tipped her head to the side. "Um, yes?"

I stuffed another bite of pizza in my mouth to avoid saying anything else stupid. But Beth's whole demeanor had shifted, back to the prickly woman she'd been when we first met. I didn't understand why my brain refused to believe that Beth was capable of all of this. That she could make delicious food, and own her own restaurant, and for it all to be so…perfect. It felt unfair somehow, that a woman as beautiful as her could run an award-winning restaurant and make it seem so *easy*. Fun even. And crap, now I felt as misogynistic as my dang manager. Of course she was capable of running her own place.

"Sorry," I groaned, running a hand over my face. "I guess I kinda hoped you were…" I weighed the pros and cons of being honest, but my virtuous upbringing won. "I don't know. The pretty face and the money behind it. I mean I knew it was your family business and I just figured—"

Beth shot off the stoop in a clatter of bracelets and a swirl of warm summer air. And boy, did she look mad. I hadn't seen someone that fired up since I left home. My spine stiffened and my heart started racing, unwelcome adrenaline coursing through my limbs.

"You figured what?" She glared down at me. "That I don't know what the fuck I'm doing. I'm not clueless. And even if I was, it doesn't change the fact that you're being an asshole. I work really fucking hard and gave up a hell of a lot to open this place. And some days I don't even know if I *like* doing this. If I even want to be here." She took a deep breath and seemed to be fighting to calm herself down. "Look, my mom ran this place as the local greasy spoon for decades. And my dad was a goddamn fisherman. We weren't exactly rolling in it. And yeah, I guess I could have gone your route, the whole degree and prestigious restaurant thing, but it really wasn't for me. And guess what? It wouldn't make this place any better. You have no idea what I've sacrificed to get here. I barely even sleep anymore. And I fucking love sleeping!"

Even though her words made sense, should have made me take back my stupid assumptions, somehow, they had the opposite effect. "Oh, sure. Having to give up your beauty rest sounds real hard." I scoffed and stood, glad I was a few inches taller than her. Suddenly we were so close I could feel the heat and anger rolling off her skin. "You have no idea what sacrifice is."

Then her lips were on mine and she was pushing me back until my body slammed against the rough wood of the cottage. Her hands fisted in the fabric of my shirt and for a long moment I was too stunned to kiss her back. Then my adrenaline and anger shifted, softened. I breathed in her taste, herbs and citrus and warm skin. My fingers drifted to brush her bare arms and I shivered to find her skin really was as soft as I'd imagined. Just as I started to relax, a soft groan slipping from my lips as they parted, Beth jerked away. Her hand flew over her mouth and her eyes flared wild, almost afraid.

"Oh my god." She groaned. "What the hell am I doing?" Her voice was muffled by her hand and she shook her head. Dang, it had been a while since I kissed anyone but I didn't think I was *that* rusty. Beth shifted away from me, shuffling backward on the flagstone path. "Um, sorry. I shouldn't have done that. Seriously, sorry. That was a mistake. I should get back to work. Enjoy the party."

And then she was gone. I was alone, head spinning, lips tingling, heart racing. The sounds of laughter and music drifted back, fuzzy and distant like a radio out of tune. The sun had dipped below the stands of scrubby pines surrounding the restaurant, leaving the sky a deep, clear blue. I lifted my thumb to my mouth, touching my lips like I was checking for proof that kiss had really happened. But I knew it had. I knew because, suddenly, everything around me was brighter, more beautiful. And a heck of a lot more confusing.

Chapter Eight

Beth

The rest of the night was a blur. I flitted in and out of conversations, refilled drinks, and resolved a minor kitchen crisis. But I felt anesthetized. Always, Adah stayed perched on the edge of my mind, but I refused to scan the crowd for her. Twice I spotted her chatting with the person she'd brought with her and my whole body seemed to levitate, hot and hollow. Our eyes met once. Adah's expression had been intense but hard to read. What the fuck had I been thinking, kissing her like that? For all I knew Jay was her partner. Adah might have brought them here on a date and I couldn't help but take her behind the restaurant and rage-kiss her. Hell, for all I knew Adah wanted nothing to do with me. She certainly seemed to think I, along with everything I'd worked so hard to build, was a phony, pretentious waste of space. So why on earth had I kissed her? Sure, she was hot. But, still, I had *some* self-respect.

I tugged the elastic from my hair and ran my fingers through it. Food service was done and I was, as usual, exhausted. Typically, though, my fatigue was purely physical: feet throbbing from standing all day, forearms sore from kneading, scalp tight from restraining my mass of hair. Tonight, I had to deal with the added bonus of being emotionally exhausted.

Most of the guests had departed, only a dozen or so remained on the dance floor and another small group hung by the bar chatting with my brother and Ahmed. Night birds chattered in the trees, their soft calls mingling with the low music. Sighing, I cleared a stack of plates from one of the farmhouse tables and started toward the kitchen. I'd given my usual servers and dishwashers the night off so I could funnel as much profit as possible into the Melinda Coulter Center.

The kitchen was dim and quiet, a peaceful reprieve. I hadn't seen Adah for a while, but still I wasn't sure if she'd left and I was hyperaware of her potential presence outside. It was totally legitimate for a grown-ass business owner to hide out in her own kitchen to avoid the woman she'd mistakenly kissed during the heat of an argument, right? Deciding that it was, I began scraping food scraps into the compost bin and hummed a few lines of my favorite Fleetwood Mac song. If Stevie Nicks couldn't soothe my soul nothing would.

Over the sound of the running water and drone of the industrial dishwasher, I registered the whine of the screen door opening. I braced myself for Nina's lecture. *You didn't even try, Beth! What's going on with you? Seriously you need to take a few days off.* I wheeled around, prepared with a sigh and invitation for my best friend to give it a rest, only to find myself face-to-face with Adah. With her hands shoved into her jean pockets, perfectly windswept hair, and intent gaze, she looked just as tough and sexy as she had that first day. Before I'd opened my mouth and ruined everything. Twice.

"Hi." Adah smirked and... Damnit why did she have to look so good?

"Hi," I replied, shaking suds off my hands and quickly drying them on a damp, questionably clean towel.

"Look, I'm really sorry, okay? What you were saying made sense. I guess it just felt easier to think that you were, I don't know, some kinda spoiled brat or something. I think I'm just jealous, plain and simple. You make this all look so effortless and I'm having a rough time, barely keeping my head above water. This all seems like it's so easy for you. Clearly you're good at this. I saw it tonight. Tasted it. Your food is great. Seriously. Even Jay had to admit that your puff pastry is better than theirs. That mille-feuille with blueberries and...wait, what else was in that?" Adah had been talking rapid fire, her words bumping into each other. She sighed and ran a hand through her hair.

"Just a Bavarian cream with some fresh mint."

Adah nodded seriously, then opened her mouth, presumably to continue on with her apology speech.

I cut her off. "I'm the one who should apologize. I had no right to kiss you like that without asking. I don't know your situation and clearly my timing could use some work."

I forced myself to meet Adah's gaze and was surprised to find her expression soft.

"My situation?" Her words were slow…almost playful.

"Well, yeah. Is Jay your partner? I'm really sorry. I wasn't thinking…" My words died in my throat as Adah stepped toward me.

"No. They aren't. I want to kiss you again." Her voice dipped low, caressed my skin. "And then I want to talk. Okay?" She waited.

"Okay." The moment the word was out of my mouth, Adah's arms came around me and her lips crushed against mine.

Earlier, I'd been too overwhelmed by the confusing twist of desire and anger to pay attention to the kiss. Now, I let myself savor the firmness of Adah's lips, her strong fingers gripping my shoulders. She tasted like the mint from the dessert with a slight undercurrent of beer as I licked into her mouth. Everywhere our skin brushed sparked with pleasure. It was as though every fiber of my being shifted, aligned with her. I was dizzy with wanting, pushing up on my tiptoes to kiss Adah harder. I fumbled with her T-shirt, trying to untuck it from her jeans. Adah smiled against my mouth and pulled away gently. I chased her lips, but she stopped me, firm grip still on my shoulders.

"We should talk." Adah dragged a rough fingertip across my cheek. Talking was pretty much dead last on the list of things I wanted to do in that moment.

"Ugh fine. If we have to. We could totally keep making out though. The choice is yours." I flashed her my best smile.

"Can we sit down?" Adah asked. "I bet you've been on your feet all day."

She was right, so I led her out of the kitchen into the small, deserted indoor dining area. The hearth was cold and the lights were off. The party limped along outside, but inside it was quiet. I gestured to a small two-top. Adah pulled out a chair, gesturing for me to sit. I wanted to laugh at her old-school manners but bit my tongue.

I laced my fingers together, elbows resting on the table, and leaned forward. "So...what do you want to talk about?"

"Alright." Adah sat up a little straighter, like a kid who'd been called on by her favorite teacher. "I have three things I want to say."

"Just three?" I couldn't contain my amusement now.

Adah rolled her eyes. "Yep. Just three. May I?"

"By all means." I made a sweeping motion with my hand.

"Uh, well okay." She cleared her throat. "One: I want to say I'm sorry. I was extra touchy tonight because this critic is apparently coming to check us out. Marcus Blanche. He's doing a profile on New England restaurants." Adah said this all Very Seriously.

I shrugged. "Yeah I know. Marcus emailed me a few weeks ago to say he'd stop by this fall. I met him last time he was up here from New York. He's a good dude."

Color rose in Adah's cheeks and her calm mask slipped again. "Of course you already knew. My dang manager made it seem like the Second Coming. Told me to tighten things up." Her knee started bouncing against mine under the table.

I wanted to lean forward and smooth back the lock of

hair that had fallen in front of Adah's anguished face. I settled for a reassuring smile instead. "It's not a big deal. Seriously. These awards are all such bullshit anyway. And what the hell did your GM mean, tighten things up? Has business been bad or something?"

Adah grimaced. "Yeah, well, that's easy to say that when you've already won them." Her voice was small. She was right, too. I didn't know what it was like to be held accountable to anyone but myself, so any accolades we got were easy to shrug off. I'd never cared about external metrics of success. But no one had ever asked me to. And I definitely should not mention that success sometimes felt like more of a burden than a gift.

"Honestly," she continued, "I don't really know what Sean meant. He's always real passive-aggressive with me. I know he thinks I'm not good enough for this job. He doesn't have the authority to fire me but sometimes I feel like he's waiting for me to mess up. And I don't know..." She shrugged. "I mean I do know I'm good at this. I run an organized kitchen, my staff are happy, and my food's good. But sometimes I don't think it's good enough. Not quite mediocre...not quite great. Like why the heck am I still paying off loans from culinary school if I can't even win a dang regional food award?" Her voice went tight.

Sympathy for Adah bloomed in my chest. Was she always this hard on herself? It seemed an exhausting burden to bear, that heavy load of self-criticism. I reached across the table, gently covering her hands with mine. "I'm not going to bullshit you. I haven't tried your food, so I can't sit here and tell you everything's going to be okay. But I'm here to help in any way I can. We aren't competition—"

Adah stiffened, ready to argue. I shook my head. "We are not. As far as I'm concerned, we need to work together. This industry sucks for women and queer folks. I'm sick of all the macho bullshit. You care about what you do, and you deserve the chance to show people what you've got. I want to see you succeed. So, look, I know Marcus. He's one of the first people that gave a shit about what we were doing here. I know what he likes. How about I come to your restaurant and try some stuff? I can think through things the way he does."

Adah narrowed her eyes, her pretty face the picture of skepticism. "Why?" She lobbed the word at me like an accusation.

I snorted. "Well, for one because you're hot."

At this she visibly relaxed, rolling her eyes and waving a dismissive hand.

"And two." I wanted to continue but was suddenly at a loss for words. What was I supposed to say? *I like you? Something about you feels right? There's a bond between us I haven't felt in a long time, if ever?* "I… I don't know, you seem good. Like a good person. Or whatever." My voice had gone all scratchy and weird. *Ugh. Really smooth, Beth.*

Whatever it was though, I felt my words resonate. Adah softened again, threaded her fingers through mine. "Thanks," she murmured, so softly I hardly heard the word in the quiet.

"So what were the other two things?" I asked, giving her hand a fast squeeze.

"What?" She paused for a moment before laughing and shaking her head. "It doesn't matter."

"It does. Tell me."

Adah groaned. "Fine. You're pretty bossy, you know that?"

"Honey, you have no idea." I winked at her, hoping it was a cute wink, not an awkward eye twitch. I usually prided myself on my ability to be charming, but with Adah I felt a little raw, a little uncertain.

"Alright. Well, I was gonna tell you that I like you. See if maybe you want to go on a date sometime?" She was a little flushed and wouldn't meet my eye.

My joy shimmered up my spine. I grinned. It had been ages since I'd been asked on an honest to god date. Easy, casual sex, sure. Locking eyes with someone across a crowded bar, definitely. I knew how to have good sex and make my partners feel good. Knew how to satisfy my needs. But this earnest, simple question threw me. It made me want.

"Shoot," Adah sighed. "Sorry. Don't feel obligated—"

"Yes," I said quickly. "I want to go on a date with you. Yes. What was thing three?"

Now Adah really was blushing. It was kind of adorable. "Uh, I wanted to tell you that you're beautiful."

Chapter Nine

Adah

"You sure you have enough tomatoes there, sweetheart?" Vanessa smirked in the direction of the two overburdened canvas bags at my feet.

I grinned, eyeing another farm stand boasting a variety of colorful heirloom, beefsteak, and delicate orange cherry tomatoes that would be perfect for the Provençal tart I'd been thinking about making all week. The South Bay farmer's market was wonderful, almost as big as my neighborhood market in Chicago, but with the relaxed, communal feel of the roadside produce stands back in Missouri. I was a little irritated with myself for not having visited earlier. I'd tagged along with Vanessa at the last minute, realizing our apartment's refrigerator was looking pretty bare and that I could check out some of the local vendors Beth loved so much.

The thought of Beth glimmered over me like foxfire. After kissing me senseless the other night, Beth had pulled my phone out of my back pocket, screwed up her face at the lock screen, handed it back to me, and rattled off her number so I could type it in. Since then, we'd been messaging whenever we had a moment to spare. Mostly we chatted about food. Beth sent me a picture of the eels her dad and brother had brought in and we went back and forth for almost an hour about the best way to prepare them. On Thursday, when Sean came in, clearly hung over and moody as all get-out, it had been a relief to vent to Beth about my manager's bad attitude. As nice as all the messages had been, I wanted to see her again. Wanted to hear her pretty laugh and feel the firm press of her body against mine.

Finally, after much prodding from Jay at the end of last night's dinner service, I'd sent Beth a weirdly formal-sounding text asking if she was free to go out with me on Monday. She didn't always respond to messages right away. Neither did I. I knew we couldn't exactly check our phones every ten minutes while running our kitchens. But it had been almost eleven hours since I'd messaged her and my whole body seemed to turn itself inside out every time I got a news update or Jay texted me asking if I'd heard back from Beth. Logically, I knew Beth had been busy the night before. The Yellow House had hosted an engagement party that Beth expected would run late. But my mind ran off on me, imagining her rolling her eyes at my text and running into the arms of her gorgeous best friend or that big guy she'd been so cozy with at the benefit the weekend before.

I yanked my phone out the pocket of my jeans. Nothing.

This hot, sticky jealousy creeping up my spine was a new feeling for me. Sure, as a kid I'd been jealous of my brothers from time to time. Well, a lot if I was honest. I'd been jealous of their clothes, of the way my father treated them, of their freedom. But I'd never really liked anyone I'd dated enough to care this much before.

"Hey, Mom, is it okay if I go play with those guys?" I startled at the sound of my son's voice, almost dropping my phone onto the sidewalk. Peter pointed to a group of kids his age playing Frisbee in the shade of one of the park's established oaks. He was so different than I'd been at his age. Peter moved through the world with a kind of confidence I'd never known: asking new friends to play with him, speaking his mind, laughing freely.

"Sure, darlin. I think I could use a coffee anyway. You want one, Vanessa?" I tipped my head in the direction of a coffee roaster's stand.

"Oh god yes. Here, give me the bags and we can sit a minute. I don't know how you stay on your feet so long."

I returned a moment later to find Vanessa reclined under a tree, her usual paperback in hand, and Peter completely integrated into the game. After a few sips of coffee roasted a little darker than I usually liked, I, again, looked at my phone. Still nothing.

"Everything okay?" Vanessa set down her book and pinned me with one of her knowing looks. "I don't know if I've ever seen you check your phone so much."

I shrugged and tried to distract myself with my coffee,

which only caused me to burn the roof of my mouth taking a too-large gulp. Goodness gracious, I was a wreck. Then my phone did buzz in my hand. A shock of nervous, electric heat pinged through me until I saw it was Mac's number on the screen, asking about taking a day off at the end of next month. I locked the screen and sighed.

"You remember Beth? From the beach or whatever." My voice sounded all wobbly and small. I cleared my throat.

Vanessa beamed liked I'd pulled out a trophy in her honor. "Of course. Such a nice girl. You know I'm pretty sure she's single. And when she moved back, some folks wouldn't stop talking about how she dates women and men now. Honestly, people need to mind their own damn business."

"Yeah. I know." I tried not to sigh. As much as I hated talking about myself, I felt like I might dang near explode if I didn't let out some of the worry buzzing around my body. "I, uh, asked her on a date last night and she hasn't responded."

"Oh, honey. I'm sure she's just busy. You know how it is. Did you leave her a message or something?"

I laughed. "Texted her. We…hung out last week when I went to that dinner and we've been talking since. Since we both have Mondays off, I figured we could… I don't even know what to do on a dang date." One week and I was already in over my head.

Vanessa nodded slowly, eyes flicking from Peter back to me. "Well how has dating gone in the past for you?" Her voice was soft, clearly not wanting to push.

As close as we'd become over the past month of Vanessa basically helping to raise my child and making my life more tolerable than it had been in years, the woman had never asked me any prying questions about my personal life. And I appreciated that. My mama and her sisters had always been nosy, swapping secrets and gossiping during Bible study. Always asking me questions I knew I couldn't answer honestly. The professional kitchens I'd worked in weren't much better, buzzing with rumors like busy beehives. Since I was little I'd just tried to keep my head down and my mouth shut. But now I wanted advice. Needed it.

"Haven't done it much," I admitted, picking at the soft grass. "Peter wasn't exactly planned and his daddy was more of a friend than a boyfriend. I was just figurin' things out and ended up having to start my life all over again." My face burned hot at the memory of Jeremy. I tried never to think of him, tried not to wonder if he even knew he had a son as wonderful as the boy teaching a new friend to do a cartwheel a few yards away from me. "After that I had a girlfriend for a little bit but we just kinda fell into it. But since I started cooking seriously I haven't had time so…"

"Okay, well, do you want to spend more time with Beth?"

"Of course. I—" I cleared my throat again to keep myself from admitting the truth. *I can't stop thinking about her.* "But what do you even do on a date?"

Vanessa leaned forward and took my hands in hers. "Look, sweetheart, it's just about getting to know her better, okay? You're a wonderful person so you don't have anything to worry about. She'd be more than lucky to spend time with you. My Amber is a single mom, too, and I'll tell you the same thing I tell my darling daughter. You need to figure out if you can trust someone enough to let them into your child's life. It takes time and that's okay." She paused, gave my hands a hard squeeze, and let them go. "As for what to do on the date…whatever the hell you want! Get a drink, grab coffee, go for a walk. Just keep it low stakes, you know?"

A strange mix of emotions tangled up in my chest. A knee-jerk desire to insist that I knew I could trust Beth. The prickle of potential rejection. And the old familiar fear of letting anyone into my life. The weight of knowing how easy it was for people to let me down. "I probably don't even have time anyway. It's unfair to ask you to watch Peter this much as it is and it's selfish of me to ignore my son—"

"Oh, for fuck's sake, Adah. Stop beating yourself up all the goddamn time." Vanessa delivered this expletive-laden command with a fond grin. "Do you want me to get a tattoo on my forehead saying how much I love watching your son? And you know you're allowed to have a life of your own. It'll make you a better parent. Balance and all that."

Her words cut through me, a sharp but welcome shock. My mama had never taken a moment for herself. She woke up before the sun, cooking and cleaning and teaching and praying without pausing for a breath. I'd never seen my mama share a cup of coffee with a friend or even sit down to read a book that wasn't the Bible. I knew better than anything I didn't want to raise Peter the way she'd raised me.

I nodded, leaned back to let the sun warm my face, shining red through my closed eyelids. "I think you just might be right."

Our usually tidy apartment was now an explosion of summer produce and Legos. In the kitchen I scrubbed, chopped, and stored food for the week ahead, setting aside the ingredients I'd bought for Bella Vista to bring over later. In the living room Peter grumbled to himself as he set to work building some gigantic Lego castle I'd bought him for his birthday the year before. His disinterest in the gift had shifted into obsession after we'd checked out a book of medieval stories at the library the week before.

"Darlin," I called over the sizzle of cubed eggplant frying in olive oil on the stove, "you want a sandwich or leftover curry from last night?"

"Curry," Peter shouted back.

"Curry what?"

"Please!" I could almost hear the eye roll in my son's voice.

I smiled, basking in a rush of warm affection for my son, and pulled the glass container of green curry out of the fridge. Peter was a good kid. I was doing my best to be a decent mom. We were gonna be just fine even if it was just the two of us. My conversation with Vanessa had smoothed out the rough edges enough that I'd started checking my phone every twenty minutes instead of every five. Still no word from Beth. Fine. That was totally a-okay. If she didn't want to go on a date with me, it was her loss. I didn't even care.

"Hey Mom," Peter called. I cut the heat on the stove and wandered into the living room.

"What's up, honey?" I lowered myself to sit across from him. The Lego castle was about a third completed and I watched as he painstakingly looked for the right piece.

"Do you know what class I'm gonna be in next year?"

"Yeah." I searched my brain for the name of his third-grade teacher. "Mr. O'Brien's class."

He heaved a wildly dramatic sigh. "Can you change it?"

"Change it? You mean put you in a different class?"

Peter nodded. "Uh-huh. Jason has Mrs. Gonzalez and he says she's nicer."

I felt confusion descend on my face. "Jason?"

Peter pinned me with one of his *duh, Mom* looks. "My friend from the park. He lives on our street."

"Sure." I picked up one of the small plastic bricks, turning it over in my hands. "I can call the school on Monday and check. I don't think they'll put you in a new class though, bud. Wanting to be with your friend might not be a good enough reason."

Silence settled between us for a long moment. Then, casual as anything, Peter asked, "How come you don't have any friends here?"

A laugh burst from my mouth. "I have friends. What about Jay?"

My son shook his head like I was a complete lost cause. "Jay was already your friend before. You told me like a million times it's important to make new friends too."

Great, now my son was throwing my own darn advice back in my face. "I did make a new friend." Why I was defending myself I wasn't quite sure. "Remember Beth from when we went to the beach with Vanessa? She's my friend too." I needed to do some reading up to learn about how and when to have this conversation with my kid. If Beth ever texted me back, that was.

Peter nodded, apparently satisfied with my friend-making abilities, and refocused on building his castle. After a minute or so I stood, hoping the eggplant hadn't gotten too oily while my son tried to fix his own mother's life.

The bright screen of my phone caught my eye and my heart did a backflip in my chest when I saw Beth's name.

Hey!! So sorry that it took me a zillion years to respond! The event last night was bananas. One of our servers was a no-show so yeah... Then I had to check out a new farm this morning so no reception. But YES! I'd love to hang out Monday. Is around noon okay for you? I can pick you up!

Trying to ignore my shaking fingers and tamp down the worry that I might seem overeager by responding right away, I quickly tapped out a reply.

Sure. Noon is good. What do you want to do?

This time, thankfully, Beth's response was immediate.

Hope you like surprises! Oh and make sure you bring a swim-suit 😄

Chapter Ten

Beth

I couldn't quite tell what was going on with my body as I eased my car along the curb to park in front of Adah's apartment. Maybe the third cup of coffee this morning had been a mistake, because my heart pounded erratically in my chest and my eyes couldn't seem to focus on anything in particular. A small voice in the back of my head reminded me that I was probably just nervous about going on an actual date with a woman I actually liked. But I didn't get nervous. Not when big-name critics came into the restaurant. Not when I'd given my phone number to the gorgeous drummer of my favorite band after one of their shows. Not even when I'd decided to open up The Yellow House. I took things in stride, did things my own way, and figured if something was meant to be the universe would work it out.

Now, though, looking up at the weathered cedar shingles siding Adah's three-flat apartment building, my throat felt gritty and hot, like I'd forgotten to drink water for a week. Forcing myself to take in a few centering breaths, I texted Adah that I was outside. As soon as I hit send though, a new wave of nerves crashed over me. Had that been rude? Would she want me to come up? Was I supposed to ring the doorbell like a goddamn prom date in a teen movie? Fuck. This was why I didn't do this whole dating thing. Too many rules and way too many chances to mess everything up. Hamlet whined in the backseat like he knew exactly how I felt.

Then there she was. Bounding down the stairs, sun catching the gold of her hair. I had to laugh because I had already guessed the exact outfit she'd be wearing: white T-shirt over her dark swimsuit, her usual workwear jeans, and a pair of heavy-looking brown boots. It was easily eighty degrees and I wondered idly if Adah even owned a pair of shorts. She was gorgeous regardless of what she wore, but I loved the simplicity of her style. She wore her basic, masculine pieces like they'd been made just for her.

I opened my door and tumbled out of the car with far less grace than I'd hoped, my sandal getting tangled on the hem of my skirt. Oh well.

"Hey." Adah stopped a couple feet short of me and pushed a hand into her hair, eyes dropping from my face to the sidewalk.

I stepped closer to her, inhaling her clean soap smell, and beamed. "Hi."

"I, uh, didn't know what we were doing but I figured nothing too fancy if I'm supposed to wear a swimsuit?"

I wanted to wrap my arms around her narrow waist and pull her close. Wanted to push up on my tiptoes and press my mouth to hers. And normally I wouldn't hesitate. But that damn nervous feeling reared its ugly head again so I fiddled with one of my bracelets instead. "Nothing fancy. Have you been up to Granite Harbor yet?" Hamlet stuck his giant head out the back window, trying to greet Adah, who looked between the two of us a little warily. "I hope it's okay I brought my dog."

Adah shrugged. "Dang, Peter's gonna be jealous. He loved that dog. Won't stop bugging me to get one since he met him." Adah eyed Hamlet for a long moment, then gently stroked the top of his head. He leaned into her touch the way I wanted to. "But no, I haven't really been anywhere yet other than your place—uh, restaurant—the other night. Too busy."

I hadn't exactly gotten out much this summer either but feigned shock anyway. "Okay well hop in. Granite Harbor is a disgustingly quaint coastal town that will be way too overrun with tourists to actually enjoy. So I'm taking you to my super-secret swim spot a few miles north of there. And I brought snacks."

As I pulled onto the highway and out of town, the tiny bit of small talk we'd exchanged about the weather and how busy the weekend rush had been died into not quite easy silence. Admittedly, I loved to talk. Not that I hated silence or anything, but I liked hearing what other people had to say. Liked finding out what made them brighten and start talking fast with big wild gestures. So, after my questions about Adah's music preferences were greeted with short, almost terse answers, I wondered if maybe I'd been mistaken about the promise of chemistry between us.

I kept my eyes on the road, admiring the expanse of clear blue sky and the quick transition from the not-quite-urban landscape of South Bay to miles of shimmering coastline. Tori Amos crooned softly through my car's less than stellar stereo system as I pulled off the highway and onto a heavily wooded county road.

"Okay," I tried again, hoping I wasn't actively making Adah miserable. "What's the worst first date question you've ever gotten?"

From the corner of my eye I saw Adah turn toward me, her eyebrows drawn together. "First date question?"

"Yeah, you know, like, *tell me about yourself* or *what's your story*. That kind of crap. Small talk questions pretending to distil you down to a simple version of yourself." I stuck my tongue out in disgust, remembering a very bad date with a very handsome man in San Francisco who had peppered me with dozens of such questions but never gave me the chance to actually answer.

"Um, I haven't really been on a lot of dates." Adah's voice was low.

"Me either." I shrugged. "Lots of hookups, I guess, but not a lot of honest to god, pick-you-up-for-dinner dates. I get bored easily, I guess. To be honest I think I've only *dated*—" I put scare quotes around the word, "—two or three people. And one was in high school so I feel like that basically doesn't count. Kevin, the dude you met and glared daggers at last weekend at the benefit."

Adah laughed, blushing a little. "Yeah. You know, just

with Peter and getting through culinary school I didn't have that much time for myself, let alone somebody else."

I wanted to ask Adah if she mostly dated women even though it couldn't have mattered less to me. I was just nosy and always liked the part of hanging out with other queer folks when we talked through our identities, swapped coming out stories, laughed about silly stereotypes. I had a feeling, though, that particular topic might spook Adah, so I steered the conversation into calmer waters.

"So you went to culinary school in Chicago, right? How did you like it?"

"Yup. I liked it fine, I suppose. It was definitely something to learn all of the fancy techniques and sauces and things I'd never even heard of growing up. I'm glad I went, because I wasn't making much as a line cook and it was nice to learn how to make something more than cornbread and chicken-fried steak."

I looked over at Adah, glad to find she'd relaxed back into her seat, the soft summer breeze ruffling her hair. "I couldn't hack it," I admitted. "Culinary school, I mean. I tried to go for pastry when I was living in California but it was all so rigid. Not my scene at all. If I had to make another fucking sugar flower, I thought I was going to have an honest to god temper tantrum."

Adah stayed quiet for a long moment and I worried I'd offended her. Then she grinned. "Yeah I can't see you listening to anyone telling you how to do…well, anything."

I had to chuckle at just how right she was. "So you cooked a lot growing up? I was always helping my mom around the café but I didn't really start liking it until high school. Until I realized I could make stuff up on my own.

Then once I decided to open The Yellow House it was cool because I could decide exactly how I wanted to do things. Grow my own food, buy from who I want, cook whatever I feel like. What got you into it? Made you like it, I mean." I was so caught up in talking that I almost missed the turn onto the mostly hidden gravel road leading to the beach. My dad had sworn me to secrecy, hoping to keep this small stretch of rocky coast from the hordes of tourists that descended on southern coastal Maine each summer.

"Yeah I did." Adah sounded a little wary. "I kinda had to, I guess. I was the only girl in the family. Six brothers. My mama needed help and, well, I guess because I'm a girl I was the one to do it. But after a while I realized I was good at it. That I liked it. We did a lot of cooking for the church, pancake breakfasts, bake sales, spaghetti suppers, that kinda thing. The kitchen ended up turning into my favorite place in the house. Quiet. Safe."

Something about the weight of the word *safe* didn't sit quite right with me, like a brick tossed into a still pond. But I knew better than to push. Instead I parked in the shade of a big pine and cut the ignition. Outside the air was alive with the rushing of wind through leaves and the chatter of birds. Inside the car was silent. Well, silent aside from Hamlet's steady panting in the backseat.

"We'll have to hike a little to get to the beach, is that okay with you?" I turned to Adah, again overcome with the desire to close the distance between us and brush my lips against hers. Her hair was trimmed closer on the sides than it had been a week ago. The thought that she'd maybe gotten her hair cut to look her best for this date flooded me with affection for her.

"Yup. I like hiking. Haven't had much time to exercise since I've been up here."

"Alright then." I leaned over the center console and gave in to the desire to press a fast kiss to Adah's cheek, clearly startling her. "Let's go."

Unsurprisingly, Adah was quiet as we walked along the narrow, overgrown path to the ocean. Hamlet bounded ahead of us, stopping every once in a while to wait for us to catch up. Questions to ask Adah ricocheted around my mind, but somehow breaking the silence between us felt almost sacrilegious. Normally I would chatter away about the restaurant, my family, or the latest podcast I'd been listening to, but I wanted to give Adah the space to talk if and when she felt ready. I let my mind drift out to the sound of the waves lapping against the rocks ahead, the sharp scent of pine mingling with the tang of salt air. I relished the warm sun on my skin and the cool patches of dappled shade. Slowly my body relaxed and my mind quieted. As we walked I scanned the forest floor, looking for wild blueberry bushes or lambs quarters. Then I spotted it. Without thinking I grabbed Adah's hand and tugged her off the barely maintained path.

"A lady slipper." I reached down to brush aside some of the pine needles obscuring the soft pink orchid. But almost as quickly as I moved, Ada's fingers closed around my wrist.

"Wait." Her voice was almost pained. "Don't pick it."

Rising to stand, I took a long look at Adah's face. Her lips were pressed into a firm line and her eyebrows crashed together. When she glanced down at me, her cheeks colored. In that moment I was overwhelmed with tenderness for her. I realized as much as she tried to be tough, she was a total softie beneath that cold exterior.

"Sorry." She huffed out a small laugh. "I looked at this article about living here and it said you shouldn't ever pick those. They take a real long time to grow back." Adah shook her head and dragged a hand over her face. "Anyway, I like it here. Reminds me of home a little." The tone of her voice shifted, embarrassment transmuting to sadness. "I mean, not the ocean obviously, but the woods. I miss the quiet."

Torn between wanting to kiss her for being so adorable, wanting to set the record straight that I hadn't been planning to pick the lady slipper, and wanting to descend on the scrap of information about her past like Hamlet going after leftovers, I nodded and took a deep breath. "Yeah I missed it up here too. Before I moved back up to Maine I was living in New Orleans. It was awesome, but nothing beats the solitude of nature." Okay, maybe I was laying it on a little too thick. I liked solitude about as much as I liked restaurants that called appetizers appe-teasers. "Did you grow up in a rural part of Missouri, then?"

Adah nodded, adjusting her backpack. "Yup. The Ozarks. Little town in the middle of nowhere. Not even in town, we had a farm up in the hills. I miss it some. Can't ever go back though."

I stopped on the path, turning to face Adah. Her cheeks were still a little flushed, like she was embarrassed she'd said anything about herself at all. "Could you tell me more? About you, I mean. Like is it okay for me to ask you questions about yourself?" The words felt a little silly as they left my mouth, but I was serious. As much as I wanted to know more about this mysterious woman, the last thing I wanted to do was push or make her feel awkward. God knew I had a talent for asking too many questions and occasionally overwhelming people. Was I doing something wrong? Clearly, she wasn't exactly comfortable with chit-chat, much less deep talks about her past.

Adah's blush deepened but she nodded. Damn, she was adorable when that tough façade slipped. I took her hand in mine and led her out to the sea.

Chapter Eleven

Adah

I couldn't look away. Never in my life had I seen something so beautiful. The sun shimmered off the water, almost turquoise where it lapped against the dark rocky shore, stretching out to a deep, flat blue. Seaweed drifted and bobbed in time with the steady beat of the current. In the distance small white sailboats glided along the horizon. The air smelled good. Clean and salty with the slight, faraway edge of someone grilling meat over charcoal.

I turned to Beth, the breeze tumbling through her hair and pressing the thin fabric of her skirt tight to her legs. Okay, she was just as beautiful as this place. But it was a close tie.

"I think the blanket and towels are in your bag," she

said, shouldering off her backpack and setting it down on a large, flat rock.

Beth's giant beast of a dog, who I now realized was about as scary as a newborn chick, made a beeline for the water, swimming a few small circles before clambering back out to shake all over us. A laugh erupted from my chest but died right away at the sight of Beth pulling her T-shirt over her head. Her red bikini was, well, small, and I had to try real hard to tear my eyes away from her smooth, creamy skin to focus on pulling the picnic blanket out of my bag.

I cleared my throat as I shook out the blanket onto the sun-warm rock. "Here?"

"Perfect." Beth raised her eyebrows suggestively but her smile was soft. "I think I need to get some sun before I swim. Are you hungry yet?"

"I could eat," I said, tugging my shirt over my head and stepping out of my jeans. I'd been glad the one bathing suit I owned, a black one-piece I'd bought when I'd been training unsuccessfully for a triathlon, still fit.

Next to me, Beth's breath hitched. I glanced at her to find her big brown eyes had gone even bigger and locked on me. She wasn't even trying to hide her desire as her lips parted and she moved a fraction closer. Half of me liked being wanted, itching to run my fingers along the curve of her hip, tighten my grip, and pull her against me. The other half of me wanted to hightail it back to the road and try my luck as a hitchhiker. She must have sensed my hesitation, because her body softened and she turned to busy herself with the food.

Dang it. I tried not to groan in frustration. Why did this always happen to me? Once I knew I liked someone, knew how much I wanted them, I clammed up. Talking was hard enough. Trying to kiss her...well, I might as well have been trying to make consommé with my hands tied and my nose plugged.

Beth sat down cross-legged and gestured for me to sit across from her. "Okay, I have prepared for us today..." Her voice was such an over-the-top version of the *listing the specials* tone, I had to laugh. "Raspberry sun tea, smoked fontina and grilled eggplant on homemade rosemary ciabatta, and a blackberry kumquat cake for dessert." She plated the food expertly on blue enamelware and slid my lunch in front of me.

I wanted to tell her more about myself. Wanted to explain why I was so dang taciturn. Wanted to let her get to know me, whatever the heck that even meant. I opened my mouth to speak, and instead of the thoughtful words I'd arranged in my head, what came out was a low, "Sorry, I guess I'm kinda nervous."

The blanket bunched between us as Beth scooted closer. "Me too. Which is actually really weird because I don't do nervous. So we're in it together." She grinned. I loved the way her smile crinkled the corners of her eyes, the way it turned her whole face into sunshine.

I took a bite of my sandwich, chewing slowly to appreciate the softness of the bread, the way the bright, herby tapenade she'd spread on the eggplant contrasted with the richness of the cheese. She really knew how to build flavors and work with texture, I had to give her that.

Setting my plate down, I took a long breath. I could do this. I could tell this woman, who I really liked, who seemed to actually like me, a few things about myself.

"Okay," I started, my voice sounding kind of shaky. "I told you I grew up in the Ozarks. My father was a pastor. A few years after my oldest brother was born, he started this church, a Pentecostal one, if you know what that is. Basically his ministry was a whole lot of gospel and a whole lot of trying to make sure everyone we met believed the same things he did." I paused to take a long sip of tea to steady my nerves and soothe my throat, which had gone all scratchy. The tea, like the sandwich, was somehow a little more delicious than I'd expected and I smiled.

"Hey, you don't have to tell me anything. Sorry if I was being nosy before. I just, like, love asking questions and sometimes I get carried away and end up acting like a total dick." Beth's hand found my forearm and gave a soft squeeze.

I shook my head. "No. I want to tell you. I mean, I hate talking about myself. But I want you to know. Anyway, long story short, my dad was a jerk and my mama didn't do anything about it. My brothers and I were all home-schooled so I guess I didn't know any different. I mean he wasn't abusive or nothing…just yelled a lot, broke stuff, made us copy Scripture for hours if he didn't like how we acted. I was the youngest, though, by kind of a lot, and by the time I was supposed to start high school the congregation had grown a whole bunch and my mama got to be too busy with church business to teach me, so I went to the public school a few towns over." A bitter laugh escaped my lips at the memory of me on my first day of ninth grade. Long blond hair that never felt right, all done up in braids that felt even worse. Homemade clothes. Wide-eyed at the sight of so many kids, so many voices, so much difference.

"I was a sight that first day, I'll tell you that. Kids weren't nice to the weird church girl. But then after a few days I met Emily. She was probably the first real friend I ever had. She was one of the only Black kids at school, and a lot of the other kids and even some of the teachers treated her like a complete outsider. It was awful. We got close and then by the time I was a junior we were, well, we were real close. My brother Tim found us together in the barn and told the rev—my dad. It wasn't pretty. I got pulled out of school, had to start working at the church full-time. Never saw Emily again." My voice got all funny and Beth gave my arm another reassuring squeeze, like she knew I needed to be reminded I was here with her and not back in the reverend's study.

"Anyway, the day I turned seventeen my mama brought Jeremy over. His daddy had grown up with the reverend. He was a missionary and they were looking to settle back down. They wanted Jeremy to court me. I guess they hoped the whole thing with Emily was a fluke. Honestly back then I kinda hoped it was, too. And Jeremy was nice. Handsome. He was probably the most interesting person I ever met since he'd lived all over. So yeah, that's how Peter, uh, happened. Turned out after a few times trying I realized I didn't really like sleeping with men, but I didn't exactly know back then that I could undo getting pregnant. I thought my mama might understand. But when I told her, well, she didn't." My eyes were dry and hot, burning so bad I had to squish them shut.

"Adah." Beth's voice was gentle and close to my ear. "I'm so sorry."

"Nah. It was fine." I cleared my throat and opened my

eyes to take in the wide expanse of ocean. "A few days after I told her I hitched a ride to St. Louis and figured it out. That's when I started cooking—line cook at a diner. It all worked out for the best."

Beth's arms slipped around me and her scent, all wood smoke and lavender, was everywhere. She pressed her lips to my temple and the combination of the gestures was shockingly intimate. Soothing. We stayed like that for a long time, close and quiet under the hot summer sun. I couldn't remember the last time someone had just held me like this. Wasn't sure if anyone ever had. Somehow, Beth knew she didn't have to say a word. Knew there was nothing to say.

Goodness knows how long we would have stayed tangled up like that if Hamlet hadn't returned from one of his swims and shaken droplets of ice-cold seawater all over us. Beth startled and laughingly told off her dog. Little by little, I seemed to come back into my own body. Standing up, I took a long moment to stretch and feel the heat of the sun on my skin. I felt odd. Tired but also somehow lighter. Maybe Jay was on to something with the whole *talking about your problems* thing.

"Should we swim?" Beth asked, pulling her tangle of hair up into a bun on the top of her head. I noticed, for the first time, a tiny tattoo on her shoulder: a series of delicately rendered stars clustered in a Y shape. I trailed my finger along it and Beth's expression shifted from thoughtful to almost comically excited. "Yes! I almost forgot. When's your birthday?"

"Sure, we can swim if you want." I shook my head and laughed. "And it's September second. Why?"

Eyebrows shooting toward her hairline, Beth clapped

her hands together and squealed. "Oh my god. Seriously? You're a Virgo? Okay well you better wife me up now because we are like bonkers compatible."

I couldn't help it, she was so ridiculous and excited and so darn cute, I pulled her into my arms and bent, pausing with my lips close to hers. Beth drew in a slow, shaky breath and I knew in that moment she and I wanted the exact same thing. Our eyes locked and my breath went shallow. "Can I kiss you?" I asked.

"Yes, please."

It started soft and gentle, my lips brushing hers, my eyes drifting shut. A small sound escaped her lips and heat unfurled low in my belly. Everything but the slide of her tongue into my mouth, the pressure of her breasts against mine through the thin fabric of my swimsuit, fell away. My hands skimmed down her body, coming to rest on her hips, pulling her impossibly closer.

When Beth's lips grazed over my cheek then down, I shivered and pulled away. Everything in me wanted to keep going. Wanted to lay her down on that picnic blanket and kiss every inch of her. But we were outside in broad daylight. Anyone could see us. Well, if anyone had been around, that was.

"Are you okay?" Beth's voice was a little hoarse.

"Yeah." The word came out harsher than I'd meant it. "Let's swim."

Without another word, Beth leapt into the ocean, popping up a few yards away from the churning water of her giant splash. Taking the safer, more sensible route, I walked over to a spot where the rock sloped gently into the water and…holy cow it was freezing. Like take-your breath-away ice cold. I couldn't help it, I shrieked. High-pitched, and loud enough to echo back to my ears, mocking me.

"Shoulda jumped in." Beth floated on her back, looking way too pleased with herself.

"Okay but is this water even safe to swim in? I don't want to die of hypothermia or something."

"It's fine once you get used to it. This is about as warm as it gets. Seriously." Beth plunged underwater again, resurfacing right back where she'd taken the plunge. "Jump in over here. Just get it over with."

I thought about staying on the rocks. Lying in the sun and maybe having another piece of cake. But I knew I couldn't resist Beth, looking like a real-life mermaid. Her hair, already escaped from the bun she'd pulled it into, streamed down her back in dark copper waves and her pale skin had an almost otherworldly glow underwater. Before I could doubt myself for another second, I jumped off the rock and into the water.

The cold cut through me, surrounded me, and then as I came up for air, settled into a tolerable, buzzing numbness. My breath came fast but I felt…good. My body felt almost liquid, like the cold had dissolved me.

"You did it." Beth wrapped her arms around my neck and then we were right back where we'd left off onshore. Pushing my fingers into the wet strands of her hair, I tipped her face up to meet mine. Her lips were cold and a little salty and perfectly soft. This time I kept my eyes open, taking in her flushed, freckled cheeks and damp lashes, searing the moment into my mind. Then her tongue grazed mine and my eyes drifted shut, my world narrowing to thick desire and tingling sensation. I lifted her up easily in the water and she wrapped her legs around my waist, both of us moaning softly at the increased contact. Her breasts pressed against me and I shifted her weight to hold her up with one hand as the other slid under the fabric of her bikini top.

"Oh god," Beth moaned into my mouth as my fingers circled her nipple, hard from the cold water and arousal. My thighs clenched and my whole body throbbed with want. I knew if she so much as touched me I wouldn't want to stop until we both came. And part of me wanted that, wanted to let go, wanted to give in to that temptation.

Instead I slipped my hand back down her stomach and moved my lips to her shoulder, peppering her skin with light kisses.

"Fuck." Her breath came fast and shallow. "I want you so much."

"Me too." My voice sounded strange, rough. "But, um, we're outside so…"

Beth rolled her eyes and released a dramatic sigh. "Fine. You're no fun at all." She tapped a kiss to the tip of my nose and dove back into the freezing water.

Running my fingers through my hair to smooth it away from my face, I took stock of myself. My fingers and toes were freezing while my insides seemed to be burning up. I was buoyant, almost fizzy, energy pinging through me. When was the last time I'd felt so present in my own body? So in control? I must have zoned out, because when I looked up, Beth was back onshore, towel drying her hair and laughing as Hamlet tried to chase a crab, the dog looking confused when it disappeared into a small crack in the rocks.

"Hey," I called, hurrying to join her in the warm afternoon sun. "No fair."

"I didn't want to disturb you. You looked very meditative."

"I was just thinking about how much I like being with you." The words came out before I could stop them, but as they left my lips, I realized the weight of their truth.

Chapter Twelve

Adah

"Whoever invented brunch should be crucified." Jay collapsed onto one of the stools along the counter looking into the kitchen. Bella Vista would be closed for the next three hours, just enough time for us to clean up and regroup for dinner service.

"Hey now. That's blasphemous to gays and Christians alike." I laughed, whipping a towel over my shoulder and rolling my neck. Brunch had been wildly busy, with an hour-long wait at the height of service. As much as I hated plating up boring iterations of lobster Benedict and realizing one of my line cooks couldn't poach an egg to save his life, it was nice to be busy. Even Sean had seemed happy by the time the last mimosa-tipsy customers stumbled out.

"Seriously though, why the fuck did we have to start doing brunch? Like, aren't we better than this? I mean, smoked salmon on waffles… That shit is gross." Jay took a long sip of coffee and I took a moment to study their face. Usually they practically glowed, radiant tan skin and bright dark eyes. But today they looked exhausted. And unhappy. I chose to ignore the jab about the salmon and waffles, a dish I thought actually worked pretty well after I'd started making the waffles with grated potato and dill.

"Everything okay?" Even though I had about ten thousand things to do to get ready for dinner, I slid onto the stool next to my friend.

"Yeah sorry for being a dick." Jay sighed and rubbed their eyes roughly. "I'm fine."

"Okay." I drew out the word, knowing Jay was about as good at keeping their emotions bottled up as I was at letting mine out.

"Fine, ugh. Remember Nina, that gorgeous woman from the dance party thing? The one who works with your enemy over at The Yellow House?" I barely had time to nod before Jay continued. "Well we hooked up and it was good. Like really good. And the next morning we did the whole breakfast together, phone number swap. I even followed her on Instagram for fuck's sake. And then nothing. I texted her to see if she wanted to get a drink the next weekend and nada. I mean, what the hell? Like you would tell me if I smell bad or something, right? First Amy, now this… Pretty soon I'm going to develop a complex." Jay laughed but there wasn't a scrap of joy in it.

I gave their shoulder a quick squeeze. "You know you're perfect in every way. And—" I leaned in to sniff their hair, which smelled a little like the kitchen but mostly like the woodsy pomade they used in it, "—you smell just fine. What happened with Amy anyway?" It had been so out of character for Jay not to talk about it that I'd been afraid to ask.

"Ugh I don't even know. When we started looking at condos she got all weird. Like I wanted to look in Rogers Park and stuff but she was dead set on all these fancy places in River North and the West Loop. A bunch of those stupid yuppie hellhole 'lofts.' Then all the sudden she starts talking about moving out to the suburbs and asking me about looking into jobs with more *financial security*. Seriously, she must have said those two words about six million times. And then she just left."

"Her loss," I said softly but the words felt too small.

Jay brightened, swiveling their stool to face me. "Hey, well if we're still lonely sad sacks by the time we're fifty, you and I can just get married. It'll be the platonic romance for the ages."

Try as I might to keep my cool, I knew my face flushed red and my whole body tensed up.

"Oh no," Jay whispered in mock horror, "don't tell me you've been in love with me this whole time."

I shoved them lightly, forcing out a hoarse laugh instead of actually speaking.

"Holy shit. No way. You hooked up with the hot witch lady, didn't you? And you didn't tell me? Some friend you are."

Now my laughter wasn't forced. "Witch lady?"

"Yeah you know she's got that whole earthy one-with-the-universe thing going on. That woman for sure owns like six tarot decks. And you totally had sex with her."

You could get a good sear on a steak if you set it on my face at that moment. I sent out a silent prayer that none of the servers clearing tables behind us heard our conversation. "No, my goodness. We kissed and then hung out a few times." My throat felt thick all of a sudden. "I think I really like her. Was planning to invite her over to have dinner with me and Peter tomorrow. Is that stupid? Maybe it's too soon. I feel like she's maybe out of my league or something."

"Um, it's stupid that you think she's out of your league," Jay scoffed. "One because the whole concept of 'leagues' is trash, and two because you're fucking brilliant and gorgeous and the best goddamn chef in the world. She should be psyched to get to know you."

I looked at my best friend for a long moment, endlessly grateful that they'd ended up in my life. "You know it ain't polite to swear."

I slid the last golden-brown pancake onto the platter and carried it out to the tiny bistro table on the porch. My son, his eyes glued to a YouTube video on his iPad, barely registered my existence. A quick glance at my phone told me his daily twenty-five minutes of screen time was up.

"Put it away." I gestured to the tablet and slid into my chair.

"But there's ten minutes left. I wanna know what the last gift is!" Peter shot me a glare but locked the screen.

"Well I suppose you'll find out tomorrow. Now eat your breakfast before it gets cold."

My son stabbed his pancake with a little too much force but didn't argue otherwise. His new friend Jason had apparently gotten him obsessed with weird videos of other kids taking electronics and toys out of boxes. I had no clue what the appeal of this stuff was but it didn't seem like it was hurting anybody. My mind wandered to my nephews, two toddlers I'd barely known before skipping town. I was sure most of, if not all, my brothers would have kids by now. Christopher's wife already had a third baby on the way when I left home. I guessed they all had big, churchgoing families by now. Did their kids watch YouTube videos or had my brothers followed in the reverend's footsteps, banning all popular culture from the sacred walls of the home? A tide of guilt swelled up hot in my throat at the thought that my son would never know his cousins.

I shook my head to clear the thought. I didn't need them and they didn't need me. I could love Peter enough for all of them.

"Do we have to clean today?" Peter groaned as he dragged a slice of strawberry through the maple syrup on his plate.

"Yep. I told you. Beth's coming over for dinner and I don't want her stepping on six hundred Legos." I paused, letting my gaze wander out to the small stretch of glittering ocean visible from our porch. "You sure you're okay with her having dinner with us? It's okay if you don't want her to…"

"Mom." Peter sighed, a very world-weary sigh for a nine-year-old. "I already told you it's fine. Besides, once I start school I'm gonna be busy. You'll need to hang out with someone other than Jay and Ms. Vanessa."

I reached across the table to ruffle his hair, which I noted was overdue for a trim. "Alright bud, once you pick up your toys and help me clean the bathroom you're free to go."

My son's whole face lit up and he rocketed out of his seat. "Okay, I'll get it done. After do you think I can go over to Jason's house? His dads said they would take us to the park today to run some soccer drills."

Leave it to my son to befriend the kid on our block with queer parents. I'd met Jason's dads a few times. They were nice, if slightly dull, guys. The kind of people who wore polo shirts and talked a lot about the weather. They were folks I'd be more than happy to chat with at playdates and school events but would probably never want to have over for a meal.

Beth, on the other hand... I couldn't wait to see her for dinner. Tonight. In my apartment. In my kitchen. Eating my food.

After our picnic we'd started talking even more, sometimes chatting on the phone for hours after we'd finished cooking for the night. My body was definitely suffering from the lack of shut-eye but I didn't mind being tired if it meant I got to hear her voice every night. She told me about her family: a boisterous, loving group that made me wish I had grown up in a different home. I told her about mine. We both griped about how busy and exhausted we were, how the summer was slipping away from us into an endless stream of unrelenting work. And we talked about food. Swapped recipes, argued about technique, and last night, bickered about what to make for dinner. The conversation, admittedly a tad frustrating because Beth refused to agree that she should sit back and relax while I did all the work, had kept a smile on my face until I drifted off to sleep. It had been the first time I'd ever been able to argue about dinner with someone who wasn't my son or a cranky restaurant manager.

Now, Beth was due over in less than a half hour. I was fine. Definitely not nervous at all. Everything was ready. The kitchen had been scrubbed within an inch of its life, the windows were thrown open to coax in the ocean breeze, and my son had managed not to track in too much mud from his soccer game. I'd even found a spare minute to stop by the Middle Eastern market on the west end of town, stocking up on too many spices and coming up with a solid meal plan for tonight.

I scrolled through my playlists for what felt like the thousandth time. Usually I turned up the Dolly Parton and Willie Nelson while cooking...but maybe Beth thought country music was trashy? I was just about to google "best music for dates" on my phone when a sharp knock sounded at the door. My spine tensed on instinct and a cold shudder danced over my skin. Then I turned and saw Beth through the window and everything went warm and soft.

Her hair was half clipped back, showing off her bright eyes and the dusting of freckles along the bridge of her nose. She wore a loose, daisy-print sundress with a flannel thrown over and a bright grin just for me.

I smiled back and pulled open the door. "You look nice," I said without thinking, cringing a little at how cheesy it sounded.

"Thanks!" Pressing up on her tiptoes, she kissed my cheek while awkwardly balancing the two canvas tote bags draped over her shoulder. "So do you. I like the shirt." She tugged on the collar of my denim button down.

"What's all this?" I gestured to the bags.

"Oh just a couple things for dinner," Beth said a little too innocently.

Peter's bedroom door banged open and my son slid on socked feet into the kitchen. Not a shy bone in his body. "Hi. Did you bring your dog?"

Beth tossed her head back, laughing. "No sorry. I didn't know if dogs were allowed at your house, so I left him at my mom's place." She stuck out her hand. "I'm Beth by the way. I don't know if we've been formally introduced."

Peter shook her hand and grinned. "Peter. Well, actually I think I'm gonna start asking people to call me Pete. I like that better."

This was news to me, but I kept silent, weirdly nervous that my son might not like Beth or the other way around. Although if Beth didn't like kids there wasn't a chance things were going to work out between us.

"Mom, can she bring her dog next time? I can take him for walks and stuff. I already asked Miss Vanessa and she said it's fine."

Trying not to cringe at the thought of my son trying to control that giant animal, I nodded.

"So should I call you Pete, then?" Beth asked, unloading bunch after bunch of greens from one of the bags.

"Uh-huh." My son bobbed his head, then cut his eyes at the vegetables. He wasn't picky but kale was not his favorite. "What's that for?"

"A salad," Beth said simply. "Want to help us cook?"

Pete backed toward his room. "No thank you. I'm working on a project and I gotta get back to it. I can show it to you later though if you want."

Beth nodded enthusiastically and turned to me as Pete disappeared into his bedroom. "What's this project?"

I groaned. "Ask him about it at dinner if you want to listen to him talk about his shrink ray prototype for a whole dang hour. Vanessa, my friend who watches him, took him to see some sci-fi movie last week and he's been obsessed with trying to build one ever since."

"Aw, that's adorable. You seem like a really good mom."

I waved my hand at the compliment and turned to my mise en place, neat rows of minced garlic, a small pile of lemon zest, freshly washed and dried herbs. "I was gonna do some pan roasted chicken with Meyer lemon jus, crispy garlic, and harissa spiced polenta." I couldn't help slipping into restaurant mode even when I made basic stuff for Pete like mac and cheese.

"Oh my god. You are such a *chef*." Beth grazed her lips over my cheek and heat crept down my neck. "Okay. Well." She squared her shoulders and made a sweeping gesture to the produce. "Today I have kale from my garden, brussels sprouts from my mom's garden, and radicchio from my brother's garden. Oh and leftover maple caneles with poached plums and some ice cream for dessert. I was going to do a salad. But maybe I should make something Pete might like better? Does he like sautéed greens more?"

"Nah. Make what you want. My rule is he has to try everything once. And if you get him to like kale, I might fall in love with you."

Gosh darn it, Adah. I clamped my mouth shut and turned sharply back to my prep work wishing I could turn back time by thirty seconds to stop myself from sounding like such a fool. I slid my knife through a shallot, neatly reducing it to perfectly symmetrical cubes.

Beth's voice behind me was all bright cheer as she spun me around to face her. "Okay then. I'd better try my best."

Chapter Thirteen

Beth

I was a terrible person. Part of me had slotted Adah into the fussy, technique heavy, but ultimately boring chef role. I'd pictured elaborate sauces and the kind of insistence on perfect uniformity that drove me up a wall. But her food was as gorgeous and wonderfully understated as she was. The chicken was perfect: buttermilk-brined and juicy, the spice complex but not overwhelming. And I didn't know what she'd done to turn polenta into the most perfectly creamy bite I'd ever taken, but I needed to find out.

"This is so good," I said, my mouth full. "What did you do to the polenta?"

Pete laughed and made a comment about my table manners being worse than his.

Adah shook her head like the question made no sense. "Just cooked it the way I always made grits at home. Let them soak and then cooked them low and slow. Sorry, I know it's nothing too fancy but..."

"Oh my god shut up, it's amazing and you know it." I winced. Probably not great form to tell your girlfriend—or whatever Adah was to me—to shut up in front of her kid. Casting a nervous glance over at Pete, I realized he'd cleaned his plate including my kale and pickled radicchio salad. Score one, Beth.

"May I be excused?" Pete asked, already scraping his chair back from the table. At the nod of Adah's head, he bounded off to his room and I took a moment to glance around the apartment. I liked it.

Adah's place was a perfect reflection of her. Neat and thoughtful. Everything in its place. The only decorations appeared to be a large, heavily annotated wall calendar and several neatly arranged drawings by Pete taped to the fridge. My house growing up had been chaos: random projects my dad was tinkering with scattered all over the kitchen table, Andrew's sports equipment strewn in a haphazard trail leading to his room, my mom's paperwork for the café forever getting lost among old newspapers and magazines.

When I'd left with nothing but a backpack and my newly acquired passport, I'd vowed to keep my life simple. Eschew the world of material comforts in exchange for freedom and novelty. Keep moving forward until I found my place. The realization that maybe I'd been running away so fast I hadn't realized how good I had it rang through me like a clear bell. Maybe I wanted to create that ideal place right here. Maybe I'd already done it. I shook my head hard and fast to shake the thoughts loose until I had some time to really sit with them.

"You okay?" Adah's eyebrows drew together in concern as she searched my face.

"Oh, shit, sorry. Yeah. I was just spacing out." I took another bite of chicken and groaned softly because it was so damn good. It would be interesting to see how much Adah's cooking changed when she was performing for an audience and trying to meet the expectations of a corporate restaurant group. "Hey, can I come in this week for lunch? I should probably check out your restaurant at some point, huh?"

Adah rubbed the back of her neck, looking suddenly and adorably nervous. "Sure. If you want. Don't feel like you have to though or anything…"

"I want to," I interrupted. "If this is any indication, I can't wait to try your menu. How's everything going anyway? Are you guys planning to change your hours after Labor Day?"

Adah tipped her head to the side like a confused, slightly intense-looking puppy. Goddamn it, everything she did was adorable. "What do you mean?"

"Oh, well a lot of the downtown restaurants that get a ton of tourist business scale down once the season ends. Like stop doing lunch or take an extra day off…that kind of thing."

A heavy, tense silence fell between us and Adah fiddled with her fork. In the distance the horn of a cruise ship in port sounded. The setting sun cast the whole kitchen in shades of rosy gold. After what felt like a solid hour of quiet but was probably less than two minutes, I slid my hand across the table and put it over Adah's. Her shoulders dropped as her gaze flicked up to meet mine. "Don't worry about it. Sorry if I made you stress out. It sounds like business has been good."

"It's been okay. We haven't been as busy for lunch and weeknight dinner service has been a mixed bag. I'll bring it up on my next conference call with the folks at the restaurant group."

I was definitely an asshole, because without thinking I rolled my eyes at the words *conference call* and *restaurant group*. But seriously, all this big business stuff had nothing to do with turning out honest food and making sure everyone stood on equal footing in the kitchen. Those assholes only cared about one thing: money. And they used weird fake hierarchies and shitty business practices to make sure they lined their pockets as much as possible.

"What?" Adah asked sharply, her body once again rigid. "Zest owns some of the best restaurants in the country. Café Eloise where I worked in Chicago has a Meridian star. And Per Diem in New York has three. Riccardo gave me a job when I had pretty much only worked in diners. The group takes pride in developing the talents of up-and-coming chefs. Not everybody has the luxury of inheriting a family business, you know."

I held up my hands. "Hey, sorry, I get it. I know you love your job and I know you're great at it. It's just, like, that stuff isn't as important to me. I tried the whole elite culinary school thing and it didn't work for me but that doesn't mean I think it's wrong for everyone."

Adah's mouth was a thin line, her eyes distant. I recognized the mask she wore over her feelings and I hated that I'd made her feel the need to put it on. Scraping my chair closer to hers I twined my arms around her neck and pushed my nose into her fresh-smelling hair.

Adah's sigh fluttered warm against my skin. "No, I'm the one who should be sorry. I didn't mean to get so defensive." She pulled back and smirked. "I think I'm just kinda jealous because your salad was so good."

While Adah talked to her son and brought him downstairs for what had begun an impromptu movie night invite from her landlady and had somehow evolved into a movie marathon and slumber party with one of his friends joining in, I finished up the dishes and suppressed the urge to snoop around the apartment. Even though I'd known Adah for a couple of months now, had talked with her on the phone late into the night, and shared a handful of dates, she was still basically a mystery to me.

Her place was without a doubt the cleanest apartment I'd ever been in. Most of the furniture looked secondhand but perfectly maintained. The small kitchen table and the four mismatched chairs around it looked like the kind of furniture my mom had scoured antique fairs for when she was still running the café. Drifting into the living room I flipped through the well-worn children's books neatly arranged in a basket next to the couch. The only picture on the wall was a large photograph in a cheap plastic frame. In it, Adah held a grinning baby Pete high in the air beneath the Gateway Arch in St. Louis. Her hair was even shorter, in a severe buzzcut that still somehow looked great with her striking features. She wore an enormous T-shirt and a pair of baggy cargo pants. I thought of her now, the easy way she inhabited her clothes, her simple sense of style, and smiled to myself.

The door creaked open and I startled backward, away from the photo, like I'd been doing something I shouldn't.

"Sorry that took so dang long. Pete's friend Jason is a real chatterbox. Kid wouldn't let me leave." Adah shut the window, drew the curtains, and sank down onto the couch.

The energy gathered thick between us as I pressed my body as close to her as physically possible without crawling into her lap. "Thanks again for dinner," I murmured, resting my head on her shoulder.

Close like this, I could feel the heat radiating off Adah. It had been an unseasonably cool day and the temperature had dropped with the setting sun but next to me Adah was like a furnace. She turned to me, her face inches from mine, and groaned. "Sorry. I don't really know what the heck I'm doing. It's been a while since I, you know…"

"Had sex?" I ventured. "Here, how does this sound? I'm going to kiss you. If you like it, we can move on from there. Sound good?"

Adah huffed out a low laugh. "I know I'm gonna like it."

Trailing a single finger up the sharp line of her jaw, I ghosted my lips over hers. The touch felt electric, like every one of my nerve endings stood at attention to feel this kiss as fully as possible. A delicious thrill raced through me. The only thing I knew in that moment was the taste of Adah's lips, warm and fresh and vital.

Adah groaned, low in the back of her throat. Her hands found my hips and tugged me fully onto her lap. Then we were kissing in earnest, soft moans and grasping hands and open mouths. I felt my pussy clench as tingling heat built and built between my legs. The roughness of Adah's hands as she pushed my flannel down off my shoulders sent goose bumps racing up my arms. All I wanted was skin and touch and everything all at once.

Almost overwhelmed as Adah's tongue caressed mine, I slid my lips lower to the soft skin at the base of her throat. Her hips bucked up against me and a whine tore from her throat. I felt almost dizzy with need. Need and something else. Something warm and light and totally new. A kind of quiet intimacy I hadn't felt in years of steamy hookups. Something I hadn't even felt with Maya. My ears buzzed hot and I buried my face in Adah's neck, so overwhelmed I was worried I was going to cry like some kind of hormone-addled teenager. Taking in deep breaths, I worked to pull myself together. *Focus, Beth.* Grounding details. The muffled sound of people laughing on the street below. The firm strength of Adah's hands on my hips. The clean soap smell of her skin.

Adah tipped my chin up to look into my face. "Honey, are you alright?"

Oh dear god, the term of endearment in her low, sweet accent was so not going to help whatever weird spell had overtaken me. Fuck. Was Mercury in retrograde or something? I hadn't checked my astrology app that morning and, clearly, I was paying the price.

Pushing out a breath I nodded and plastered on a grin. "Yeah, sorry. I just got…"

"You're beautiful," she breathed. "I don't know what I did to deserve you. You're so…" She shook her head. "Heck, I don't even have an actual bed." She chuckled, gesturing to the futon under us.

Some of the unwelcome anxiety in my stomach eased

and this time my laugh was genuine. "Damn, if you only knew… I've definitely done the deed in way worse settings."

Adah's lips found my earlobe and I moaned, all humor evaporating, leaving only burning need in its wake. "Will you take off your dress?" Her question carried a commanding edge that ignited my body all over again. My hands felt heavy and sluggish as I stood and fumbled with the back zipper and slid the dress down to pool at my feet. I hadn't bothered with a bra and the cool air pebbled my nipples. The roughness of her hands on me, palming my breasts before skimming down to my hips and pulling me back onto her, was exactly what I needed. Well, not exactly. I wanted to feel her skin against mine.

"Is this okay?" I paused, my fingers poised at the top button of her shirt.

Adah nodded slowly and as I fumbled with the buttons, I realized why so many characters in movies and romance novels tore off each other's clothes. I was desperate to see her. And when I finally managed to get her shirt off, it was more than worth the wait. She was all hard planes and sinewy muscle. Two unexpected tattoos stood out against her pale skin: one a small series of numbers and letters above her hip that I guessed marked longitude and latitude, the other a beautifully done black and gray botanical curving up her ribs and disappearing beneath the dark fabric of her sports bra.

As she shed her jeans with efficient movements, I trailed my fingers over the lines of ink. "What is this? It's beautiful."

"Witch hazel. Grows all over back home," she said simply, lying down on the couch and gesturing for me to lie on top of her.

Then I was lost in her. This was more than just desire, though. It was closeness. It was something that felt an awful lot like care. We moved together, kissing furiously, trying and failing to keep quiet. I discovered she loved when I licked into her mouth, and she found the spot behind my ear that drove me wild with need. Then Adah shifted and my clit ground against her thigh and my whole body burned. I could feel my own wetness through my underwear rubbing her skin and the sensation turned me on even more. Adah clearly liked it too because she groaned and arched up, grinding back against me. We moved together faster, hands grasping, moans growing steadier and louder. My nipples dragged against the fabric of Adah's sports bra and I sighed with pleasure as my internal muscles clenched tight.

Twined together, our hips found their rhythm, our breaths came hard and shallow. My lips tingled from kissing and pleasure gathered in my belly. My skin was flushed hot, probably red and mottled. A few strands of Adah's hair fell across her forehead, bobbing in time with her movements. I was climbing fast, everything inside me going warm and tight and full. Adah reached to palm my breast as her lips claimed mine again.

"Fuck, I'm close," I breathed, my voice high and needy.

At this Adah pinched my nipple hard and the slight edge of pain pushed me right over the edge. My orgasm crashed through me, my whole body going rigid, as pulse after pulse of hot and cold pleasure radiated outward. Adah was still moving against me, then she groaned and bit my neck. With one last rough thrust against my thigh she collapsed into me.

I felt pliant and satisfied as I peppered Adah's face with light kisses. She smiled and sifted her fingers through my hair, which I was pretty sure was a tangled mess. If we stayed in this position much longer, I would probably lose all feeling in my arm but it was more than worth it.

"You're amazing," Adah whispered, her voice serious. She pressed a kiss to my forehead and then that same weird overwhelmed feeling returned in a rush. I wanted to play it off, make a joke or maybe even dash to the bathroom before fleeing to my car. Instead I squeezed my eyes shut and let myself bask in the warmth of her affection.

Chapter Fourteen

Adah

Sunlight filtered through the leaves casting dappled shadows over Beth's face. She looked way too cute: face screwed up in concentration, curls springing out of a braid, big cream-colored sweater riding up as she stretched to reach a particularly perfect-looking Honeycrisp.

"Want me to get it?" I tried not to sound as amused as I felt.

She shot me a look that my mama would have been proud of and started back up, this time jumping to try to reach it. I wasn't that much taller than her, maybe only three or four inches, but it was just enough for me to reach up, grab the apple, and set it gently in her basket. Beth rolled her eyes before dropping a quick kiss onto my cheek.

"You really needed that one, huh?" I laughed. I'd already filled a whole bushel basket with apples. Beth, on the other hand, apparently only chose the fairest apples of them all for the individual apple tartes she was making for a big autumn feast at The Yellow House.

"Yes," she said in a mock prissy tone. "I want to celebrate the peak bounty of the season."

Now it was my turn to roll my eyes. She shouldn't have been able to get away with saying that kind of stuff, but somehow she did. "Is that right?" I asked, stepping closer to her. She tipped her face up to mine, desire clear as day in her pretty brown eyes. Dang. I could not get enough of this woman. Since the first night we spent together we'd found any excuse to meet, to steal a few minutes alone together. I couldn't recall a single time in my life that had been so charged, so exciting. So right.

Then my kid came tearing out of the greenery like the devil himself was hot on his heels. Despite the fact that we were at an apple orchard in Maine on a beautiful October afternoon, my eyes immediately darted around, looking for danger. Which was stupid, I knew. But old habits died hard and all that.

"Bees!" Pete stopped just short of hiding behind my legs. "You didn't tell me this place was gonna be full of bees."

"Sorry, honey. Are you afraid of bees? You're safe, okay?" Beth's voice was calm and gentle, soothing me as much as I assumed it did my son. "A lot of the farms I work with have beehives. They're just after the apple blossoms, not looking to get you. And if one does land on you, just stand really still and it'll fly away when it's ready."

"No way. One was for sure chasing me." Pete looked

over his shoulder like the bee might be behind him, biding its time until it could attack.

Beth nodded, furrowing her brow seriously. "Well it might have been confused since you look so much like an apple blossom." She winked. Pete tried to scoff but couldn't hide his smile.

"My mama kept bees too. I never got stung." As soon as the words left my mouth, I wanted to push them back in. My past wasn't a secret to Pete. He'd seen a photo of Jeremy and I told him the occasional story about growing up on the farm. Still, the last thing I wanted to talk about now was my family. The word didn't even sit right in my brain anymore. They were just people I used to know from a place that I wanted to forget.

"Why?" Pete asked, looking genuinely interested.

"Why didn't they sting me?"

"No. How come your mom had bees?" Pete rolled his eyes.

"Oh, well, we had a big garden and bees helped pollinate everything so we got bigger yields. And we harvested the honey. My brothers always used to make me do it." For the love of all things holy, why couldn't I keep my mouth shut? His uncles were a big old question mark to Pete and I tried my hardest not to bring them up.

"How many brothers did you have again?"

Did. Past tense. It made sense. As far as Pete was concerned that whole part of my life was dead and buried. For the most part he was right. "Six." My voice was a wobbly mess. I cleared my throat hard.

"I wish we had a big family." Pete sighed and scuffed

the toe of his sneaker into the grass. "Being an only child is boring. Jason's dads said they might adopt another kid."

The pain struck hard and deep, as my son's words settled uneasily in the pit of my stomach. Had I deprived him of important things, necessary things, because I couldn't get it together enough to give him a stable life? Beth's hand found my shoulder. Her touch was a lighting rod I hadn't known I needed. Grounding reassurance. "Are you kidding?" Beth asked, her voice easy and bright. "My brother and I used to fight so much I wished he'd never been born. He's okay now though. Besides you have a wicked great family. Your mom here's okay, but Ms. Vanessa? Jay? They're amazing. Didn't Jay take you guys to Legoland last weekend?"

And just like that the tough part of the conversation was over. Pete yammered on about our pilgrimage to Boston to visit his own personal version of the holy land until he got distracted by a family walking by with cider donuts and scampered off to buy some of his own. Adrenaline and embarrassment warred for control of my body. *Deep breath in. Count to ten.* Nothing worked.

Bracing myself for the coming questions from Beth, I shifted my gaze to the trees, scanning for another perfect apple that might distract her enough to avoid this conversation. What was I supposed to say? Yes, my son knows next to nothing about his entire extended family and might not ever meet his dad. No, I have no idea what I'm doing. But yeah, I'm probably failing as a mother.

"Hey." Beth didn't touch me. Her voice was low but not laced with the kind of cloyingly sweet pity I couldn't bear hearing. "What do you need right now?"

The question startled me so much, my thoughts seemed

to grind to a halt. I had no clue. I did know that my eyes fizzed with tears and *that* was not happening. I shook my head and raked my hands through my hair. This was fine. I was fine. Nothing to worry about. "Sorry," I mumbled. "I'm alright. Just, uh, I don't really want my family to know where I am. I don't like thinking about that stuff."

Beth nodded slowly, her eyes locked with mine. "Can I hug you?"

I laughed and pulled her into my arms. And darn if it didn't make me feel a thousand times better.

Both Jay and Mac had insisted, for what felt like the twentieth time in the past week, that I take Monday night off. Finally relenting, I felt at loose ends. Listless. I wasn't really used to having time to myself that wasn't spent with my son. As I'd wandered out of the kitchen into the warm, early afternoon light, I'd decided to text Beth and see if she wanted to have dinner with Pete and me. She'd responded right away, in a flurry of exclamation points and grinning emojis that she would come get me in twenty minutes. And she had, her little beat-up car screeching around the corner, some kind of frantic flamenco music blasting from the speakers.

Since we had about two hours to kill before Pete's school let out for the day, we walked down to the small beach on the far end of town. Aside from a few old men fishing and a mom and daughter looking for shells, we were alone with the swaying seagrass and soft rush of water. Conversation flowed easy between us. Beth told me about her time in New Orleans: about the woman she'd almost moved in with, about the tangle of ferns and vines spilling from her tiny apartment's balcony, about late nights at her girlfriend's jazz club. And I told her about St. Louis: about meeting Dorothy—my first and only serious girlfriend—about learning to be a mom, about my grimy basement studio, about early mornings at the diner learning to poach the perfect egg.

Beth was in the middle of telling me about how she and her brother had spent countless late nights watching YouTube tutorials to learn how to transform the neglected hearth at her mom's café into The Yellow House's fancy wood burning oven, when her phone started buzzing loudly where it rested on the ground between our feet. A picture of an older woman with long hair pulled back in a braid and a bright smile flashed up on the screen.

"Oh shit!" Beth grabbed the phone and scrambled to answer it. "Hey Mom. I know. I know. I'm with Adah." She rolled her eyes dramatically at me. The very enthusiastic sound of a woman's voice poured from the speaker.

Beth pulled the phone away from her ear and covered the bottom. "I totally forgot that my mom and dad are headed down to Boston tonight for a concert. Any chance you want to come with me to pick up Hamlet from my parents before we get Pete? Will Vanessa care about you having a dog at your place?"

Heat flooded my face at the thought of meeting Beth's mother. I'd heard about her from Beth and she sounded like a kind, if slightly kooky, woman. My hesitation must have shown in my face, because Beth's hand covered mine and her expression softened.

"Hey, you can totally wait in the car if you want."

In the background I faintly made out the sound of her mom saying "No she cannot. I want to meet this girl!"

I shook my head. "No it's fine. It's totally okay. And Vanessa won't mind at all. Heck, Pete's gonna be over the moon."

Beth's childhood home was less than a mile away from The Yellow House, down a heavily wooded road leading in the direction of the ocean. In fact the house was right on the water, a small cedar-sided colonial with a mess of buoys, wind chimes, and a canoe hanging from the roof of the covered porch. The garden was a riot of colorful blooms and herbs. Some of the sunflowers along the back of a vegetable bed were almost certainly taller than me. The front door was painted ocean blue and adorned with a seashell wreath. As we walked up the paved path to the door I noticed Beth's name carved into the cement in curvy cursive, and her brother Andrew's name next to it in blocky print. It was the kind of house I knew I would have loved to grow up in. Just the kind of house I'd pictured producing a woman like Beth Summers.

Beth turned to me, looking uncharacteristically nervous. "Okay, just to warn you my mom is…kind of a lot. Like I'm really sorry if she says something weird or sort of offensive. Her heart is in the right place, she just has no filter and—"

"I heard that, Elizabeth." Mrs. Summers tugged open the door and shook her head at her daughter. "I do too have a filter. It's only the older I get the less I choose to use it."

Beth's mom looked a lot like her daughter. Her hair was a little shorter than Beth's, but still fell past her shoulders in copper-colored waves shot through with silver. Her face was tanned and lovely, her features sharp in a way that made her look like a fairy queen from one of Pete's old storybooks. She wore a pair of overalls over a striped T-shirt and no shoes. I noticed her toenails were painted a shocking shade of purple. I liked her right away.

"Adah." She said my name so warmly I wasn't even startled when she pulled me into a hug that smelled like freshly turned soil and clean laundry. "I have heard so much about you." She held me out at arm's length. "And holy shit you are gorgeous. My daughter wasn't kidding."

"Mom," Beth groaned. "You can let her go now."

"Is Pete in the car?" Mrs. Summers looked over my shoulder.

"Oh no, ma'am. He's at school until three."

"Right, right. School. Ma'am bullshit. Call me Robin. That's too bad though. My daughter here has told me lots about you and your kiddo. He sounds like a sweetheart. You three will have to come over whenever you have a night off. Which—" she waved between us, "—I know, I know, hardly happens. And I'm sure you like to have the time to yourselves. But I can make you my lobster pot pie. I promise it'll be worth putting up with my husband."

I thought the lobster pot pie sounded great and was about to say so when Hamlet came bounding out the house and nearly tackled Beth. His tail wagged wildly and within about two seconds everyone was coated in slobber. The laugh bubbling from my chest surprised me.

"Okay, Mom, well we need to go pick up Pete. Have fun at the concert though. And thank you for watching my baby."

"Honey, I know I sound like a broken record but…"

"Yes." Beth sighed fondly. "I need to work less. I hear you loud and clear."

Mrs. Summers's clear blue eyes fell on me and I stood up a bit taller. "Both of you girls need to relax more. Elizabeth tells me how much you work, too, my dear."

It felt nice to be on the receiving end of such a well-meaning maternal lecture. I nodded. "You're right, ma'am—uh, Robin."

Despite Beth's best attempts to leave, the three of us stood chatting on the porch for a few minutes before Robin invited Beth and me inside for some iced tea and banana bread. It occurred to me then how strange it was that I'd been to Beth's family's house before I'd been to her home. She'd invited me over a few times but it hadn't worked out with our schedules and Pete's school and increasingly busy social calendar. I was sure in that moment, though, that Beth's place would feel like home. What little I knew of where she grew up and the business she'd built had me sure that whatever space she'd created herself would be a perfect reflection of her. Bright, a little chaotic, and fully welcoming.

Beth must have successfully declined her mom's invitation for snacks because before I knew it Robin was thrusting a grocery bag full of zucchini and greens into my arms and two foil-wrapped loaves of banana bread into Beth's hands.

"Mom, you know I literally bake for a living, right?" Beth laughed, accepting the food nonetheless.

"I do. But I also know your brother tells me you eat nothing but old bread and leftovers that are about to go into the compost. Adah, tell her she needs to take better care of herself. This girl used to be the queen of...what did you call it, honey, self-care?"

"We're leaving now. Thank you, Mom." Beth brushed a kiss over her mom's cheek and I almost wanted to do the same.

After Pete quite literally jumped for joy at the sight of Hamlet waiting with me and Beth outside his school, the four of us walked the few blocks to the apartment together. The crisp autumn air smelled like cinnamon from the bakery a few blocks away and some of the stores along the main cobbled street had put out cutesy arrangements of pumpkins and chrysanthemums. And was it just me or did everyone in this town seem to own a dang plaid scarf? Maybe I should get one for Pete.

My son was talking a mile a minute about the book report his teacher, Mr. O'Brien, had assigned as we clomped up the stairs to the apartment. He'd ended up loving his teacher, a very energetic guy in his early twenties that made me feel about a thousand years old every time I talked to him. I was proud of my son, though, for branching out and making even more new friends at his school. Which reminded me, I needed to call Jason's dads back to make some kind of playdate. As I turned the key in the lock, Hamlet somehow managed to squeeze his gigantic body in front of me and bounded into the kitchen.

"Sorry," Beth said through a laugh. "He always has to be first."

"Mom, do you think I could take Hamlet to the park?" Pete shrugged off his backpack and kicked his shoes into the middle of the floor. I pinned him with a long look and he hurried to hang his backpack on the back of a kitchen chair and at least relocate his shoes to the mat by the door so we wouldn't trip on them and break our necks.

"Weren't you just talking about how much homework you have?" I washed my hands at the sink and started pulling a few things for dinner out of the fridge. Nothing fancy. Pete had been asking for spaghetti and meatballs for weeks, so I'd picked up the ingredients at the little Italian market around the corner.

"Yeah." He heaved a dramatic sigh and threw his body into the kitchen chair where he'd slung his backpack.

"Here," Beth said, sitting down next to him. "Why don't I sit with you while you get started on your book report? I have some work I need get caught up on too. Once we're done maybe we can all go over to the park. Or even the dog beach if you want."

An easy quiet fell over the kitchen as I got to work on dinner prep. I was surprised Beth hadn't tried to help but I was glad she hadn't. I wanted to cook for her. I wanted to take care of her. Shaking my head at my sappy thoughts, I began chopping the onion, carrots, and celery for the mirepoix.

I slid easily into my typical super-focused, forget-the-world-around-me cooking mode. The rhythms of chopping and predictability of heat and fat transforming into something new calmed me. Then the sound of Pete laughing uproariously pulled my attention away from the tomato sauce.

"That doesn't sound like a British accent at *all*." Pete shook his head at Beth. She shrugged and started reading out loud from a book from Pete's school library in an accent that sounded a little like the crocodile guy from Australia and a little like an old-timey mobster from the movies I'd never been allowed to see as a kid. My lips twitched up, but I narrowed my eyes at my son.

"Peter David Campbell. Are you making Beth read you that book? You should be doing your own homework."

Beth stopped reading and rolled her eyes at me, fondly I hoped. "No, Chef Grumpypants. He started laughing at this line from the book so I asked to read it and, well, this book is really good so I started reading out loud."

"In that weird as hel—heck voice." Pete caught himself before I made him put a quarter in the swear jar.

The two of them started laughing again and I couldn't hide my smile.

It turned out Beth did her darnedest to help out with dinner. Pete had decided to head to the park with Jason and Hamlet in tow, promising to be back in exactly a half hour. For a few minutes Beth stayed seated at the kitchen table, filling the room with lighthearted chitchat. But as I started to wash the tender greens from her mother's garden, Beth's arms came around me from behind and she buried her nose in the crook of my neck.

"What are we thinking for salad?" Beth's voice was warm and low, sending a small shiver rippling across my skin.

Drying my hands on a clean dishtowel, I turned and brushed a kiss over her cheek. Then another to her lips. She was so soft. I couldn't get enough of the feel of every inch of her against me.

"How about you relax, huh?" I kissed her again. She smiled against my lips and shook her head.

"No thanks. I was thinking we could do a nice lemon vinaigrette and some blistered cherry tomatoes? Does Pete like fennel, because I could quick pickle…"

I pressed a single finger to her lips and grinned at her. "Sit down." I dropped my voice a touch.

Beth's eyes went wide for a fraction of a second before she scoffed. "You play dirty, Campbell." With a dramatic sigh she hopped up on the counter, sitting too close to my cutting board for comfort. After a moment she let out an audible gasp and picked up her phone. "Shit. I totally forgot to mention it to you!" She angled her phone toward me, but all I could make out was an email on the screen.

"Mention what?" I asked, wiping my hands on a clean towel and coming close to her to look at the message.

"You might already know about this but if not you guys should totally sign up. Might be a good way to connect with more of the locals as the season ends. Not that you need the prize money." She raised her eyebrows and tipped her chin down.

I decided to let that one slide. Plus she was right. Riccardo had more money than he knew what to do with. "Sign up for what? That font is so dang small I can't read it."

"Oh, sorry. It's an email from the Port Catherine Business Association. Autumn Fest is at the end of the month. When I was growing up it used to be kind of a cheesy thing they put on to try to get the last little bit of tourist money they could before it got too cold for anyone to want to visit. But I guess a few years ago it got featured on one of those Cuisine Channel shows, you know that one with the dude who eats all the weird stuff?"

Beth paused and I shook my head. I'd never followed the

cooking shows. Never had the time or interest. I quickly checked on the sauce, which was slowly reducing to a perfect silkiness.

"Anyway, he came up to try the truly disgusting lobster tomalley candy our neighbor Dan used to make. Since then it's become kind of a foodie thing. People in town with nothing better to do, such as my father, judge a competition for best seafood supper. The prize this year for first place is three thousand dollars. That money should definitely be going to the food pantry but I'm gonna enter since I could really use some cash to expand our dining room."

I could feel my confusion register on my face. "If you want to win why would you want me to enter?"

Beth shrieked with laughter. "Damn, you're awfully confident." She slid down off the counter and brushed her lips over mine. "I'm winning this one. Hands down. Just thought I'd try to make it a little more of a challenge for myself." Her fingers fluttered up the back of my neck and into my hair. A hot shock of desire coursed through me. Desire for Beth. And desire to win.

I covered her mouth with mine, savoring the taste of her lips. As I pulled away I whispered low in her ear, "You're going down, Summers."

Try as I might, I couldn't get my focus back. The normal level of longing I felt in her presence had been cranked up by the thought of competing with her. Beth's gaze followed me around the kitchen, and I found myself seeking out any small excuse to touch her. The meatballs were simmering in their sauce, the pasta water was on to boil, and my salad prep was done. I crossed the small kitchen to stand between her knees.

"I see you went the Caesar route for the salad. Classic. I'll allow it."

"It's Pete's favorite. Been a while since I made it for him." I shrugged, not admitting it was my favorite too.

Beth brushed my hair back from my face and scooted closer to me. "He's really lucky to have you. We both are."

All I could do was kiss her, but her words kept me smiling all through dinner.

As Pete cleared the plates, Hamlet hot on his heels, he paused to look back at me and Beth. She'd pulled her chair up close to mine as we got into it about the merits of white chocolate. Beth argued that in small amounts, good quality white chocolate could elevate the flavors of other ingredients in desserts. Since I knew better, I argued it should be banned as a hideously sweet toxic substance.

"Are you sleeping over, Beth?" Pete asked, setting the plates next to the sink. His eyes flicked from the two of us to the kitchen window. The sky was almost dark, the deep blue right before night.

"Oh." Beth's cheeks pinked. "Um, I—"

"I have sleepovers all the time. Well not all the time, but I slept over at Jason's house and it was really fun. One of his dads even let us stay up late to watch *Saturday Night Live*." He shot a sheepish glance in my direction. I pressed my lips together. A little TV wasn't going to hurt the kid.

"Anyway," Pete continued, "you should sleep over if you want. If that's okay, Mom."

I couldn't help it. I laughed. Probably louder than I'd laughed in years. Pete and Beth exchanged an *is she okay* look. "Of course she can. Beth, if you want to have a sleepover, by all means."

Pete insisted we watch an episode of his new favorite show, some weird half-animated program about animals. Beth snuggled up close to me on the couch, the three of us huddled around my iPad since I hadn't ever bothered to buy an actual TV. I'd never really gone out of my way to buy one since the last thing I wanted was my son zoning out to mindless garbage. But I remembered Dorothy, the first woman I ever really dated when I moved to St. Louis, telling me about her family movie nights growing up. Her dad would make "hamburger pizza," a downright gross dish Dorothy loved to re-create. Her mom would rent a few movies and she and her sister would argue over which one to watch. They'd done it every Friday. I'd dang near burned up with jealousy when she told me about it, picturing her goofy dad and his collection of loud tourist T-shirts and her cool, collected mom snuggled up on the couch with Dorothy and her sister. But now I wondered if Pete and I couldn't do something like that, too. Maybe even with Beth. Just without the hamburger pizza.

Once Pete's head started bobbing down and snapping up, the telltale sign he was pretending to be awake, I shuffled him into his bedroom for a speedy version of his bedtime routine. Hamlet nosed his way in and I didn't even bother to kick up a fuss when the dog jumped onto Pete's bed and snuffled to sleep at the foot. When I came out, Beth sat on the couch, flipping through the romance novel I'd picked up at the grocery store to read when I couldn't fall asleep.

"That's some steamy stuff." She laughed, fanning her face with the book. As much as I liked her, it still seemed unfair that someone that pretty could also be so darn likeable and excellent in the kitchen.

"Sure is. They get busy on the beach, though, and that doesn't seem like it would really be that nice. Too much sand." I slipped the book out of her hands and pulled her in close.

"Hmm, I don't know, we almost fu—uh, had sex on the beach and it was pretty great. Then again, it was a rocky beach."

I scoffed and had to try real hard not to ruffle her hair. It was a little wilder than usual today and I wanted run my fingers through it. Fist my hand at the back of her neck and pull her down onto my lap... Okay. Not good thoughts when my son could barge out of his room at any minute. Glad as I was to have found Vanessa and such a convenient location to the restaurant, the apartment really lacked privacy.

I pulled out the bed and the wrinkled, mismatched sheets I kept in a basket under the side table. We made quick work of making up the bed, a task I usually hated when I came home from work so exhausted I could fall asleep standing up. Beth followed me into the tiny bathroom and laughed when I told her all I did for my "skincare routine" (her words) was wash my face with a little soap and rub on some of the same lotion I used all over my body.

"Next time I come over I'm at least bringing you some rosehip oil. And some witch hazel. For god's sake, Adah, you have the plant tattooed on your body. The least you could do is use it as a toner for your face." Her voice was light and teasing enough that I didn't feel silly for having no earthly idea how to take care of my own skin. It definitely wasn't something my mama taught me.

As I pushed an extra toothbrush out of its plastic packaging and set it in the cup mounted over the sink, my body flashed with a hot tingle of awareness. This was comfortable. Beth next to me, rummaging through my tiny basket of toiletries in search of "decent moisturizer." Our eyes meeting in the mirror as we brushed our teeth. The easy way she cuddled up next to me in the dark. It was all right.

"Alright, chef, that's the last of it. Have a good week now." Martin, my favorite of our produce suppliers, tipped the last crate of apples off his dolly and gave me a jaunty wave. With the help of Mac and our prep cook Sam, I hauled the order into the walk-in and started picking through the greens, winter squash, and a big bushel of Gala apples. A smile twitched my lips up as I noticed the bruises and bumps on a few of them, remembering how Beth had cradled each apple she'd picked like a newborn baby. We'd spent the drive home talking through recipe concepts and I'd come up with the idea for a new menu item: apple and root vegetable tagine to pair with the mackerel we'd been getting in for the past few weeks.

My mind was a million miles away...well, maybe fifteen miles at a certain farm-to-table restaurant, firmly fixed on a certain redheaded restauranteur. I must have been pretty dang distracted thinking about Beth, because I completely missed Sean coming into the walk-in. But when I looked up, there he was, arms folded over his chest, irritation clear as a bell on his face. My heartbeat picked up and I hated myself for it. There was no reason this man should make me nervous. No reason his showing up in the walk-in should remind me of the reverend coming into the kitchen through the screen door ready to yell at the first person he stumbled upon.

"Can I talk to you for a minute, Adah?"

"Sure." I didn't stop pulling containers of lobster stock that hadn't been labeled with a date off the shelf. Whatever nonsense Sean wanted to talk to me about could wait. I needed to talk to Mac about starting up a better system for keeping the pantry organized and making sure we dated every single item. We'd been wasting more food than I liked, and I wanted the kitchen staff to find a solution that would work for everyone.

"In my office." Sean turned to leave, assuming I would follow.

"We can talk here. Got a lot to do." My eyes stayed fixed on the neatly organized jars of preserved lemons and roasted red peppers.

"Maybe you need to manage your time better. If you don't have time to talk about the kitchen you run are you sure you have time for that little competition you entered?" His anger cracked through his usual smarmy professionalism. I almost liked him better angry. At least angry he was honest. Sean cleared his throat loudly. "Have you even taken a look at last week's numbers?"

He knew I reviewed the numbers every night. Trying not to sigh, I looked up from the work I actually needed to do. "Yup. I saw that things have been slowing up a bit. A lot less tourists coming through. That's why I entered the contest. Good exposure for the restaurant with people who might come in more than one time. I was thinking we could—"

Sean held up a hand and it took a heck of a lot of self-control for me not to smack it down. "I already talked to Ric about it. It's a profit issue. So basically, we're spending too much on supplies." He eyed the produce boxes between us. "We need to lower our operating costs and the best way to do that will be changing our vendors. I know this whole 'local food' thing is having its moment, but most people can't tell the difference anyway. I have a meeting set up with our rep from Wesco for tomorrow afternoon to expand their service. In the next few weeks we're going to be phasing out our other distributors."

I was a little surprised when, instead of being engulfed by a haze of mind-numbing red rage, my first thought was of Beth. Of the way she would undoubtedly stomp her foot and launch into a whole speech about why sourcing food locally mattered to the environment and community. I could practically see her face getting all flushed as she gesticulated wildly, starting in on the ways big food suppliers monopolize the food market and hurt workers. A smile crept over my face and I shook my head.

"Do you really think that's the best solution?" I asked, looking my idiot manager right in the eye. "Because it seems to me like most of our loss is coming from weekday lunch service. I don't think a lot of the local folks have the time for a three course sit-down lunch."

"You can leave the business stuff to me, Adah. I know what I'm doing here, okay? You stick to the kitchen and I'll take care of the rest."

And there was that explosion of anger. My throat clenched tight and hot and I wanted nothing more than to push Sean out of the way and run out the back door. Keep on running until I felt okay again. "Well, our menus and

website all talk about our commitment to the finest ingredients and the freshest food. Heck, Sean, we're charging
thirty-five bucks for a piece of fish and a few fancy veggies
here. They at least gotta be good ones." I hated myself for
being so darn inarticulate. I hated how every time I got
mad my accent reared back up. It was always going to be
easy to dismiss the dumb hick who hadn't even managed to
finish high school. Planting my feet firmly on the ground,
I lifted my chin to meet Sean's gaze. "This is good food.
And it's my menu." *My kitchen*.

"None of that has to change. We'll still be serving the
same stuff, just cheaper on our end. Which means we'll be
making more money." He was speaking slowly now, like
I was too stupid to understand the basic concept of profit.
"And speaking of, I think Marcus is going to be coming
soon so I did talk to Ric about tweaking the menu. Fresh-
ening things up a little." With this delightful comment,
Sean turned on his stupid fancy-shoe heel and stalked out
of the kitchen.

My anger went with him, leaving only exhaustion and
sadness churning it its wake. I knew when I took this job
that it wouldn't be easy. Accepting the role of executive
chef meant dealing with endless headaches and putting out
both real and figurative fires. I understood that working
for a restaurant group meant dealing with a wide variety
of people who saw the world different from me. But this
feeling was new. This felt personal and unfair in a way I
didn't quite know what to do with. Maybe being a good
boss meant having to grit my teeth and deal with giving up
control sometimes. I wasn't really sure. What I did know,

though, was that this job gave me and Pete full benefits and a steady income and it was going to take a lot more than my manager being an idiot for me to give that up.

Chapter Fifteen

Beth

It honestly wasn't fair for someone to be as hot as Adah Campbell. I watched as she set up her table at the Fifth Annual Port Catherine Autumn Fest. Crisp button-down shirt with a perfectly starched navy blue apron. Hair pushed back with a neatly folded bandanna tied around her head. That laser focus. She was not going to win this, but she was going to look hot as hell while she lost. When she'd told me she planned to make sous vide lobster tail it had taken a lot of effort not to scoff into the phone. If people in Port Catherine hated one thing it was overly fancy preparations of lobster. I liked her idea of doing a Maine potato gratin and tarragon beurre blanc, but I doubted the people of my hometown would agree.

The other competition ranged from a cocky chef from South Bay, who loved bragging about his conquests in the kitchen almost as much as he loved hitting on his front of house staff, to Dana Whitfield, my old preschool teacher who had already seemed old twenty-five years ago and made the same chowder for every local cook-off in southern Maine. It was a pretty great chowder.

My prep was done and I had chosen to make a simple dish I could execute flawlessly with my eyes closed. Sea bream caught by my next-door neighbor, brushed with some excellent olive oil, would be roasted over applewood and served over a bed of delicata squash, crispy garlic, and crumbled bacon. I usually felt like adding bacon into dishes was a cheap thrill, but I knew folks in Port Catherine would love it. I set down my knife, washed my hands at the big communal sink they'd rigged up, and wandered over to Adah. She was bent over her work station, one of the big plastic tables set up along the waterfront in town, furiously chopping tarragon. Behind her the reflections of fluffy white clouds shone in the deep blue, perfectly still port. Dozens of small lobster boats dotted the water. The view had always been gorgeous but it had nothing on Adah.

"What'd you decide on?" Adah asked, not even looking up from her prep. The back of my neck heated but it had nothing to do with the early afternoon sunshine. Damn, why did her focus do it for me?

I explained my dish and gave her a quick rundown of the other competition and judges. "So the first judge, the guy with the Santa beard, is Jim Davis. Used to own this really awful dive bar that my dad and the other lobstermen loved. He sold it last year to this couple from New

York who turned it into a wine bar. Honestly, the wine bar kind of rocks but people in town love to bitch about it. The lady with the super-long hair owns the local food co-op. She's a sweetheart and grows some pretty great pot. And the other guy, the one with the fancy sneakers…him I don't know." I worried about this new judge, a dude about my age who had Brooklyn Transplant written all over his designer workwear.

Adah looked up and flashed me what I could only describe as a cocky grin. My stomach flipped and if I didn't think it might get us both disqualified from the competition I would have kissed her then and there.

"I think my food will speak for itself. You better get to it, Summers." She winked and returned her attention to her prep work.

Two hours later my food was perfectly plated and lined up on the judges' table. I had to admit Adah's dish was gorgeous. The lobster was clearly perfectly cooked, even if I did think sous vide was an idiotic way to prepare food. And when I'd set my dish down next to hers the smell of the tarragon beurre blanc may or may not have made my mouth water. But food like that wasn't about to win big in Port Catherine. My dad, for example, routinely made fun of people for eating nothing but a lobster tail and was wholly convinced that the only right way to consume seafood was the day it was caught and doused in melted butter, ideally chased with a cold beer. Still, my heart seemed to thud to a halt as Judge Brooklyn stood up to announce the results.

I caught Adah's eye across the sea of people still finishing their paper plates of food. Her stony façade crumbled only momentarily as the corner of her gorgeous lips lifted in a small smile. Then she clasped her hands in front of her and brought her full attention to the judges' table.

"So we're all super grateful for these amazing chefs cooking up some of the most dope dishes we've eaten all year." Judge Brooklyn beamed out at the crowd. Dope dishes? I tried not to roll my eyes as he continued to speak. "I'm so proud to be a part of this awesome town and very grateful that I got to try all this awesome food." Again I caught Adah's eye and mouthed the word *awesome*, then pointed to myself. She rolled her eyes and bit her lip.

"Today's winner captured the exciting future we hope to see for this town. Modern, creative, and..." I knew what he was going to say. "Awesome. Without further ado, I'm pumped to announce that the winner of the Fifth Annual Port Catherine Autumn Fest cook-off is Chef Adah Campbell from Bella Vista in South Bay. Her dish was not only the judge favorite but the crowd favorite, as well. Congrats, dude!"

The crowd erupted into applause and a weird mix of pride and anger bubbled up in me. Adah's face was impassive as she strode up to the table to accept the check and pose for photos with the judges and various local officials. On autopilot I strode over to the buffet tables and grabbed a plate of lobster tail. Even lukewarm it was excellent. The flavors were perfectly balanced, the slight sweetness of the tarragon cutting through the richness of the potatoes and shellfish. I wanted to toss the food into the garbage but it was so tasty I wanted to finish every overly fancy bite. Well damn it all to hell.

"Nice there, Beth." Jim sauntered over, his beard full of

crumbs. "Maybe next year you'll take first. Bacon was just a little overpowering for the fish, we thought."

I managed a tiny smile and watched as he grabbed a second plate of Adah's lobster.

Next time I saw Adah I was going to either strangle her or kiss her senseless... Okay it would definitely be the latter. But I couldn't eat another bite of that damned delicious lobster.

The sky stretched open overhead, so bright and clear I wanted to tip my head back and stare up into its depths. A flock of honking geese flew south in a perfect V formation. As much as I wanted to watch them until they disappeared, the shoppers and tourists along Bay Street might not appreciate the weird lady standing stock still on the sidewalk, gawking at the sky. But it had been a while since I'd paused to appreciate a perfect New England autumn afternoon. The sun cast everything in shades of gold, the shadows dancing long and lean over the brick sidewalk and cobbled streets.

I turned the corner and there I was. Bella Vista. Adah's restaurant. I'd put off my promise to check the place out because, honestly, I was worried I wouldn't like it. And, okay, I was still kind of pissed off about losing the competition in my own damn town. Plus the last thing I wanted was to take out a loan for the dining room. That money wouldn't have solved all my problems but it would have been a sizable drop in the bucket. Adah hadn't said a word about it and her stupid honor made me like her and hate her even more.

Despite my sour grapes, a quick look at the offerings

on Bella Vista's website had me worried for Adah. A good number of the dishes sounded wonderful, but Marcus did not mess around when it came to seasonality. If a restaurant claimed to buy from local producers, the menu damn well better reflect it. Not so at Bella Vista, where I'd seen a watermelon and feta salad and a number of eggplant dishes being offered. Not exactly in season in mid-autumn in Maine when overnight temperatures were already dipping down into the thirties at night.

I rolled my neck, pulled a long, even breath of crisp ocean air into my lungs, and pulled open the imposing wrought iron door. Inside, Bella Vista was quiet and undeniably stunning. The place looked less like the nicer restaurants around South Bay, places with exposed brick walls and big communal tables, and more like the elegant places I'd tried cooking at a few times throughout my travels. Next to the host stand the wall was covered in living moss and flowers. The dining room, quiet though it was, was gorgeous, with dark wood floors, large abstract seascapes on the walls, and modern metal light fixtures that had probably been custom made. The air smelled like fresh-cut lilies and new construction. So much money and effort for a space that probably intimidated half the locals in town.

I thought back to the remodel that had turned Summers's Corner Café into The Yellow House: my dad, Andrew, and me working long hours in the hot sun, scouring antique markets and salvage yards all over the state, the way the edges of my fingernails had been caked with yellow paint for days after I repainted the cottage. Our dining room was cramped and got pretty damn stuffy in the summer. But I liked it. It felt right.

Following the host to a table in front of the window, I craned my head toward the kitchen, which was open to the dining room and boasted an empty row of chef's tables overlooking the action. The kitchen orbited around Adah, movement circling her calm presence. She lifted her head and our eyes met. A small smile bloomed on her face and she turned to say something to the woman next to her. I hadn't even sat down in my sleek black wooden chair before Adah was crossing the dining room, looking more excited than I'd ever seen her. Her cheeks were flushed and her pretty green eyes were bright. My heart seemed to slow down then speed up as heat crept up my neck into my cheeks.

"You came." Adah offered an awkward but very adorable wave. "I was starting to wonder if you ever would. Thought maybe you were still licking your wounds." She grinned and any last ounce of competitive anger I'd been carrying dissolved.

I couldn't exactly tell her I'd been dodging this visit, so I smiled and gestured to the space around me. "Water under the bridge." I shrugged. "This place is gorgeous. I don't even remember what used to be in here. It must have been a huge reno project."

Adah nodded, smoothing her hands down the front of her spotless whites. "Yup. I think it used to be an old produce distribution center, but it'd been abandoned for a long time. Ric, the owner, hired a whole architecture and design company to redo the place."

I'd seen Adah taciturn and stiff before, but I didn't think I'd ever seen her this…nervous. She shifted her weight from foot to foot and kept rubbing the back of her neck. I was searching for something reassuring to say when a giggle cut through the heavy quiet of the dining room. Adah glanced back and groaned. Jay and the woman I'd seen Adah talking to earlier were falling all over each other in a fit of laughter. When they caught my eye, they both laughed harder and waved. I laughed to myself.

"Oh goodness." Adah dragged a hand over her face. "I'm sorry in advance. I think those two actually thrive on my embarrassment." Her voice was fond.

"Hey, Beth," Jay called across the room as they emerged from the kitchen. Two of the older couples seated at the adjacent tables shot us curious glances. "Thanks for finally gracing us with your presence." They winked in a way that should have been cheesy, but somehow was nothing but charming. Their thick, dark hair was a little sweat-damp and pushed back with a stretchy red headband, making them look like a soccer player fresh off the field.

"I'm Mac." A woman with even curlier hair than me and gorgeous eyebrows extended her hand. "Heard a lot about you."

Adah muttered under her breath and Mac clapped a hand on her shoulder. A weird, hot *something* twisted in the pit of my stomach. It took me a breathless moment to catalogue the feeling. Jealously. For what was maybe the first time in my life, I was jealous. The emotion would pass, surely. I knew my jealously was misplaced and silly. Adah and I were both adults capable of complex emotions and...being in the presence of unfairly gorgeous sous-chefs.

"So what can we get ya?" Jay asked, a wild grin spreading over their face.

"Just fuck me up on your favorites." I laughed. Adah chuckled too.

"Thank the lord Sean isn't here today." Jay rolled their eyes.

"How many times does the dude need to meet with wine distributors? He's gonna show up more wasted than usual and give front of house hell." Mac shook her head, looking resigned and frustrated.

At this, Adah bristled, shoulders set and jaw tight. "If he says anything tell me. I won't tolerate that. Not from him, not from no one."

Seeing her step up for her staff like that, seeing how much she cared, shifted my jealousy into a low, pulsing desire. Why had I waited so long to see her at work? She was so competent and gorgeous, and I needed to cool it before I embarrassed myself.

Thankfully Jay interrupted my increasingly dirty thoughts with a dark look and a shake of their head. "I'm sure soon enough we'll be getting all of our wine from Wesco too. It's gonna suck next week when we stop getting shipments from Bayside Seafood. I was just starting to get close to asking out the delivery girl."

Adah buried her face in her hands. "Alright, you two. Back to work." She surprised the hell out of me by pressing a fast kiss to the top of my head. "We'll be right out with your food."

The rest of the meal went about as I'd expected. The food was a little fussier than I would have liked but it was damn good. The beet salad with blackberries was the low point, seeing as blackberries had been out of season for a solid two months and they tasted like nothing but damp pulp. But the highlight of the meal, maybe a highlight of my life, was Adah hand-delivering, then sitting down to watch me eat, the best Sicilian seafood stew I'd ever tasted. And I'd spent a few months in Sicily. Then again, maybe those intense green eyes watching my every bite made the food taste better. Either way, as I stepped out into the crisp evening air, I was sure of two things: Adah Campbell was an excellent chef, and Marcus was not going to like those blackberries.

The cold was a force unto itself. Biting wind blew off the water, the kind of damp chill only possible this close to the sea. But the night was clear. The distant lull of foghorns and buoy bells soothed me as my boots rang out against the cobblestone streets. Tipping my head back, I took in the bright wash of stars and watched as the cloud of my breath dissipated into the dark. I loved the almost industrial smell of the old port cities in New England: all seaweed and tar. Aside from my visit a few days earlier to Bella Vista and my regular stays at Adah's apartment, situated where the T-shirt tourist lanes met the shabbier workaday streets, I hardly came into town anymore. I was as surprised as any-one at how much I'd come to love the sleepy quiet of Port Catherine, the familiar smell of home.

I'd been looking forward to climbing right into the bath, then right into bed after an almost sixteen-hour shift, but Adah asked me to meet her for a drink after she finished work. Something about her text had pricked my concern. She didn't usually do spontaneous, late-night meetings. Lately she'd been working longer days than even me, and the time we spent together was always scheduled in advance. Something was wrong. And the wrongness thickened when Adah suggested we meet at Oliver's, an industry dive that catered to the harder-living members of our profession.

Taking a final breath of cold night air, I pushed open the windowless, unmarked door and went inside. The bar was quiet still. Most folks came to Oliver's at the end of the night. I spotted Adah right away, hunched over her drink and bathed in blue neon light. My hand on her back, meant to soothe, made her jump and go tense.

"What's up?" I asked the question innocently enough, but hoped she might tell me what was actually bothering her. Because something was clearly going on. While I would never describe Adah as a particularly relaxed person, now she radiated tension. Her jawline was tight and sharp enough to cut. Her expression was flat, still.

"Nothin'." She pulled out the stool next to her and gestured for me to sit. I did. Then when she stayed silent I flagged the bartender, a young guy with elaborate facial hair, and ordered a gin and tonic. He made it quickly and sloppily and it tasted watery. I pushed it away and scooted closer to Adah.

"Is Pete with Vanessa tonight?" I tried a new approach, knowing Adah usually lit up when talking about her son.

But she just shook her head. "Nah. He's over at his friend's house. Birthday slumber party for some kid in his class."

Okay, this was good. A full sentence. I could work with that. "Oh was it Jason's birthday? One of his dads, is Samir his name? Anyway he came in a few days ago to buy a cake. He's so quiet, have you ever noticed that? I liked that about him. Do you ever notice how loud some guys can be? I feel like I'm always telling Andrew to take it down about six hundred decibels when we're in the kitchen together."

"No. It's some other kid's birthday." Adah took a long sip of her beer. She'd peeled the label off then torn the whole thing to shreds. Shreds she now started arranging into a neat row in front of her.

While I fundamentally didn't believe in the existence of awkward silences, the quiet that settled between us was not exactly comfortable. I took another sip of my awful drink and tried yet again to lighten things up. While I had only known Adah for a few months, I was already certain that if I directly asked her what was wrong, she would only add a few more bricks to the walls around her.

"Nina was in a weird mood today," I mused. Actually, now that I thought about it, my usually chipper best friend had been off for the past month or so. I'd simply been too busy with the ever-growing onslaught of customers and too fixated on my new relationship to actually stop and think about her. "She's been really quiet lately, which is so not like her. Cooking her heart out...but that's it. Huh. Note to self: tomorrow stop being such a self-absorbed asshole and talk to your best friend."

"Hey now." Adah shook her head and pushed a stray curl behind my ear. Warmth spread through me and I arched into her touch. "Don't say that about yourself. You're busy but you don't have a selfish bone in you. And I know you've been sitting there trying to figure out how to ask me what's wrong without spooking me."

I snorted out a laugh, the tension easing in my shoulders. Adah seemed to relax too. I ran my palm over the skin of her forearm where her sleeve was rolled up. "You're not wrong."

"You think it has anything to do with Jay?" Adah's question startled me.

"Jay? Why would Jay have anything to do with this?" I'd only met Jay at the queer dance party, but Adah talked about them often, always with a fondness that made me glad she had such a wonderful person in her life. I was having a hard time, though, connecting the dots between Adah's best friend and mine.

Adah nodded and shot me a slightly confused look. "Yup. They hooked up with Nina and then Nina kinda left them hanging. You know, said she'd call and never did."

My disbelief was strong enough to quickly snap into a messy, directionless anger. "No way. Nina wouldn't ghost someone. She's not an asshole. Besides, she tells me when she, like, buys a new pair of socks, so I think she might have mentioned hooking up with the bff of the person I'm dating. It was probably someone else from the party."

Adah shook her head but shrugged, clearly not wanting to get into it. "I'm pretty sure. But anyway, maybe just ask Nina what's going on."

I narrowed my eyes at Adah. Even though I'd seen her dozens of times, had held her in my arms, had woken up next to her, I couldn't get over how gorgeous she was. That perfect balance of tough and soft. The way her face lit up when she finally let that stoic mask slip away. But smoking hot or no, I was so not letting her get away with deflecting.

"Nice try there, slick." I bumped my knee against hers under the bar. "Something is clearly going on with *you.*

Don't try to throw me off the scent with this Nina business."

Adah laughed, resigned. "You brought that up. But okay, fine. Can we take a walk, though? Mac insisted I check this place out but…" She glanced from the greasy paneled walls to the group of loud guys who'd just stumbled in.

"Yeah. A walk sounds good." Nodding emphatically, I shrugged on my coat.

The wind had picked up in the half hour or so we'd been in the bar and as I followed Adah down the uneven brick sidewalk I wished she would take my hand, cuddle in close. Her heavy work jacket looked a hell of a lot warmer than the beautiful embroidered wool peacoat I'd spent half my savings on at a market in London years ago. But at least the silence was easy between us now as we navigated to the waterfront path, busy with runners and dog walkers on sunny days, now desolate and still. We were headed in the direction of Adah's apartment and I hoped we would go straight there instead of lingering in the chilly air. Stepping into a pool of orange streetlight glow, I realized how tired Adah looked. Her shoulders were up, her hands stuffed into her pockets, eyes trained to the ground. Trying not to sigh, I gazed out at the ocean. Lights glittered on the opposite side of the bay and the moon reflected bright white on the black water.

"It's cold," I said, officially scraping the bottom of the conversational barrel. I was relieved when, in response, Adah's arms came around me. She smelled like the kitchen still, like warm spices and browned butter, but under it I could smell her. Clean and fresh and, now, achingly familiar. A scent that clung to my skin and made me flush with heat and grin to myself like an idiot. Without thinking I burrowed into her, craving the closeness missing between us all night.

I was frustrated with myself for not being better at navigating this. I knew things weren't easy for Adah. Being a single mom was hard enough. Pile on the fact that her workplace seemed to be growing more toxic by the hour, and the writhing pit of trauma that she kept locked away deep, I was impressed that the woman even managed to get out of bed in the morning. So much of me wanted to swoop in and fix it. All of me felt her pain too deeply and wanted to draw it out of her by any means necessary. I could suggest therapy. I could berate her with questions until she finally cracked and answered them. I wanted to devote myself wholly to making her happy.

But I didn't know how. So I stayed silent, listening to the wind and the sea. Then I tipped my face up to Adah's and pressed my mouth to hers.

The kiss seemed to startle her but then she pulled me closer, held me tight. At least I knew this. The language of her body, I understood. I deepened the kiss, gripping the rough fabric of her coat, relishing the warmth of her skin. What started as gentle grew hungry and then Adah was tugging me fast the few blocks to her apartment. The heels of my boots rang out against the cobblestones and into the night.

As soon as the door clicked shut behind me Adah pushed my coat down and claimed my mouth in a bruising kiss. Gone was her usual trepidation. Tonight, Adah was in control and I let myself drift in her current. My back hit the kitchen wall with a hard thump, and it took me a moment to remember that Pete was at a friend's house for the night. We were alone. No need to be quiet or careful. Desire shivered down my spine leaving me clumsy and wanting. All I knew was Adah's arms around me, her mouth on my neck, the soft moans in my throat. The ache between my legs grew, until my whole body pulsed with scorching need. We were both still fully dressed but I knew if Adah so much as rubbed me through my tights I would come.

Unwilling to break the kiss even for a moment, I reached to undo the buttons on Adah's shirt, my fingers trembling and slipping. Adah broke away, smiled, and shook her head slowly. "Pull your tights down." Her voice was warm and commanding and perfect.

My pussy clenched as I rolled the clingy fabric down my legs. Our eyes met. Her pupils were blown wide, her cheeks flushed. Then the touch almost painfully light, her fingers trailed up the bare skin of my thighs. I was on fire, unable to do anything but wait for Adah to make me feel good.

"Please," I whined.

Pushing my panties to the side, Adah's fingers plunged into me in one smooth, hard thrust. My muscles clenched around her and an electric jolt of pleasure twisted in my stomach. Fuck, I was wet. Everything felt sensitized and swollen and completely perfect. She slid out of me, spreading slickness onto my clit, rubbing in small, tight circles. Just as I predicted, I came fast and hard. Everything went white. I felt my orgasm everywhere, hot sparks dancing in my throat and stomach. I collapsed against Adah, my bones turned liquid.

"You're so beautiful." She pressed her lips to my cheek, reigniting my desire. "I love watching you come."

Suddenly, the need to touch Adah was overwhelming. I wanted to run my hands, my lips, my tongue over every inch of her gorgeous skin. "Can I touch you now, please?"

"Of course." She cupped my face and kissed me thoroughly before pulling me into the living room. The futon was still pulled out as a bed, neatly made with a red wool blanket and deep blue sheets. She turned on the small, old-school stereo on the sideboard and the room filled with soft music. Something low and longing—a country artist I didn't recognize.

I undressed quickly and slid under the covers. The apartment was cold. I watched as Adah revealed herself, shedding her heavy jeans and belt, efficiently undoing the rest of the buttons on her shirt. She lay down next to me and I snuggled into her, grateful for her warmth. Because of our hectic schedules and most of our date time including Pete, it was rare that Adah and I had time to go slow and enjoy each other. Mostly, it had been hurried make-outs and getting off fast. I knew she liked making me come, but with the exception of a down-the-pants, over-the-underwear rubbing and some top-notch thigh grinding, I hadn't had the chance to touch her. Now I wanted to make her feel good. Make her forget, at least for a few minutes, whatever had been weighing her down all night.

I ghosted my lips over her chest, from the thin skin of her collarbone down to flick my tongue over her nipple. Adah's breasts were small and perfect in my hands. She gasped when my teeth grazed her, arching up into me. I smiled against her belly, kissing down the smooth planes of her hips. As much as I wanted to push her thighs apart and bury my nose into the small patch of pubic hair between them, I paused and looked up at her. Her arm was over her eyes, hair mussed, chest heaving. She seemed to sense my gaze on her and sat up a little.

"Do you like penetration?" The question felt clinical, but I had to ask. Plenty of people didn't. It was always best to read the recipe before you started cooking.

A small wrinkle formed between Adah's straight eyebrows and she sat all the way up. "Not really." Her voice carried an edge of something that sounded too much like apology.

"Whatever you're comfortable with is perfect," I whispered, smoothing her hair back and kissing her temple softly. "Tell me what you like, what you don't like... I promise you're not going to offend me." I winked.

Adah smiled softly, shifting to press her mouth to mine. My heart constricted. That same weird, overwhelmed feeling took over again and I wanted to squeeze her close. I needed to get a fucking grip. To distract myself I pushed Adah back down into the pillows and focused on her eyes. That gorgeous soft green. I had never wanted so badly to kiss someone's eyes before. Okay, clearly this wasn't helping. Her breasts. Focus. I kissed down her neck again, nipping and licking her until she started moaning steadily and her hands fisted the sheets.

"Beth." Adah breathed my name and my whole body clenched with need. Fuck. "Can you please..."

"Tell me what you want, baby." I kissed her sharp hip bone, grateful for the distraction because where the hell had that term of endearment come from?

Adah half laughed, half groaned. "I'm not used to this much talking, you know."

"Well get used to it. I like hearing from you." I swirled my fingers over her clit, keeping my touch feather soft. Her gasp brought a smile to my lips even as my whole body lit up with desire. I wanted nothing more than to make her feel as comfortable and cared for as I did in her presence. "Is this what you want? My fingers?" I dropped my lips back to her stomach, kissing just as gently as I'd touched her. "Or do you want me to eat your pussy?"

"That." Adah's voice was raw now and I felt her clench at my words. "Please, that."

I started slow, dragging the point of my tongue up and down to spread her wetness. I tasted salt and the sweet tang of her desire. Adah's hands tangled into my hair, and she ground against my mouth. My own body felt flushed and desperate but I focused on Adah. Listened carefully to the cadence of her moans and her rhythmic cries of pleasure, shifting the angle and pressure to get it just right. And when I did, she went rigid and silent against my mouth, her grip on my hair just shy of painful. I was so turned on simply feeling her that I almost came myself.

As she relaxed, I nuzzled against her smooth, muscular thighs. Slowly kissing my way back up until I could plaster myself against her, part of me wanted to keep going. Wanted to see how many times we could make each other come, maybe breaking for a late-night snack. But my body had other ideas. Adah's arms around me and the warm press of her skin lulled me into the kind of satisfied, hazy half-sleep I absolutely adored. It was like falling asleep in the perfect patch of summer sun.

The rumble of Adah's voice roused me and I blinked my eyes open, wondering how long I'd been dozing. "Sorry, what?" I asked, taking a deep breath through my nose and rubbing my face roughly.

"Oh nothin', sorry, honey. Go back to sleep." Adah kissed my forehead and then I was awake and turned on. Why the hell did that do it for me?

"No. I'm up. What is it? Are you finally ready to tell me what's been bugging you all night?" I was half teasing but Adah nodded seriously.

"Yeah. It's not a big deal, just…" She trailed off and her fingers tangled into my hair. I wondered if touching me soothed her. I hoped so. "Work stuff. Right before the, um, cook-off…before you came in, Sean told me he wanted us to change vendors. Like keep saying that we are 'committed to the finest ingredients' but actually start buying more from Wesco."

I bristled, ready to smack that fucking asshole back to whatever pretentious cocktail lounge he'd been shaken up in. But Adah wasn't finished.

"I didn't really know what to say, you know? Like, yeah, in theory I'm in control of purchasing but Sean does the budget and he's our connection to corporate for the most part. But then the next day he told me that he'd canceled all of our contracts with local suppliers. We ended up losing some money because he didn't bother to read the fine print. Now we get pretty much all of our food from Wesco." She shook her head.

"Fuck! Are you fucking serious? You guys charge like forty-five dollars a plate! That's highway robbery. Not to mention…"

Adah surprised me by laughing her warm, low laugh

and claiming my mouth in a feverish kiss. "You are really something, you know that?"

Heat bloomed on my face but I shrugged, all easy nonchalance. "There's more to this sordid tale, isn't there?"

"You bet. I guess Sean got wind that Marcus is due in town any day now. So this morning I get into work and what do you know. The whole dang menu has been overhauled. He said Ric and the rest of the partners approved it but..." She bit her lip. "That was my menu. It was good food. But that little snake had been developing something with the chef at Per Diem, our sister restaurant in New York. It's all this weird foam and gel...that molecular gastronomy junk, which I kind of thought was over and done with." She sighed and her weariness seeped into my bones. "Anyway, I hate the new menu. But what the heck can I do? It's already approved and up on the website, so that's that, I suppose."

I tried, I really did, to rein myself in. Logically, I knew exploding into a fiery ball of righteous indignation was useless. What Adah needed was to be heard and supported. But, unfortunately for both of us, my passion boiled over like an unwatched pot of milk.

"You have to be fucking kidding me." I sat up, blood rushing to my head and cool air striking my skin as the sheet slipped down. "I would say I'm surprised but if my time at the Gourmet Institute in Sonoma taught me anything, it is that this industry is fueled by pure, unadulterated bullshit." And now I was on a tear. My brother used to call them my spirals of doom. I liked to think of them as passionate speeches. Either way. "I don't know what you expected, frankly, working with people like that. It's all about the bottom line. Who gives a shit about the local economy, right? What the fuck does it matter that the farmers in this state are desperately poor? As long as we can call it innovative and make sure some random assholes from, like, LA like it, that's the important thing. Plus Marcus is going to hate that." Somewhere in the back of my mind an alarm bell sounded and I forced my stupid mouth shut.

Adah didn't look mad. She, surprise, surprise, looked totally impassive. "Our food was good before Sean made all these changes, though. You said you liked it when you came in the other day." A tiny glimmer of hurt shone at the edge of her words. It should have stopped me. It didn't.

"Well yeah, your food is great. You're clearly a talented chef. I mean, you honestly can make a delicious plate of food, honey. I was so fucking jealous when you won the cook-off. But you deserved it." *Good, keep going down this path, Beth. Remember you want to be nice to this woman you cannot stop thinking about. Your job here is to help her feel better, not to throw water on a grease fire.* "But, like, the restaurant itself is so designer and slick. Who needs that in Maine? And all that super delicate plating... I don't know. I just think food should be more honest. But if Marcus was going to have an issue with your sourcing before, he sure as shit isn't going to like it now. I mean, how dumb do you all think your customers are?" And great, I had been a complete and total asshole. Definitely a spiral of doom.

Before I could formulate a half-decent apology, Adah was up and out of bed. The music cut abruptly and she tugged her briefs up without meeting my eye. "It's late.

I'm just gonna wash up real quick." The soft click of the bathroom door closing echoed in my ears until I drifted into an uneasy sleep.

Chapter Sixteen

Adah

It had been a long time since I'd been this tired. Even in the early days of Pete reverse cycling at the same time I worked the morning shift at the Sunshine Diner, I hadn't been this darn exhausted. Now, learning a whole new menu, dusting off techniques I hadn't much cared about during culinary school, and helping Pete finish up his stupid family tree school project had me honest to goodness feeling like I could nod off on my feet at any given moment.

Sean had it on good authority, or so he claimed, that Marcus would be coming to review us by the end of the week, which meant he'd been in rare form, hovering over my every move. And not just mine. He'd told Jay they cracked eggs wrong and called Mac sweetheart so many times she threatened to quit if he did it again. At that I'd told him calmly to get the heck out of my kitchen until he learned how to treat his coworkers with respect. The new menu was a total joke: so fiddly and dull that no one seemed to like cooking in our kitchen anymore. Plus, I'd gotten up at five this morning to make sure I had my son's meal prep squared away before heading into the restaurant to catch up on inventory. Thank heavens it was Monday. I could toss leftover lasagna in the oven, stretch out on the couch, and read with Pete until we both dozed off around sunset.

But as I lumbered up the weathered wooden steps to the apartment, the steady thump of pop music drilled right into my skull. Usually the young couple that lived above us was quiet as a pair of church mice. It was just my luck that they picked today to have some kind of noisy celebration. A loud peal of laughter drifted on the cool evening air and I felt my jaw tighten. That was Pete's laugh. Maybe he and Vanessa were doing another one of the calisthenic workouts she'd become fond of. I pulled open the door, trying to figure out a polite way to ask Vanessa to turn it down, only to come face-to-face with Beth.

The source of the shrill music was Beth's sticker-covered laptop, open on the counter. Behind her, Vanessa and Pete were dancing and laughing. The tension in my jaw radiated down into my throat, my shoulders, lodging hot in my chest.

"What are you doing here?" My voice was a harsh crack. Pete and Vanessa stopped dancing. Confusion overtook the smile on Beth's face.

"Oh, um." Beth wiped her hands, which were dusted in flour, on her jeans.

"Sorry, hon, I should have texted you." Vanessa waved me inside. I realized I was still standing in the doorway, letting the cold rush into the kitchen. "Beth stopped by to surprise you. When Pete and I got home from school we saw the poor thing waiting on your porch and…" Vanessa kept talking. But my head was throbbing now, every heavy bass note making my heart race faster, my head pound harder.

Deep breath. The kitchen smelled good. Toasty and rich with the smells of herbs and cheese. *Focus.* But I couldn't. Shards of worries and memories rattled around in my mind. Would Vanessa let just anyone in here? Would I get home from work one day to find the reverend sitting at my table, that slick smile turning the lock to let him into my house?

Without thinking, I snapped the laptop shut, plunging the kitchen into quiet.

"We made pizza, Mom." Pete's voice was bright, but his gaze bounced from me to Beth to Vanessa like he was trying to find the source of tension. I'd had plenty of practice at that particular game when I was his age.

This was when I was supposed to smile. Shrug off my coat and ruffle my son's hair and say thank you. Maybe kiss Beth's cheek. Instead I stood, teeth grinding, eyes trained to the floor. I'd missed a spot last time I'd scrubbed the tile. A small patch of gray stood out against the gleaming white. Hot anger roared through me and I bit my lip hard enough to taste blood. But why the heck was I angry?

"Sorry, I hope it's okay. I just, um, wanted to surprise you." Beth's voice was small.

"Thanks." My reply was automatic and harsh.

Vanessa cleared her throat and grabbed her jacket from where it hung on the back of a kitchen chair. "Well, I've got last night's *Game of Thrones* and Chinese leftovers with my name on them. You all set, Addie?" I usually loved the silly nickname Vanessa had bestowed on me. Now it raised my hackles. I nodded and let her leave without another word.

I didn't miss the confused look Pete shot to Beth and my body didn't forget to surge with guilt at the mess I'd made. For no reason at all I was making my own kid feel nervous. I was no better than the reverend. My stomach clenched. I needed to go outside, to pull as much fresh autumn air into the back of my throat as possible. To fill myself with fresh and clean and push out all the bad. Then I saw Pete's hands. The flash of pink glittery polish on his nails catching the golden afternoon light.

The words came out before I could stop them. "Take it off." A flat command. I'd been doing this all wrong. Focusing on all the wrong things. All that mattered was my son. Not chive foams and cubes of white wine gelée. Not Marcus Blanche. Not even Beth.

What was I going to do when Pete came home from school with tear tracks on his cheeks because kids could take any scrap of difference and shape it into an excuse to be cruel? When Jason and the other kids didn't want to play with him anymore. When teachers pulled me aside to ask if everything was okay at home. *It ain't right.* The reverend's voice filled my ears.

"What?" Again my son looked to Beth instead of me.

"Your nails," I snapped. "Take that crap off."

"Do we have nail polish remover?" Pete asked, genuinely confused.

We didn't. I hadn't painted my nails once in my life. I shook my head. "I need to talk to Beth." I pushed out onto the porch, hoping like heck she would follow. I couldn't stay in that room another second. But the slap of cold air on my face did little to calm me down.

As soon as Beth tugged the door shut behind her, I rounded on her. My anger was huge and scary. Her arms were crossed over her chest, whether to keep warm or shield herself from me, I didn't know.

"What the fuck is wrong with you?" I wasn't sure if I was being quiet but I couldn't really bring myself to care. "What the hell were you thinking coming over here without telling me?"

She flinched back like I'd slapped her full across the face. "I'm really sorry. I just wanted to do something nice for you after the other night. I know I was a total asshole and you seemed so stressed so... I don't know. I really didn't mean to upset you. I can leave if you want." Beth's eyes went wide and glassy. The look on her face was pure hurt. It should have stopped me, but it didn't.

"And painting his nails! You don't just do that to someone's kid without asking." I rubbed my hands through my hair, giving it a quick, hard tug. "Do you have any idea what the kids at school are gonna say? He's already the new kid. He doesn't need to go in there looking like a freak." Unbidden my brothers' taunts rushed back to me. Their laughter anytime I tried to get away with borrowing their clothes. Their shock and disgust when I cut off the hair I'd hated for so long.

"Sorry, he said he liked mine and I had the polish in my bag. But honey, I don't think his friends will say anything. And even if they do, do you really want him buying into all that heteronormative patriarchal bullshit? I think if kids know how to communicate and push back—"

I cut her off, raising my hands. "You have no idea what you're talking about."

Beth's shoulders dropped and she nodded slowly, her eyes so intent on my face I felt like she could see clear into me. "You're right," she said. "I'm not a parent. And I'm not really visibly queer so I don't know what it's like to navigate that stuff. But, Adah, you are both. I mean, how can you get upset about painted nails when you don't worry about conforming to gender norms either? And I'm so sorry if I overstepped. I really am. I just wanted to have a fun night in and…"

She kept talking but I didn't listen. I couldn't. Her words went distant and dull. My focus shifted away, out to the twist of purple and gold clouds on the horizon. I wanted to flow out to meet them, to feel nothing. Instead, guilt clogged my throat, expanding until it almost filled me right up.

The kitchen door banged open and Pete poked his head out, face a mask of worry. My body startled. Had we been shouting? What the heck had I even said? I knew Beth had been quiet. I knew I hadn't. An apology situated itself on the tip of my tongue but Pete spoke first. "Sorry, I think the pizzas might be…"

With a tiny yelp, Beth darted inside and I followed. The kitchen wasn't quite choked with smoke but it was hazy and acrid with it. Thankfully, the fire alarm hadn't gone off yet. Wrenching the window open wide, I shouted for Pete to prop open the door. Beth switched off the oven and when I turned, I saw the two beautifully formed pizzas she'd made were charred through. She transferred them to the cutting board on the counter and the three of us stared at the remains of our dinner for a long moment. I could have salvaged the evening. Could have spit out that apology and pulled the lasagna out of the fridge. Could have asked Beth to stay. Instead when she offered to run to the Italian market down the street to replace the pizzas, I shook my head.

I'd never seen Beth like this before. She seemed unusually panicked: eyes wide, frantic. I realized then, how much I relied on her calm. Now, in its absence, my panic grew too big. I wanted her to touch me, to brush her cool, rough fingers over my cheek and tell me everything was fine. I wanted her to clean up this whole mess that I'd made but I didn't know how to ask.

"Adah." She said my name so gently it almost broke me clean in two. "I'm really sorry. What can I do?" She did touch me then, but so tentatively it made me feel worse.

"You know what... I'm real tired. Have to get up early tomorrow."

I didn't know if I was thankful or miserable when Beth nodded, said goodbye to Pete, and left without another word.

Wednesday lunch service was dead. Not a single customer walked through the door for the first hour we were open. Sure, it was snowing outside. But we'd never been completely empty before. The kitchen was silent. I'd sent two of my line cooks home and was considering telling Mac she could take the rest of the afternoon off too, when Jay slapped the metal prep table and groaned.

Mac looked up from her dinner mise, half startled, half amused.

"You know you're killing us, right?"

The last thing I wanted was to be short with my staff, not to mention the only person who seemed capable of putting up with me. So I rolled my shoulders back and took a deep breath before setting down my knife and looking at Jay. "I can't help it that we're still doing this dang lunch service. I told Sean…"

"No, dummy." Jay crossed the kitchen to put their hands on my shoulders. "I mean you. You're so goddamn miserable it's like someone let a bunch of angry, taciturn rain clouds in here."

I felt my face heat. I had been…unhappy since Beth left on Monday. She'd texted a few times. Long, sincere apologies. But when I didn't respond she stopped. I didn't know what to say.

"Sorry. Just some personal stuff." I tried for a casual shrug but it felt robotic.

"Yeah no shit, Sherlock. Did you and Beth break up?"

My stomach flipped. Had we? Had my cruelty and silence cut the cord that tied us together? Was it that easy? I picked up a clean towel and started wiping the already spotless stainless steel in front of me.

"Maybe she doesn't want to talk about it," Mac said behind me.

"Well too fucking bad. I'm worried, you know, Adah. I haven't seen you like this since…" They trailed off. The last time I'd felt like this, numb and scooped out, had been after the reverend had shown up at my old apartment and scared me half to death.

"It's nothing like that," I murmured. Mac didn't know about my past and she didn't need to. That was private. Ancient history. Closed.

"Okay so you and Beth broke up. Or got in a fight. Or something is wrong with Pete. You can tell me, babe."

"I don't know." I groaned into my hands. "I guess we broke up? She came over to surprise me and was there with Pete when I got home. I wasn't expecting it and I lost it. I barely remember what I said but it wasn't good."

Jay made a sympathetic face. "Okay, well that kind of sounds like a fight. Did you two talk about it after?"

My guilt was so big I thought it might split my skin trying to burst out of me. "No. She texted me a few times but I didn't respond. I mean, what the heck am I supposed to say? I don't know how to do this."

"Well you could start with apologizing for snapping at her." Jay's voice was insistent but not unkind. "Are you sure everything's okay with you because I'm—"

Jay's words died on their lips, however, as one of our servers came barreling into the kitchen. His pale cheeks were flushed and his eyes flashed wide, darting from me to Mac, then back to the dining room. I searched my mind for the guy's name. A good number of the front of house people Sean had originally hired had been college kids, chosen more for their looks than their experience waiting tables. This guy… Tim, that was his name, was a little older and far more competent. Too bad for him business had been so slow since he started that he was probably barely pulling in enough tip money to eat anything other than our family meals.

"Everything okay, Tim?" I asked. The guy looked like he'd seen a ghost.

"Yes, chef. I just thought you should know right away that Marcus Blanche is here. Sean showed us all a picture of him and well..." Tim gestured to our best table by the window, where a stylishly dressed man with salt and pepper hair perused the menu. "That's him."

My stomach curdled and my legs buckled. He was the only person in the dining room. Why the heck had he come for lunch? I didn't like anything about the new menus, but the lunch service was downright awful. And eating in silence, save for the awful, sleazy sounding electronica Sean insisted on playing, would make it even worse.

After a moment of feeling sorry for myself and letting all my worries in, I closed the barn door and trapped them there. I needed to focus. Needed to serve this man the best dang meal I could possibly cook.

"Bring him out a glass of the '02 Le Mesnil Blanc de Blancs, on the house, and then come right back. Sound good?"

Tim nodded seriously and turned on his heel.

Jay and Mac didn't say a word. They got to work. We had talked about our plan for when Marcus finally showed up and we executed it flawlessly. Jay started on forming fresh pita, the dough studded with sumac and nigella seeds. We had some ready to go, but these would arrive to Marcus fresh from the oven. When I glanced over at Mac's station, she was already arranging the crispy onions on top of the tuna tartare with preserved lemon and Aleppo pepper we planned to serve as an amuse-bouche.

I checked her plating, perfect as usual, and lifted the bone china bowl off the pass.

I quieted the noise in my head. There was no more fight with Beth, no more worrying about my son, no more fussing over what Sean was going to say. There was me, and the food, and the guest. Marcus Blanche. Taking a deep, even breath, I walked out into the dining room. I had to admit, although it was a little over the top for my tastes, our restaurant was lovely. Near the front door stood a small table covered in a careful arrangement of autumn flowers and greenery. The soapstone bar, even empty, was striking. The floors were rough-hewn wood stained a matte black, the walls a deep terra cotta.

Marcus sat at the center table in front of the windows overlooking the port. He gazed out the window at the admittedly beautiful view. In the distance a few tugboats chugged out to sea. Bruised slate clouds hung heavy over the dark water.

I'd seen pictures of Marcus before, had read larger-than-life profiles detailing his childhood in Lagos and culinary training in Paris, but he seemed smaller in person. He was thin with the kind of gentle presence that made me want to sit with him in easy quiet. His clothes were nice in the way that rich people's clothes always were, simple but beautifully made. He must have felt me looking at him because he turned to me and offered a soft smile.

"Ah, you must be Chef Campbell." His voice was musical, with a light British accent.

"Yes sir. It's a pleasure to meet you. Thank you so much for joining us this afternoon."

"Oh please call me Marcus. And the pleasure is all mine.

This is a lovely space you have here." He glanced around the dead empty restaurant and it took everything in me not to apologize for the oppressive quiet.

"Thank you. We're proud of it." I paused, smiled, glanced at his water glass to make sure it was still full. "Have you had a moment to look over the menu, or would you like a little more time?" A bolt of inspiration hit me then. A special. I could offer him something good. Something interesting. Something that was mine. A dish I'd been dying to make with some of the sea bass we'd gotten in floated to the surface of my mind. I mentally checked our pantry—we had everything I needed to make it. "I did want to tell you about a special we have today." Another pause. The last thing I wanted to do was rattle off the details of a dish he had no interest in hearing about.

Thankfully, he perked up, dark brown eyes lifting from the menu to lock with mine. "Please."

I raced back into the kitchen, heart hammering in my chest. Mac and Jay turned, both of their faces tense. Idly, I wondered where Sean was, why he wasn't out there schmoozing with Marcus and ruining the man's meal with his terrible, borderline offensive jokes. He'd been showing up later and later, looking puffy and exhausted. Whatever the reason for his absence, I was grateful for it.

"Okay." I washed my hands quickly and called Marcus's order over my shoulder. "I need one brussels sprout salad, one scallop. Jay, when the pita's done run it out to Marcus yourself and charm the pants off him."

Jay barked out a laugh behind me. "You got it, chef."

"Um, chef." Mac's voice was heavy with confusion. "Did he not do a main or…"

My lips twitched up. I looked around my kitchen. It was still mine. I had my best friend in the world here and a take-no-prisoners sous-chef. "We're gonna do a special."

Chapter Seventeen

Beth

Quinces were a fascinating fruit. Knobby and yellow on the outside, hard and tart inside, when exposed to the magic of heat they transmuted into a soft, sensual pink bursting with flavor. I contemplated the pounds of quince we'd gotten from Snakeroot Orchard. Maybe a cake would be best. It was November now, officially cold. Outside the trees were nearly bare of their russet and ochre leaves. Frost etched the windowpane. Guests would appreciate winter spices, the floral bite of wildflower honey, and a bit of almond flour melding into the kind of warming dessert folks wanted when they came in from the snow. Then again, poached quince with a thick, creamy custard could be good too.

I wrapped my arms around myself and heaved an overly

dramatic sigh. It was all well and good to plan next week's menu, but what I really wanted was to hear back from Adah. It had been more than two weeks since my disastrous pizza party. I'd texted a few times. I'd even worked up the nerve to call and leave a very pathetic voicemail. But if Adah didn't want to hear from me, I had to respect her boundaries. Even if I didn't understand them.

I did understand that I had fucked up. Something about me showing up out of the blue had been a major trigger for Adah. There was no mistaking the terror flashing in her eyes, the way she seemed to retreat so far into herself she wasn't there with me at all. I'd felt her pain like a hot brand on my own skin. Sure, she'd been kind of a jerk. But I wanted to talk it through, wanted to understand, wanted to help her in any way I could.

My body felt hollow, hulled out, and sick with sadness I didn't want to acknowledge. For the first time I'd known in my bones that everything was right. That she and I fit together. That she was my person. It was more than the fact that I wanted to tear her very practical clothes off every time I saw her. More than the arguing over recipes and teasing her about her the fact that she'd seemingly never listened to music made after 1980. Something fit. I saw a bright, clear future with Adah. It pained me to think of it now but I'd imagined getting into the habit of helping Pete with his homework in the evenings, picking him up from school and stopping for an ice cream on the way home. I'd hoped to finally show Adah my house, to wrap her in comfort and set her at ease in every way possible. I wanted the chance to show her how much I cared.

The back door clattered open and Nina brought a swirl

of snowflakes and snap of cold air into the kitchen with her. At first glance, I thought her face was red from the cold. Like me, she was pale and tended to flush easily. Then I saw her puffy eyes and pained expression. I opened my arms and she came into them willingly, her tears immediately wetting the fabric of my shirt.

"Sweetheart, what's wrong?" I ran a soothing hand over her hair.

"I'm so sorry, Beth." Nina's voice was raw and tiny.

The heartbreak in my usually sunshiney friend's voice sent a tremor of worry through me. Nina had seemed decidedly off for the past few months. The few times I'd tried to check in with her, though, she brushed me aside. Was she sick? Had something happened to her family? Had I done something unkind or spent too much time talking about my new relationship? Gripping her shoulders tight, I pushed Nina back and stared into the deep gray of her eyes.

"You're going to hate me." She dropped her gaze to the floor.

My worry shifted then. Fear wrapped its fingers around my throat and when I spoke my voice sounded forced. "I could never hate you. Tell me what's going on, okay?"

Nina sniffled and rubbed her eyes, leaving dark streaks of mascara on her cheeks and hands. "I just checked our email and we had a personal note from Marcus saying we won. People from *Gourmand* are coming in next week to do the photo shoot and interview you." She paused, clearly waiting for my reaction.

My thoughts scattered. I should have been trying to connect the dots as to why this good news was making Nina weep. Instead, though, concern for Adah flooded my mind.

She would be devastated. And this award definitely wasn't going to help my case for winning her back.

"Did he say who else they listed for the top five?" My mouth moved ahead of my brain. I said a silent prayer to the universe that Bella Vista had at least been awarded a spot.

Nina nodded. "Yeah he included a link to the announcement on their website. I'm pretty sure there was one other place in Maine…some B&B way up north. Obviously Ninth Street in Boston came in second. And some other new place that opened up in Cambridge. I forget the other one though…"

I yanked my phone out of my pocket and thumbed over to my email app. The message from Marcus was lengthy but I didn't even skim it. I would read and reply later. My breath stuttered to a halt as I clicked the link and waited for the article to load. Damn spotty cell service.

Then there it was. The five best restaurants in New England with The Yellow House right at the top. I didn't even read the review. I already knew what we'd served Marcus: the same fall vegetable and venison tourtière we'd served all of our other customers that day. He'd ordered an extra side of our blistered endive and homemade fromage blanc toast, a kale and buttercup squash salad, and a slice of tarte tatin for dessert. My eyes flicked over the glowing reviews of a French-style inn near Elkhead Lake, gushing descriptions of the elegant Italian place in Cambridge, recycled praise for Ninth Street, and then… My stomach dropped. The number five spot had gone to a family-run Vietnamese restaurant in New Haven. I kept scrolling, past the flashing ads, down to the bottom. I wanted to punch the air. He'd mentioned Bella Vista among a list of notable dishes to try.

While Bella Vista's watered-down molecular gastronomy ap-proach feels out of context among the coastal charm of South Bay, Chef Adah Campbell's baked sea bass with a fresh za'atar salsa verde was a bright spot in an otherwise unexciting menu.

"He mentioned Adah!" I chirped, waving my phone at Nina.

Nina's eyebrows crashed together. "Aren't you excited about us winning? Now we've really made it. This is a re-ally big fucking deal, Beth." She said this in a monotone, like she couldn't be less happy about the news.

I lifted a shoulder. Of course, it felt good to know that people liked our food. But I hadn't opened The Yellow House to cater to critics. And besides, we were already so overbooked the new wave of publicity was probably going to drive me into an early grave—death by shaping pastry. Plus, I still hadn't come up with a funding solution for the dining room expansion problem, which was now more dire than ever. "I mean obviously it's awesome, but Adah's going to be so upset. She really wanted to win this and…"

"Jesus Christ!" Nina snapped. "Can you stop talking about Adah for like two seconds? I get it, you're in love, everything worked out perfectly for you. You got the life you wanted." Nina's voice broke and tears slid down her cheeks, one after the other.

As much as I wanted to push back—to remind Nina that Adah wouldn't even talk to me, that I'd never been sure I wanted this life, that I was still so scared and over-whelmed I wanted to run away—I knew now wasn't the time for that. Nina and I had never fought, not even when we decided to stop hooking up and stayed friends. "Tell me what's wrong." I leaned against the prep table and tried to project as much calm as possible.

"I'm leaving," Nina murmured. "I wanted to tell you earlier but then you seemed so happy and then all this award stuff came up and now we won and I've probably fucked everything up for you."

"Hold on, honey, slow down. What do you mean you're leaving?"

Nina buried her face in her hands and shook her head. She'd always been dramatic, my best friend. I crossed the small kitchen and pried her hands away from her flushed cheeks.

"I just feel so stuck here, you know? Like, you left. You got to travel and date around and see shit. I don't know, like, I'm gonna be thirty next year and what the hell have I even accomplished? This town feels so small now and I just didn't know what to do. So when I saw this opening at a winery in Bordeaux, I applied. I didn't think they'd have any interest in me but they want me to start in the new year. So basically I'm completely fucking you over because we're about to get even busier and you'll be down a chef and you and I both know you'll take a zillion years to hire someone." She started twirling her hair around her finger, something she'd always done when she was nervous. Nina was almost never nervous. "And, well, I hooked up with Jay. You know, the pastry chef that works with your girlfriend." This last part was uttered in the kind of hushed whisper I would have expected from a deadly secret, not a revelation of a onetime sexual encounter I already knew about.

I waited for her to elaborate, to bring a little clarity to

this jumble of thoughts and feelings, but when she didn't, I decided now was the time for comfort. I hated the thought that Nina had twisted herself into knots trying to hide these things from me when really all I cared about was her happiness, whatever shape it took. "First, I mean it when I say I could never hate you. You know that. And I'm so thankful you worked with me but it doesn't mean you're chained to this kitchen forever. I'm sorry you felt like you couldn't tell me and I'm really sorry if I've been distracted lately because of Adah." At the mention of her name hot panic twisted through my chest. Maybe she wouldn't ever talk to me again. Maybe this award would push us so far apart I wouldn't be able to find my way back to her...

Not now. Focus on your friend and save your pity-party for your few hours of tossing and turning and failing to fall asleep.

"And I'm a little confused," I said belatedly. "What does you hooking up with Jay have to do with this though? Was it really so bad you want to skip town?"

Nina huffed out a small laugh. "No. Pretty much the opposite to be honest. They were so fucking cute and nice and perfect and I'm just not ready for..." She gestured wildly at me.

"Ready for what?" I chuckled.

Now it was time for the dramatic eye roll. "Oh you know. The whole stupid in love, settled down, it's destiny thing you and Miss Hot Butch Adah have going on. I could tell that's what Jay wanted too. You know, a capital R relationship: making breakfast together, camping trips, and all that shit. After I slept with them I started thinking about what I really wanted and I realized I've never really gone after it, you know?"

Nina's words ignited the spark in my chest I'd spent the last week trying to extinguish. I needed to try. I was done running. I wanted stay here. With Adah. I owed it to both of us to try to salvage this relationship from the burning wreck I'd turned it into. Moving on instinct alone, I spun on my heel and darted to the tiny closet I'd turned into an office and grabbed my jacket off the coatrack. When I returned to the kitchen, digging around in my coat pocket for my car keys, Nina's eyebrows had shot to her hairline and confusion had eclipsed worry on her face.

"I love you and I'm proud of you and I know you're going to kick ass in Bordeaux. But right now I have to take care of something, okay? Can you get Grace to finish this?" I waved my hand at the pile of quince and mess of spices I'd pulled from the pantry.

"Wait what? Where are you going? Beth—"

The click of the door behind me cut off Nina's words. Heart in my throat, blood rushing hard and fast in my veins, I trudged through the knee-deep snow to my car. It was time to make things right with Adah.

The adrenaline rush wore off just as I stepped into the warm, dry air of Bella Vista's dining room. I'd only been in for the one lunch, but even a cursory glance revealed just how much money was being lavished on the restaurant. A large floral arrangement of chrysanthemums and twigs dominated the entryway. A bowl of matchbooks with the restaurant's name on them sat on the host stand. The bottles of top-shelf liquor behind the bar gleamed, softly lit in shades of blue from below. The place was dead empty.

"Good afternoon, table for one?" A pretty young woman

offered me a practiced smile. I realized I probably looked like a disaster: staring into space at the restaurant entrance, hair coated with snow and escaping from its braid, coat buttoned up all wrong. I needed to focus on Adah. On making things right between us. My mind felt blurry and sluggish though, every doubt that had been plaguing me for weeks returning in full force.

"Ma'am, can I help you?" The hostess sounded unsure now.

"Oh." I gave myself a little shake and patted my hair self-consciously. "I'm so sorry. I kinda zoned out there for a second. I'm a, um, friend of Chef Campbell's. Is she in?"

The woman laughed. "Of course she is. Chef Campbell practically lives here." She seemed to catch herself then, and ran another assessing gaze over me. I probably should have changed out of my flour-dusted jeans and kitchen clogs. "She might be busy though. Let me just check with our manager…"

"No need." An overly hearty voice called from behind her as Sean came into view. I hadn't gotten a good feeling from him the first time we'd met and Adah's stories about the general manager further soured his energy. "Miss Summers! To what do we owe the pleasure? I must congratulate you on the big award. You should be thrilled. We were certainly disappointed by the snub, but who gets into this business for the critics anyway?" His smile was a little forced, like he'd practiced the act of smiling dozens of times but never experienced actual joy. Yeah, bad energy for sure. Poor Adah, having to put up with this creep day in and out.

"It's definitely exciting, but like you said, critics aren't why I'm in business. I'd like to talk to Ad—Chef Campbell please."

Sean's whole demeanor changed then, the smile shifting from obsequious to slimy. His gaze slithered down my body then back to meet my eyes. "Ah, you ladies are pretty close, then? Hey, no judgement from me." He held up his hands.

I brushed past him without another word, happy that I was probably tracking snow and salt all over his stupid fancy black floors. The kitchen was a gleaming, silent spaceship, all spotless stainless steel and white tile. I found Adah immediately, her quiet confidence palpable even from across the room. She was beautiful. The overwhelmed feeling came back and like egg whites and sugar suddenly transforming into a perfect meringue, I knew what it was. Love. I was wildly in love with Chef Adah Campbell.

Her head flicked up from the prep work in front of her and our eyes locked. My whole body flushed hot and cold, prickling with awareness. I wanted to pull her into my arms, wrap her up tight, and leech away all of her sorrow. The first flicker of surprise over her features settled into a mask of stony indifference. Adah turned, murmured something to Jay, and crossed the kitchen toward me.

"Hi. Sorry for showing up randomly like this. I guess thinking things through really isn't my strong suit. I realize that it's probably kind of weird of me to show up at your workplace like this. If you want me to go I totally can. I'll respect your space. I'm just so sorry about the other day and I really care about you a lot." The words I'd rehearsed on my drive over tangled together as they rushed out of me in a jumbled mess. My hands were trembling.

Adah sighed and gestured to the walk-in. "Let's talk in

here." The flatness of her voice worried me. She closed the metal door softly behind us and the clatter of pans in the kitchen dulled. I glanced around at the orderly rows of produce and neatly labeled fish tubs and smiled to myself. My girl ran a tight ship.

"You saw the list, huh? Guess congratulations are in order." A tiny glimmer of hurt shone through her apathetic mask.

The urge to touch Adah boiled over. I knew, though, that I needed to follow her lead, that pushing any harder might break us irrevocably. I clasped my hands behind my back and willed myself to radiate empathy and care. "Honey, you know I don't care about that stuff. I'm so sorry. I know you were really eager to get some good press. And Marcus did mention one of your dishes, that counts for something, right? Anyway, regardless you have to know you're an amazing chef, no matter what some random dude says."

Adah crossed her arms over her chest. A long, taut band of silence stretched between us. My stomach clenched. I'd done it again. Said the wrong thing. I wanted to slap myself across the face. How did I always manage to fuck up? I needed to think things through for once, not just cannonball into problems and expect things to align themselves in the wake of my chaos.

"Well," she bit out, "I don't expect you to understand why this 'stuff' matters to me." She looked past me then, staring hard at the walk-in door like the only thing she wanted was to get back to work.

I looked at Adah for a long moment. Her chef whites perfectly starched, her hair pushed back with a rolled-up red bandanna, her posture so tense she looked spring-loaded. Maybe I'd been fooling myself this whole time. Maybe what I'd thought was the blossom of a relationship had only been a distraction for Adah. I'd been falling in love while she'd wanted out all along. My throat tightened and my nose fizzed with unshed tears.

"You could tell me, you know," I whispered, my voice dangerously close to breaking. "I get that it's hard for you to talk about how you feel. I really do. But I want to listen. I want to help you. I love feelings talk. It's, like, my specialty. Seriously, I understand that I'll never be able to change all the horrible shit that happened to you and I can't even imagine how hard everything has been in your life. Don't you think it might help to talk though? To me or to Jay or to a therapist. To someone. You can't keep working yourself into the ground and pretending that's going to make all your feelings disappear." My voice had gotten loud, filling the small space. I drew in a centering breath and closed my eyes. "Look, I really lo—care about you a lot. And now I feel crazy because it kind of seems like the whole time I thought we were…something, and you didn't. What do I even mean to you?"

The silence was unbearable. Blood roared in my ears as I waited and waited for Adah's response. She stared blankly at the door behind me, through me like I didn't even exist. When she opened her mouth to speak my heart pounded hard in my chest and my legs felt like they might give out under me.

"I really need to get back to work."

Chapter Eighteen

Adah

Turns out ten days without more than a few hours of sleep a night will catch up to you. Jay had been talking goodness knew how long, pacing my tiny kitchen, but I hadn't heard a word they'd said. It was like I was underwater trying to listen to distant words on dry land. Every night had been the same: working myself to the point of exhaustion, collapsing into bed, and spending the next few hours in the dark missing Beth and feeling sorry for myself. But I'd been awful. If I'd thought I messed up before, there was no going back now.

To make matters worse, since losing out on the award, things had gone south at Bella Vista. Sean hadn't exactly been a ray of sunshine to work with before, but now he was openly hostile to me in the kitchen. He was convinced that I'd messed up the menu dishes on purpose to make my special look good, and in doing so, lost us the spot we deserved. I didn't even have the energy to argue. All I could do was show up, cook the food I didn't care about, collect my paycheck, and take the few moments of joy I could find with my son.

I jolted back to the present at the soft touch of Jay's hand on my shoulder. My vision had blurred as I stared into space and I rubbed my eyes roughly. "Sorry," I muttered, "what were you saying?"

Jay shook their head and slid into the kitchen chair across from me. Worry filled their face and my heart dropped. I was in for yet another big talk I didn't know how to handle.

"You have to tell me what's wrong. I know this is about more than the award. Maybe about more than Beth, even?" Their voice was pitched low, more serious than I'd heard them speak in a long time.

Unbidden, my mama's words echoed through my head: *you always have the choice, darlin, and you need to find the strength to do what's right.* I shook my head. I didn't know what right meant anymore. It wasn't the rigid moral code I'd grown up with. And clearly wasn't what I'd been doing, pushing problems down and assuming they would decompose once I'd buried them deep enough.

"I don't think Beth is ever gonna talk to me again. And I know it's my dang fault." Saying the words wasn't easy. But the minute I said them out loud, something in me felt the tiniest bit lighter. Maybe Beth was right that talking would help me feel better. I had, after a particularly rough night tossing and turning on the pull-out bed, even looked up the names of a few counselors in town and bookmarked their contact information on my laptop. But the thought of calling them up, of admitting something was wrong, of talking about everything, made me honest to goodness nauseous. Where would I even start? Too much in my life was a tangled mess for me to even think about pulling the first thread.

"Can you tell me what happened? What did she say when she came to the restaurant the other day?" Jay put their hands over mine on the table and the warmth of their skin seeped into me.

"I don't even know. I'm no good."

"Well, we both know that's not true so maybe you could give me a little more to work with here. She looked pretty shaken up when she left."

I pulled my hand out from under Jay's to take a long sip of my coffee. It had gone tepid but I could hardly taste it anyway. "Yeah. I never apologized in the first place after losing it on her with the whole pizza thing. Never responded to her texts because I didn't know what to say. Then when she showed up I was, I don't know, real mad about the award. I know she deserves the win. She works darn hard at what she does. But I had thought, maybe, just this one time we'd get a little recognition too."

"Okay." Jay drew out the word. "But what did you say to her?"

I shrugged, resigned. "Nothing. She was real sweet, apologized for things she hadn't even done wrong and I basically told her to get out. Haven't heard a peep from her since. Not that I should. I wouldn't want to talk to me either."

Jay shook their head with a pitying expression that would have aggravated me if I didn't like them so much. "Do you want to see her again?"

"Of course. I love her." The words tumbled out before I could stop them, before my brain would even process what I'd been about to say. But the moment I said it, I knew it was true. I loved her. Thinking of seeing Beth again—hearing her soothing voice and the clatter of her bracelets and crystal necklaces, smelling the lavender and spicy incense on the warm undertone of her skin, feeling her body close to mine—I couldn't help but grin. Even though the past few months had been hard, in some ways harder and scarier than anything I'd done before, she'd made me feel capable. With Beth by my side I really did feel like I could do anything I set my mind to.

"I'm pretty sure there's a simple solution to your problem, bud. Pick that up—" Jay smirked and gestured to my phone on the table, "—and give her a call. Hell, text her if you don't think you're up to the whole talking on the phone thing. Ask her to meet for a coffee and... Talk. To. Her."

"I know," I groaned. "But she doesn't need someone like me. I'm a dang mess."

"True," Jay said through a laugh.

"Really though, Beth deserves someone better than me. Somebody who doesn't lose their cool over every little thing." The thought of the past few months with Beth being nothing more than a new line in my long list of failures made my stomach churn. The fear of losing her for good slammed into me hard, leaving me reeling. I couldn't let her disappear from my life. And I really didn't want her to disappear from Pete's life either. Although he hadn't said it, I knew he missed her. After all, unlike me, my son wasn't used to running and hiding. He was used to people sticking around. Used to love.

Jay gripped my hands again, all traces of laughter gone from their face. "No. Don't start with that. Yes, I think you need to do some work around letting your emotions in and talking about how you feel. But you went through some shit, Adah. It's going to have an effect on you. And you're lucky enough to have people in your life who care about you and want to help in any way we can." They looked at me for a long moment, their gaze so intense I could almost feel it on my skin. "You deserve to be loved. You know that, right? Both of us do."

Tears welled in my eyes, blurring my vision, but I blinked them back and willed them away. I knew Jay was right. I knew I should thank them. Instead, all I could do was nod.

Jay stood and shuffled over to my fridge, heavy wool socks sliding on the freshly scrubbed tile. If I thought I cleaned a lot when things were okay, it had nothing on the levels of sanitary my house could reach when I was miserable. The condiments neatly arranged in the fridge door rattled and a spill of yellow light fell on the gleaming floor as Jay tugged open the fridge. It was snowing outside again, heavy dark clouds churning over the water and casting the whole city in a gray gloom.

"Jesus Christ your fridge is more organized than the damn walk-in. I think you missed out on a career in the military. That's a stereotype, right, that folks in the military are super neat? I mean, these are in alphabetical order." They opened the lid of a container of leftover vegetable stew, contemplated it for a moment, then shoved it back into the refrigerator. "You need to eat something. It's not good for your bones if you subsist on nothing but black coffee and self-loathing."

I scoffed. "I had toast this morning. And Pete and I went out for pizza…a few days ago."

"How about I make you an omelet and tell you about my date." They waggled their perfectly groomed eyebrows at me and launched into a convoluted story about meeting up with a woman from a dating app at a coffee shop. It turned out the coffee shop had two locations, one in South Bay and one in Port Catherine, and they'd shown up at the same place in two different towns. Then the woman had been really intense about scheduling their second date before they'd even talked for twenty minutes. I tried hard to listen and laugh at the right times, but at the mere mention of her hometown, my mind kept drifting to Beth. What would she say if I called her? Would she even want to hear from me now, after the way I'd acted?

My phone buzzing on the table jarred me from my thoughts and a spark of hope ignited in my chest at the thought that maybe, somehow, Beth was calling me. Then I glanced at the screen and that spark extinguished real quick. It was Riccardo. The boss I hadn't heard from directly since Sean changed up our menu and suppliers. My face felt frozen as I swiped to answer and lifted the phone to my ear. Getting fired was not going to make the mess of my life any dang easier.

"Adah, how are you, my dear? It's been far too long. I'm so sorry for going missing on you. Clotilde and I were in St. Barth for a few weeks. Had to get out of this horrible weather. I bet you're wishing for some sunshine now, too, no?" Riccardo's breezy tone was a welcome relief. I sagged back in my chair.

Jay whipped around from the stove, whisper-screaming, "Who is it?"

I shook my head and cleared my throat. "Hi, Ric, nice to hear from you." I ran through the pleasantries of asking about his trip and whether he had any big plans for the holidays. Jay, however, was not deterred by my efforts to focus on my conversation with my boss and waved a Post-it note in front of my face reading *PUT HIM ON SPEAKER!* I lightly batted them away and hunched in on my phone, trying to keep my voice even and the background of the call free of Jay's antics.

"So," Riccardo said heavily and my whole body seemed to drop through the floor, "I know you saw the article. Such a shame we lost out on the award."

"Yes. Sir, I'm so sorry, I did everything I could—"

"You have nothing to apologize for, Adah. Marcus did reach out to me directly to compliment your off-menu dish." Another heavy sigh. "I'm a big enough man to admit that I made a mistake."

I breathed a sigh of relief, my list of ideas for turning Bella Vista around ready on my tongue. But before I could say a word, Riccardo continued.

"You've seen the numbers. What we're doing just isn't profitable. Clearly when the tourist trade dies down, so does business. I'm thinking we'll have to do a complete overhaul. Tone things down a bit to draw more people in."

Beth's words about scaling back for the winter echoed in my head. I'd been so confident that I'd known the right path. And now I had nothing but failure to show for my arrogance. "Sorry," I cut in, "but what do you mean? Because I have some ideas." I hoped my worry didn't show in my voice. Across the kitchen I caught Jay's eye, their face the picture of incredulity.

"Oh darling, didn't Sean tell you?" Riccardo sounded genuinely surprised.

"No, Sean didn't tell me anything," I ground out.

"Oh, well, I'm thinking of going in a different direction. Closing for a few weeks in the new year, changing up the space a little. Going for more of a fast casual approach. And making some changes to the kitchen staff." This last sentence came out fast, clearly not news Ric had wanted to deliver to me personally.

I knew what this meant. My job was gone. There was no reason to pay my salary and benefits when a brand-new culinary school grad could churn out an overly fancy menu of sandwiches and salads. Dang it, Beth had been right all along, these jerks really didn't care about anything but the bottom line.

"Do I still have a job?" I sounded like a scared little girl. Heck, I felt like a scared little girl. If this didn't work out, if I'd uprooted my whole life, my son's life, just to fail, I didn't know what I was going to do with myself. Out of the corner of my eye I saw Jay making frantic motions but I focused hard on the table in front of me, the nicks and divots in the soft pine surface. Pete and I had spotted this table on the curb in our neighborhood back in Chicago, racing home to get the car to load it into, grateful we'd no longer be eating picnic-style on the floor of our apartment.

"Oh of course, my dear." Riccardo's words cut the strings of tension holding me upright and I sagged with relief. "But you're expensive. I know you care deeply about the food, that's why I hired you. And I know you're worth it." I felt another *but* coming. I'd been exhausted before this conversation, after it ended I expected to be laid out comatose on my kitchen floor. "If I'm honest I think your talents are being wasted up there. You should come back to Chicago. We miss you at Café Eloise. And I'd love to take you on as executive chef. Sean recommended someone to run things at Bella Vista as we, I'll be frank, dumb things down. This guy is just out of school and...well, he has different standards for running a kitchen."

I ended the call a moment later, perfectly polite. Riccardo promised to check in with me in a few weeks once he'd made final decisions. My heart seemed to be racing hard against my rib cage and struggling to beat at the same time. Logically, I knew I was still sitting in my kitchen, in the apartment that was just starting to feel something like home. Soon I'd have to get myself up and bundled to pick up Pete from a school he'd grown to love. A gust of wind off the water rattled the frost-etched windows. I felt disembodied and numb. I knew I should be angry, maybe panicked, but my mind was strangely blank. There was nothing I could do. The decision was out of my hands.

"This is trash. I'm quitting." Jay's outrage pulled me back to myself. Clearly, they'd heard most of the call.

Then the panic came in a tingling wave. I was hot, my skin suddenly two sizes too tight. I was going to have to run again. Leave everything behind. I wouldn't wake up to the low foghorns in the bay or the shrill cries of gulls. I wouldn't hear Vanessa downstairs shout-singing along to Madonna. I would lose the closest thing I'd ever had to a real mother. Pete was going to lose his family all over again. And I was going to lose the woman I loved for good.

"I don't want to leave," I whispered.

Jay's eyes practically popped out of their head. "You can't be serious. You want to keep working with Sean after he fucked you over like this? Because I can guarantee you that this whole 'fast casual' thing was that idiot's idea."

I shook my head slowly, like the motion might clear my blurred thoughts. "I don't know. I guess I have to take things one day at a time. See what happens."

If Jay weren't as docile as a lamb, I think they would have physically shaken me in that moment. Instead they pushed a beautifully made omelet across the table to me and mumbled that I needed to eat. The kitchen was silent for a long moment as I cut into the carefully folded eggs and cheese, willing myself to chew and swallow. Jay was an excellent cook in addition to being a truly gifted baker, but the dish could have been a gas station burrito long-forgotten in the back of a warmer for all I enjoyed it.

Once I'd taken a few bites, Jay continued their combination pep-talk-rant. "You know you don't have to keep your head down and take whatever shit Sean and Ric pile on you, right? You're an excellent chef. Another place would snap you up in a hot second. No matter what you do, I'm giving my notice tomorrow. There are about a million bakeries in South Bay. Hell, I'll work at a coffee shop again before I work for that piece of shit snake. You know he wouldn't have done this to you if you were yet another big macho dudebro. He doesn't want people to shake things up and you fucked with the hierarchy that keeps him on top because you're such a stoic motherfucker and you actually treat everyone with respect." They paused and stole a bite of eggs. "You know what? I'm going to email him my two weeks now. I don't owe him anything and I'm sick of making melon sorbet in the middle of fucking winter. No one wants to eat it!"

We both smiled then. Jay had been shocked and appalled by the new dessert menu Zest had come up with. Instead of their thoughtfully made takes on Greek and Middle Eastern desserts, they were now expected to churn out complicated petit fours, a variety of powders and foams, and sorbets that no one ever ordered.

Then, without warning, Jay launched out of their seat, the kitchen chair tipping back and clattering to the floor. My heart started back up with its fast, heavy beating and my eyes darted around the kitchen for the source of the commotion. But Jay was beaming, pacing in front of the stove. "I don't know why I didn't think of this before." Their fever-pitch, excited words reminded me of Beth getting geared up for one of her passionate rants and I tried to ignore the fresh wave of sadness washing over me. "We'll open up our own place. This city desperately needs a good, high-quality neighborhood diner. Right now folks have to choose between tourist traps and the old-timer greasy spoons. We could make everything from scratch and do a nicer dinner service. What do you think?" They were nearly vibrating with excitement.

The idea sounded about as practical to me as opening up a restaurant on the moon and my reluctance must have shown on my face. Jay shrugged and mumbled that it was just one idea before righting their chair and sinking back into it. But the more I thought about the idea, the better it seemed. Realistically, it would be almost impossible to get together the money, but I wondered what it would be like to work for myself. To have control over my own menu. To be able to bounce ideas off of Beth. I realized then, how much I'd been underestimating her the whole time. I'd assumed what she did, despite seeing her in action, was somehow easier than my work. In reality, though, the opposite was probably true. She just made it look effortless because she was that amazing.

After a restless night of tossing and turning, fears about my future racing through my head, I slipped out of bed before the sun came up. My body felt full-up with crackling energy. After a series of push-ups and planks did nothing to dispel it, I decided to make Pete a big breakfast before school. Most mornings we were in a hurry to get out of the house by seven so I could get him to his before-school program and get into the kitchen before anyone else arrived. I loved the quiet calm of my space, taking care of any loose ends before the chaos of the day began. Now, I decided, I wouldn't bother with going in early. Pete could go to school at nine and I would head into the restaurant after. It was high time the two of us enjoyed a leisurely breakfast together.

A half hour later my son had demolished two large helpings of biscuits and gravy and was eyeing the stove for leftovers. His appetite had skyrocketed the past few months, which meant a growth spurt and a trip to Goodwill for a whole bunch of new clothes would be soon to follow. I pushed my plate over to him and he attacked it like a hungry coyote. I took a huge gulp of coffee, hoping the steady stream of caffeine would make me at least semi-functional for whatever awful scenario waited for me at work.

"Mom," Pete said through a mouthful of food. I gestured for him to swallow before continuing. "Did you and Beth break up?"

The question hit me square in the chest, surprising me so much I answered honestly. "Yeah, honey, I think we did." I hated that he'd gotten to know her, that he'd gotten close to her, only for me to screw everything up. And now I was failing as a parent too. Fantastic.

"You don't seem very happy." He looked at me for a long time and I had to wonder what he saw. I knew I looked tired, my face gaunt and hair a rumpled mess.

After shoveling a few more bites into his mouth Pete scraped back his chair and headed to his room to get ready for school. I sat at the table, my coffee going cold as I tried to figure out how to fix this disaster I'd gotten myself into.

Enough snow had fallen overnight that I was surprised Pete's school hadn't closed. But I had to hand it to the city of South Bay. The roads were plowed clear and salted, the sidewalks shoveled. The fresh snow glimmered in the weak morning sun, almost pretty. I trudged the half mile from Pete's school to the restaurant, past cute tourist stores selling homemade jam and nautical memorabilia. It wasn't even a week after Thanksgiving but already the town had put up a giant Christmas tree made of lobster traps, pine boughs, and twinkle lights. All around me people were heading into work, clutching cardboard cups of coffee, bundled up in heavy scarves and hats. I'd forgotten both and the wind blew icy snowflakes down the collar of my coat, making my whole body shudder.

As much as my sluggish brain wanted to toil over what to do and what to say when I got into the kitchen, it was like my thoughts were moving through molasses. What I did know was that spontaneously quitting like Jay had would be a huge risk. I had just managed to switch out of financial survival mode, opening a savings account and putting money into it regularly for the first time in my life. On the other hand, that account did mean I had a little cushion. And if I swallowed my pride, I could probably land another job in South Bay within a few weeks. It wouldn't be anything fancy, but it would be money, a chance to take stock of what I wanted and how I wanted to move forward. At the end of the day, what mattered was Pete. Right now I was barely spending time with him and when I was home I was so exhausted and distracted I could barely pull together the gumption to help him with his homework, much less play marathon games of Go Fish and War like we used to. What was the point of missing out on my kid growing up for a job I might lose anyway?

I must have really been out of it because when I looked up from the steady blur of white and gray, I was at Bella Vista. The kitchen door was already propped open and inside I could make out the clatter of pans and distant buzz of the sports radio the prep cooks listened to when I wasn't around. No quiet time for contemplation this morning.

Neither Mac nor Jay was in when I rounded the corner, still buttoning my whites. But Sean was. And the silky smile on his face rocked a chill down my spine. It was like the reverend's placid calm right before he sent his fist through the wall.

"Well good morning, Adah. In a little late today, are

we?" He was using his front of house voice, overly hearty and weirdly emotionless at the same time. When I didn't say anything a tiny cloud of irritation passed over his face, but he soldiered on. "Ric told me you two talked yesterday."

I nodded briskly and dropped my shoulders, never breaking eye contact. I was done with his games. "Yup. He told me he was gonna take some time to figure out next steps. We talked through a few ideas I have for turning things around." This last part was a lie, but Sean didn't need to know that.

He smiled his creepy shark grin that didn't reach his eyes. "I do too. I shared a few of them with Ric this morning. He and I decided you should stay on."

My jaw actually dropped as his words registered. Was it possible I'd been wrong about Sean this whole time? That I'd been reading bad intentions into his behavior when really he was just trying to do right by the restaurant? Maybe my hair-trigger negative first impression of him had been wrong.

"In a more...supportive capacity," he continued. Okay, heck no. I hadn't been wrong at all. I wanted to go back in time a few seconds, pluck that thought out of my brain, and throw it right into the garbage disposal. Sean was a bad egg through and through. "You did well in that role at Café Eloise. I think you shine when someone else...a better team player, is running the show. Does that make sense? If we just bring in a guy with a fresher take—"

I lifted a hand to cut him off. The fog lifted and I knew exactly what I needed to say. "Thank you for the generous offer, Sean, but I don't think that's the right role for me." I gave myself the pleasure of pausing and looking at his splotchy potato face getting angry for a moment. "I quit." I savored the power of those two words. "Honestly, I've had enough of you trying to make this place as uncomfortable for me as you could. Bella Vista isn't the kind of environment I want to work in and you have a whole lot to do with that. But good luck with the whole fast casual thing. Hope it does real well for you."

When I walked out the door a few minutes later, knives and a small handful of my things stuffed into a canvas tote bag, I felt lighter. Free in a way I hadn't since I left home all those years ago. And I knew where I was going next.

Chapter Nineteen

Beth

About ninety-nine percent of the time I wished computers had never been invented. Sure, dog videos and the whole limitless access to information thing were great... but at what cost? Having to deal with social media, endless emails, and now, apparently, setting up an online reservation system, made me want to go back in time and stop Al Gore from inventing the internet. Really, it shouldn't have been that hard. All I wanted was to add a button to our stupid piece of garbage website that people could click on to reserve a table.

After the Best of New England feature officially ran in print copies of *Gourmand* a week ago, our phone had, no lie, not stopped ringing. I thought poor Ahmed's ear was going to fall off, he spent so much time sweet-talking into that flour-crusted cordless. After a few nights of parking lot Tetris and hordes of angry people from Boston and even New York lined up in the snow and getting mad about our first-come-first-served policy, we realized something needed to change. A woman had actually cried when she realized she wouldn't be able to join us for dinner last night. So, a reservation system it was. Since we'd posted on our Instagram this morning that we were now open to reservations, we'd already booked out for the entire rest of the month.

Without a doubt, this was the moment where the whole *having a business plan* thing might have been a good idea. Staking my ability to expand my business on winning a paltry sum of cash in a local food festival probably hadn't been the best example of thinking ahead. As it stood, I had no earthly idea how to deal with this volume of business. And with Nina leaving at the end of December, I was starting to panic. No, not panic. I trusted the path I'd chosen. Besides, my favorite astrologer's yearly overview for Taurus had promised that this was the year I would settle into the groove that was right for me. And seeing as it was late fall I was kind of running out of time…everything was going to be just fine. So what, I was back to officially running on day-old bread, tepid coffee, and catnaps. Who cared that my mom and dad were basically taking full-time care of my dog? No big deal that I'd managed to destroy the best relationship I'd had with the only woman I'd ever truly loved. I shoved that last thought down to the very bottom drawer in my mind and locked it up tight. If I let myself think about Adah I would start crying again, and I wasn't quite sure if my body had enough liquid left in reserve to support another weep session.

I stood, shook out my hands, and shuffled out of my tiny mess of an office to the equally tiny, but very visually pleasing, dining room. When The Yellow House had still been Summers's Corner Café, the space had been perfect for my mom's needs. A few tables for folks to camp out at and chat, a bar overlooking the hearth (then purely ornamental and crowded with family photos, dried flowers, and a creepy taxidermy owl). Now Ahmed had to weave through tightly crowded two tops clustered around the big, communal farmhouse table. Even before the latest award things had been…cozy. Now, with the addition of a few more stools at the bar and a lot more guests hoping to crowd around the big weathered wooden table, it just wasn't working. In fact, if the fire marshal, my dad's old baseball buddy, happened to stop by, even he might not be able to look the other way at the tight quarters.

No doubt about it, we needed to expand. Really, we needed to build a whole new dining room and turn the entire cottage into an expanded kitchen. But that meant money that I didn't have. And no way was I raising the prices so high folks in town couldn't afford to eat with us. And the idea of an investor telling me how to run my business made me want to preemptively scream. But as soon as more customers started pouring in, the energy in the kitchen had been a little more charged than I preferred. Even though my brother and Eitan liked to make fun of me about it, I swore up and down that any stress we carried in our bodies would come through in the food. There was no denying that I was radiating stress at the moment. But I also had barely been cooking with all of this administrative bullshit on my plate. I sent a silent prayer of thanks to the universe for sending Grace my way. She'd been the one to bake the tarte tatin with rice and chestnut flour crust that Marcus devoted two whole paragraphs to and the one to keep things positive and fresh in the kitchen since we'd gotten so horribly busy.

I was just settling back down in front of my laptop, neck and shoulders already tense with the knowledge I was in for at least three more rounds of accidentally almost ruining The Yellow House's website, when Andrew knocked gently on my office door.

"You okay in here, sis? You're grumbling an awful lot. We're opening up soon and I don't want you freaking people out." My brother leaned his towering body against the door frame. Normally he would have jumped on the opportunity to tease me, but his voice was soft and flat.

I waved the concern away, glancing back to the screen in front of me. "Oh, you know technology and I don't get along. I'm still trying to do this stupid reservation thingie." What was I supposed to do with all these lines of weird code? Probably not change it, right? How had I even gotten here? I hit the back button...and great, I was back to square one. Again.

"Why don't you have Eitan take a look at it? He used to be some kind of big tech guy out in California." Something about the energy in the room shifted at the mention of my newish hire. I glanced up at Andrew again. His hands were stuffed into the pockets of his work pants, eyes fixed determinedly on the floor. Something was up with my brother. And great, now I'd missed Nina's life crisis, my brother was upset about something, I'd imploded my relationship, and I hadn't even taken the time to really get to know Eitan. I was a fucking mess.

"Good idea," I murmured, narrowing my eyes at Andrew, expecting his usual retort that I needed to stop trying to read his mind. When it didn't come, I asked, "Seriously bro, what's going on with you? Is everything okay?"

Andrew stood up straight and lifted his hands like I'd made an accusation. The silence between us was tense for a long moment. Then he sighed and rubbed his palm over his close-cropped dark hair. "I, uh, well—" His gaze, once again, fixated on the wide-plank pine floorboards. I mean, sure the floors were lovely, but not worth staring at for that long.

"Hey, you can tell me." I kept my voice gentle. It was so strange seeing my big, laid-back brother this bent out of shape. Something was definitely out of whack cosmically. Then, just to prove my point, my phone alarm chimed loudly, cutting through the quiet and any chance of getting to the bottom of this latest dilemma. Shit. It was time to proof the sourdough and check in with Nina about dinner service.

"Nah. It's cool. I'll ask you about it some other time." Andrew sagged in clear relief and turned to go so fast he was basically a blur of flannel.

After sending a quick text to Ahmed and Eitan about the two of them meeting with me at some point this afternoon to go over this cursed reservation system, I closed my laptop with a little too much force and stalked into the kitchen. I tried, I really did, to switch off my brain and get into the right baking flow. Wash my hands and appreciate the warmth of the water on my skin. Breathe in the smell of yeast and butter and the ever-present earthy scent of the fire.

But as she had each and every time I set myself to the meditative rhythms of baking, Adah slipped into my mind. But now the blank expression she'd worn last time I saw her overshadowed the sound of her warm, low laugh. The flat intonation of her voice as she pushed me away clouded over the taste of her lips, the silky feel of her hair slipping through my fingers, the fierce concentration in her eyes as she cooked.

I wanted it all back: the plans I'd made to take Adah and Pete up north to Moose Lake, the dreams of waking up slowly with Adah next to me in my bed, the meals we could have made together.

And now my face pulsed hot and I'd managed to completely overwork the dough I'd been kneading. Distantly, I heard the sound of boots crunching through the thin crust of ice that had formed over the snow the night before. Probably the first customer of the day, showing up early in hopes of beating the line. I stared into the fire for a long moment, watching as hot white gave way to yellow, up to a soft flickering orange glow. For the thousandth time since I'd walked out of the kitchen at Bella Vista I wondered if there was anything I could do to make it right. But I'd done enough to make it wrong. Adah had been crystal clear that she did not want me in her life. This would be my routine now: never-ending work and a sadness that I knew would fade but not disappear with time.

The back door banged open, a gust of biting winter air rushing into the kitchen. And with it came Adah. Every fiber of my being went still. I was pretty sure I stopped breathing. All I could do was stare at her, searing every detail into my mind: the dusting of fresh snow on the shoulders of her heavy brown work coat, the strands of wheat-colored hair poking out of her knit beanie, the nervous expression on her beautiful face. She took a deep breath like she was about to say something but instead of words Adah closed the distance between us in two strides and kissed me. Her cold fingers cupped my cheek, tipping my face up to meet hers. I breathed her in, a smell I'd missed on a cellular level. She tasted like peppermint and coffee and the fresh edge of cold air. I couldn't even think. All I could do was feel as I melted against her, relief flooding me. She groaned softly as I deepened the kiss and I hadn't even realized how much I'd missed those sounds.

Then my brain switched back on and I jerked away. "What the fuck?" I snapped, surprised at the anger in my own voice. "I thought you didn't want this." I gestured between us.

For a moment Adah's face went blank, a dark cloud passing over the sun. But then she crumpled, her eyes squeezing shut as tears slipped silently down her cheeks. She was flushed and so tense it looked like it hurt. Tentatively I reached out and ran my fingers up her arm. Adah's body went slack and she pulled me into a hard, tight hug. I could feel her crying into my hair as I wrapped my arms around her, rubbing her back in big, soothing circles. Slowly, her breathing evened out and her grip on me loosened slightly.

"Sorry," she said softly as she pulled away, tugging off her beanie and running her fingers through her hair. It was a little messy but she couldn't have looked more beautiful if she'd tried.

I tried to untangle the knot of my own feelings, teasing out the threads of anger and relief. "I need you to talk to me," I said evenly, done with the routine of trying to tap-dance around Adah's feelings and still managing to mess everything up anyway.

"I know." Adah nodded, dropping her shoulders and looking me dead in the eye like she was steeling herself over for a fight. "I don't know what the heck to say. I understand if you can't forgive me. Hell, I don't think I would forgive me if I were you. I just…" She sighed and rubbed a hand over her hair again, the bravado act officially gone. Her voice went soft. "I really am sorry, Beth. I was unfair to you. I was so scared. This is all new to me, I guess. And when I realized my life might change, I wanted to back off. It's like you got to be too important to me and then all the stuff with work—"

My exasperation with her using the work excuse must have flickered over my face because Adah raised her hands, showing me her palms, and shook her head. "I know it ain't an excuse. This is on me. I think I need to, I don't know, work on myself. Anyway, I have an appointment with a therapist lady next week to help me figure this stuff out. Or at least make it better. Sorry I don't know what I'm sayin'. I had a whole speech planned out and I'm messin' it up." As usual, Adah's accent got thicker when she was upset. "Anyway, long story short, I was afraid to trust you and that's dumb because I already do trust you more than anyone else I ever met. I know I did a heck of a job showing you that and I get it if you don't want to see me anymore after how foolish I acted." Color rose high on her cheeks again as her voice started to break.

"Come here." I opened my arms to her again and she returned to them willingly. Some tension lingered between us, some things still left unsaid, but I knew as her arms twined around me that everything was going to be alright.

"You're too good for me," Adah murmured into my hair.

"Hush." I gripped her shoulders to push her back and look at her face. The face that had flitted on the edges of my dreams for weeks, now here in front of me. "That's not true and you know it. But what I know is that you and I need to have a conversation. A big, long one with lots of honesty and feelings, okay?"

A small smile twitched up the corners of Adah's lips. "If we have to," she said through a laugh.

"We do. Now I'm going to get you a cup of tea and go check in with my brother and Grace. Then we can finish this conversation at my place?" I phrased this last bit as a question because as much as I wanted to show Adah my house and, maybe if things went well, my bed, I wanted her to know doing this in public was an option too.

Adah nodded, looking a little dazed, and I hurried around the kitchen, making her a cup of chamomile lavender tea, writing out a few notes so Grace and Nina could pick up where I left off with prep, and finally, dashing into the dining room where my brother and Eitan appeared to be locked in a heated argument. They stopped talking the moment their eyes landed on me, so I was one hundred percent certain they'd been both listening to and discussing my conversation with Adah.

"Okay I know you were both listening to me reunite

with Adah, so I don't have to tell you I'm taking the rest of the day off. Where's Nina?" I couldn't quite hide my grin.

Oh my god, Eitan mouthed, flashing me a thumbs-up before reporting that Nina and Grace were picking up our order of root vegetables and winter greens from LaCour Farm.

Where Eitan was all soft smiles and clear happiness on my behalf, my brother's face was stormy, his hands shoved into his pockets. "It's none of my business…"

"But?" I sighed, wishing I could fast-forward through this conversation and get back to kissing my girlfriend. The word made me want to smile. Because that's what Adah was to me again. What I wanted her to be, well, forever.

"Just, I don't want to see you all bummed out again, Beth. You've been like a different person since she dumped you. And when someone shows you over and over again that they can't commit to an actual relationship, you should probably learn your lesson." This last sentence came out a little harsh, and a lot out of place.

I cocked my head to the side. "She didn't really dump me. And—" I held up my hands. Clearly something was going on with Andrew but now was not the time to start chipping away at that impenetrable wall. "Look, are you guys going to be fine without me tonight or what?"

Eitan's firm "absolutely, just go" and Andrew's flat "no" collided in the air. Eitan shot my brother a stern look then made a dramatic shooing motion. "We can take care of it. Go get your girl."

I needed to figure out how Adah did it. How with an abashed grin and a few murmured words she managed to peel away all my defenses. Part of me still wanted to be mad at her. I wanted to deliver the angry rant that had been snaking through my head every night when my body desperately wanted to power down and sleep. Instead, on the short, snowy drive from The Yellow House to my place, Adah's tight grip on my hand rendered me as soft and wobbly as freshly made custard.

As I fumbled with shaking hands to unlock my front door, the strangeness of the moment slammed into me. This would be the first time Adah saw my place. I'd imagined bringing her here so many times: making her favorite meal (which I had only just learned was, of all things, baked mac and cheese), lighting some candles and playing some good music, maybe even giving her a massage before driving her wild in bed. What I had not imaged was my damn dog pinning her against the wall with a full-body *please pet me* lean and my house being an utter disaster.

To Adah, someone who I was relatively certain cleaned significant portions of her apartment with a toothbrush and bleach, my home must have looked like the den of a very sloppy beast. My couch was a nest of tangled blankets and pillows, spun together with night after night of restless tossing and turning when my bed felt too big and too lonely. Every surface was cluttered with mostly full coffee mugs and crumpled, scribbled notes for my long-overdue business plan. My very lovely antique farmhouse table was completely hidden beneath a pile of unfolded, but thankfully clean, laundry. And my mom must have gotten marrow chews from the butcher for Hamlet again, meaning my bright kilim rug was actually scattered with honest to god bones.

"Sorry it's such a disaster," I muttered, sounding stupidly nervous. "Things have been wild the past week, so I haven't been around much."

Thankfully Adah was too focused on rubbing Hamlet's exposed belly to focus on the awful state of my home. "Who takes care of this guy all day?" Adah asked, moving on to scratch his muzzle. It was weirdly nice to see her bonding with my dog.

"My mom. Although she's been giving me shit about how much I've been working since the award. Seriously, we're booked out for like two months now that we're taking reservations. I might as well just give Hammie to my mom and dad at this point. They've been a godsend but if I never hear the words 'work-life balance' again it'll be too soon." And great. I'd done it again. Basically humble-bragging about my supportive family and how busy we were as the result of an award Adah had desperately wanted to win. "Fuck. Sorry. I'm an idiot." I just barely resisted the urge to smack myself in the forehead.

Adah, to my surprise, just huffed out a low laugh and shook her head. "You're not. It's alright. You're allowed to complain, you know."

"Right. So…" The words hung between us, a clear but awkward as hell invitation for us to continue our Big Relationship Conversation. When the words didn't start flowing immediately, I busied myself with lighting the woodstove and finally hanging Adah's coat on my very overburdened coatrack. Both Adah and Hamlet followed me into the kitchen as I filled the kettle with fresh water and set it onto the flame. Because herbal tea would totally fix this whole situation, right?

"Your place is really..." Adah looked around, a small smile on her lips. "Colorful."

"You can say messy," I laughed. But looking around at the butter yellow walls, riot of batik throw pillows on my turquoise couch, and cluster of potted herbs, succulents, and Christmas cacti in full bloom on the greenhouse window Andrew installed for me, I supposed she was right about the colorful thing too.

Adah took a seat at one of the stools pulled up to my kitchen island, looking weirdly at ease. After another span of horrible silence in which I contemplated: turning on some Dolly Parton because I knew she would put Adah in a good mood, launching into one of my tirades, and skipping the whole talking part in favor of sliding into Adah's lap and kissing her senseless (I mean, seriously had she worn that western-style denim shirt just to fuck with me?) I finally landed on the tactful "ready for the feelings talk now?"

"Not really but we're gonna do it anyway, huh?" Adah smiled wanly at me and I sank down onto the stool next to her, dragging it close enough our knees touched, her dark clean denim against my wash-worn, flour-dusted jeans. She took a sip of tea then sighed. "I know I told you about my dad and all, but I guess I didn't realize how much all that stuff stayed with me. I mean, I knew. Like I'm jumpy as all get-out and still have all these weird hang-ups. I know that. But when you showed up to surprise me that night it got pretty bad. Overwhelming. A couple years after I moved to Chicago, the reverend and my oldest brother showed up at my place. I hadn't heard a peep from any of them in years. I didn't think they knew where I was. Even now I don't know how they figured it out. But he knew all about

Pete and Jeremy and, well, everything. He kept saying he was gonna take Pete back and raise him proper. Yelled so much the neighbor called the cops."

As deeply as I felt Adah's pain, as much as my heart raced and then shattered for her, I knew that empathy wasn't enough. There was nothing I could give her but love and understanding. Space to feel and a willingness to listen. I slid my hands slowly over the butcher block to cover hers and squeezed. Hot tears slipped down my cheeks and I tasted salt on my lips.

"Anyway, I know I didn't handle it right. I know I shoulda talked to you instead of clamming up and getting mad. I know I have to work on it and I want you to, maybe, help me?"

The tentativeness in her voice broke me and I slid off my chair and wrapped my arms clumsily around her. "Baby, of course. I love you so much. I know it's hard for you to tell me how you feel but I promise I'm on your side, okay? Always."

Adah's nod was firm, her face beautiful and serious. "I know. You made me feel, make me feel, safer than I ever did before. It was, well, it was hell not talking to you, letting you go like that. It's what I always did. Run away. But I don't want to anymore because I really love you too. A lot. And I know I have to prove it." Her face was so intent and earnest a fresh wave of affection crashed over me. Affection and heat. Now that the air was clear between us, I wanted Adah more than ever.

I brushed a fast kiss over her lips, stood, and pulled Adah to her feet. "Okay. Well now I think it's time I reward you for all that talking, don't you think?"

Chapter Twenty

Adah

I had been awfully quiet since telling her I loved her. It had been scary. No one in my family said it growing up and I'd never really been with anybody long enough to feel it. Sure, I loved my son with an unwavering fierceness I knew in my bones. But he was a part of me. And I loved Jay to the moon and back. Heck, I loved Vanessa in a way I probably hadn't loved my own mama. But this was different. Loving Beth was both a choice and an inevitability. I'd been running this whole time and had only just now figured out my destination.

When the surge of adrenaline from telling the truth and rush of fear that she might not be able to forgive me finally dissolved into relief, I hadn't quite known what to do with myself. I'd sat at Beth's kitchen counter, dazed, looking around her house. It was a perfect reflection of her: bright and colorful, with plants and crystals and half-melted candles everywhere. It smelled just like her too, warm and spicy and herbal. I loved it just as much as I loved her. Beth was right, though, the place could use a good tidying.

"Did you run out of your weekly allotment of words or something?" Beth glanced back at me, amusement dancing in her eyes, as we climbed the narrow stairs up to her bedroom.

Belatedly I realized the woman I loved was still standing on the step in front of me, amusement quickly giving way to concern on her pretty face. I couldn't believe she still wanted me. That someone this perfect existed. That we'd found each other. That she actually wanted to put up with my miserable self. Reaching to brush away a small streak of flour on her soft, pale cheek I shook my head. "No. I got a couple left." I wanted to kiss her again, so I did. Her mouth was warm and familiar. My stomach flipped as the kiss got hotter, hungrier. Beth moaned into my mouth and my thighs clenched, desire lancing down from my lips to my crotch. I ran my hands down the rough knit of Beth's oversized wool sweater. I needed to feel her skin against mine. To touch every freckle and curve I'd been missing.

"As much as I want you to fuck me right here, I don't think you'll appreciate the audience." Beth chuckled, her breath tickling my face. I turned to find Hamlet waiting patiently a few steps below me, his big dopey head cocked to the side.

We scrambled up the stairs, laughing and closing the door to keep the dog out of Beth's room. The space was big and airy, with colorful tapestries on the walls and more plants hanging from the ceiling than I could count. Pale afternoon sunlight poured through big windows, which overlooked the snow-glazed woods around her house.

As soon as the door clicked shut behind us, I pushed Beth hard up against it and crushed my mouth to hers. She opened to me right away, her hands fumbling for the buttons on my shirt. I grabbed her wrists and pinned them together over her head, pulling a high, wavering whimper from her.

"I missed you," I whispered against her ear, then dragged my tongue down to the base of her throat. When I bit lightly at the thin, pale skin there Beth bucked hard against me, testing my grip on her hands. She was so beautiful like this: pink creeping up from her collarbones to her cheeks, auburn hair a tangle around her face, brown eyes bright and fixed on me. A fresh wave of heat throbbed through my body, but that could wait. I wanted to watch Beth come undone.

"Tell me what you want." My voice was surprisingly low and commanding. The usual mean little self-conscious whisper that showed up when I had sex wasn't invited anymore. All that mattered was making Beth feel how much I loved her any way I could.

"You," she moaned as I palmed her breasts through the thick fabric of her sweater. I loved that Beth never seemed to bother with bras. Her breasts were small and firm and perfect in my hands.

"You got me, baby. But tell me how you want me."

"Fuck. I want you everywhere. You can do anything. Please."

Beth's words sent an unexpected hot bolt of pleasure down

my spine. I didn't even have to think about what I wanted to do. I did it. I tugged her sweater and the flour-dusted gray T-shirt she wore underneath it over her head. Next went her jeans and black panties, pulled roughly down then kicked off as I pushed her down onto her brightly colored quilt. As much as I wanted to bury myself in her right away, I knew Beth liked it when I took my time. Our eyes met as I hovered over her, my hands on either side of her pushing me up.

"Hey, Adah," Beth said my name softly and, once again, I wasn't really ready for what her voice did to me. "Just so you know, I really love you a lot. Like so much. I don't even know how to put it into words. God, it feels really good to say it. Like I used to feel this sometimes at weird moments, like when I watched you make me coffee one time and you were so fucking serious about it. So many times I would feel this, I don't know, big feeling and I didn't know what was going on. I knew I wanted you so much…" She shook her head, hair rasping against the blanket. "Anyway, I guess I wanted to tell you I'm really happy."

"Me too," I said simply, hoping my words carried everything I meant. Draping my body over hers, I brushed my lips gently over her forehead. Something in the tenderness of the gesture seemed to ignite both of us because Beth swore under her breath and I was suddenly almost dizzy with wanting her.

I went slow, licking and biting down her neck to her nipples. Flicking my tongue over the firm, taut skin seemed to be torture for both of us because after a moment, Beth groaned and started whining the word *please* over and over until I slipped a finger inside of her. She was so wet, clenching hot around me the moment I slipped in. I pulled out slowly, spreading slickness over her clit then pushing back in with a second finger as I used my other hand to haul her closer against me. Our mouths found each other, her tongue sliding against mine as she moaned. Belatedly, I realized I was still fully dressed, her naked skin dragging against the rough fabric of my jeans and shirt. Beth didn't seem to mind though, so I didn't stop.

Instead I pulled my lips away from hers for a moment and pinned her with a long, serious look. "What do you want, honey?"

Beth's channel tightened around my fingers and she squeezed her eyes shut, her long eyelashes fluttering against her flushed cheeks. "Harder," she whined. Then, "More."

I plunged a third finger inside her and started pumping in and out of her rough and fast, curving up to the spot I knew drove her wild. Beth must have liked that because she started babbling a stream of curses and my name and the word *yes* over and over until she arched up and froze, clenching and pulsing around my hand. As she came down, I returned to myself and realized just how much I wanted her to touch me too. But not yet. Instead, I pushed up onto my side and smiled at her, totally unable to hide how dang happy I was. Beth smiled too.

"You sure do talk a lot." I laughed and nuzzled my nose against hers.

"Oh shut up. Well, actually don't. Please keep talking to me. But I know you like it." Then she got a wicked gleam in her eye and rolled fast as a lighting flash to lie on top of me. "You like it when I beg you to fuck me. How I want you so deep inside me I'll be sore the next day. How hot it is when you eat my pussy and look up at me like I'm the only thing in the whole world that matters."

No way was I proud of the tiny, strangled squeak that popped out of my mouth at the sound of her sweet voice saying those filthy words. But I couldn't help it. I sat up, tugged my shirt over my head, and shucked my jeans fast as anything. Beth seemed pretty dang pleased with herself, but I didn't care. I just wanted her to touch me. And she did. Just the way I wanted her to: slipping her hot mouth down from my chest to my stomach to where I wanted her most. I loved the way she breathed me in. The way the very tip of her tongue flicked over my clitoris, sending sparks and flashes of hot and cold over my skin. The way she knew just the moment to move hard and fast against me to make my world dissolve into a swath of bright white light.

We kept it up for a long time: kissing and touching and coming and talking until we were both sweat-soaked and twisted up in Beth's soft flannel sheets. I was rubbing her back in slow circles, wondering how anyone's skin could possibly be that smooth, when I realized I never told her the biggest, okay, well maybe second biggest, admission of the day. The words tumbled from my mouth since I had no dang idea how to bring it up casually. "I quit. This morning. I meant to tell you that earlier but I guess I forgot."

Beth froze under my hand then turned to face me. Her face was pure, vivid joy. I grinned too and wrapped my arms around her, drawing her in close as the reality of what I'd just said really sank in. I was free. I didn't have to go back to Bella Vista. I didn't have to feel like I was failing at a game where the rules kept changing. And things were going to be just fine. I knew that now.

"Tell me everything." Beth gave me a fast, full-body squeeze as she wrapped her arms and legs around me. "I know you're going to want to skimp on the details but, one, I love quitting stories and, two, those motherfuckers had it coming and I want to picture the look on Sean's face when you told him to go to hell. Well, I know you probably didn't say that, but whatever."

I did my best to be as specific as possible as I told Beth about showing up that morning to find Sean waiting for me with his fake job offer. When I recounted my very short quitting speech, Beth actually punched the air and whooped.

"Congratulations. Seriously. It was, like, a Herculean effort to stop myself from begging you to quit every time I saw you the past few months. And I know I wasn't great about hiding my feelings about the way that shit-monster ran your restaurant. But he was treating you like some kind of... I don't even know. He was treating you really badly and I did not like it one bit."

I laughed so loud I almost surprised myself. "Yeah, you didn't really hide that, honey. And I know I let people do that sometimes. I'll work on it. I promise."

Beth let out a very unhappy groan next to me and buried her face in my neck. "No. That's his fault, not yours. Jesus. You can't blame yourself for some misogynistic idiot being a jerk to you." Her voice was muffled against my skin but that didn't mask her obvious frustration. Then she softened and shifted her face up to kiss me. "Sorry, I really don't want you to think you did anything wrong here, but I don't need to get all ranty about it. But if you want, I can put you in touch with a few of my friends who might be looking for good, talented chefs. Probably nothing too fancy but it would be solid work and a lot more free-form than your last jobs."

Her words were still taking a moment to process: the idea of finding a new job I actually might be happy at, the thought of being able to stay in South Bay and settle my life on my own terms, igniting something like a tiny flame of hope in my chest.

Then Beth launched herself out of bed. Before her bare feet even hit the floor, it seemed she was already pacing around the bedroom talking a mile a minute. Vaguely I made out the words *restaurant* and *inn* and *event space*. She yanked her hair up into a bun, a sure sign she was settling in for a good, old-fashioned lecture. Her mouth opened, then snapped shut and she gestured wildly between the two of us. A grin spread over her face before she launched back into bed and started kissing me wildly, still halfway trying to talk so fast the words blended together. I could not keep up with this wonderful woman.

"What in the world is going on with you?" I asked through a laugh as Beth continued to squirm against me.

"This might be the only time in history I ask you to just not talk and hear me out, okay?" Beth waited until I nodded to continue.

"So, I spent all morning trying to figure out this stupid online reservation system. Oh shit, I totally forgot that I was supposed to meet with Ahmed and Eitan later. Anyway, yeah, so since the *Gourmand* feature, we've been wildly busy. Like we literally have to turn dozens of people away every night. It's bananas. Our Instagram kinda blew up too after the feature. Obviously, I'm completely overwhelmed. I hate that kind of chaos." She paused, nodding seriously.

"Yesterday Ahmed and I decided to open up reservations and no joke, we're booked out through the new year. But that's not really what I envisioned for The Yellow House, you know? I didn't want it to be this fancy destination place. I want it to be a good place for people to eat. That's all." She delivered this all at a fever-pitch pace then looked at me expectantly, as if I could follow her swarm of thoughts. One stray strand of hair that had already escaped her top-knot was now being twisted so tightly around her index finger I worried she was going to cut off circulation.

"We need to expand. I've been thinking about it for a while. Like more than making the dining room a little bigger or whatever. Events are my happy place and I'd love to be able to do more of them. Like good events...weddings, grad parties, family reunions...that kind of thing. We could maybe even build an inn over by the pond. What do you think, four or five rooms and a kind of country B&B vibe? It seems like a lot of folks are going to be traveling to Port Catherine to eat with us so that might be a good idea. That old stone barn back there could be salvageable. That would be wicked cool. I could do events and Grace could take on more of our baking program." Another definitive nod.

"Honestly, I think she's better than I am anyway. She baked the stuff Marcus liked so much. That tarte tatin was amazing. I mean, adding sesame oil and ginger to the dough...holy shit. And yes! Andrew could expand the farm. He's been dying to get chickens and goats and build a real greenhouse for ages. I bet with the Williams Award and all this good press I could probably get a loan to build up the business, right? I had thought that money from the competition that you totally kicked my ass at might have helped but I need more. So, maybe even an investor? But the idea of some rich weirdo calling the shots kinda makes me sick."

At this point Beth finally paused, her gaze fixed on the snowy landscape outside the window. As hard as it had been to follow the twists and turns in her rapid-fire monologue, I had to admit I really loved the way her brain worked. She talked through all of the stuff I kept shut up tight in my brain. I opened my mouth to agree that she might not take too kindly to working with a lot of the types of people that invested in restaurants when she started right back up.

"We for sure need more than just a bigger dining room. Adding like five tables isn't going to do jack. I bet if we added onto the existing cottage, maybe put on a big kind of solarium porch thing, that might not be too expensive. I can talk to my dad and Andrew about it. But then the kitchen would need to be bigger. I bet we could do a small addition on the back, though, just knock out that wall next to the fireplace and push it back to give us a bigger work-space, maybe add another range. That way we could seat more than, like, twenty people a night. And you could totally be our head chef!"

"Okay, hold up," I practically shouted…if shouting meant raising my voice just loud enough to be heard over the deep intake of breath indicating Beth was gearing up for round three of this speech. "You have a chef. Nina. Your best friend. No way am I stepping on her toes. I'll figure out another job. Besides, the last thing I need is to get in the way of something that's been working so well for you."

As ridiculous as the idea was, Beth's fierceness, the re-alization that she cared about me enough to bring me into the paradise she'd created, warmed me through. Which was saying something because as the sweat cooled on my skin I started to realize how dang cold Beth's bedroom was. Did she heat this whole cottage with one woodstove? How had she not frozen to death in this awful Maine winter?

Beth simmered with a bright energy I couldn't quite understand. Never in my life had I seen someone actually embody the phrase *fired up*, but she sure did. Her eyes darted from me, to her phone on the nightstand, to the windows, then back to my face. Every inch of her seemed electric. I wondered if I might not feel a spark if I reached out and touched her.

"Nina's leaving." Beth's face fell a little as she spoke. "She told me a few days ago that she's moving to France next month and I kind of didn't let myself think about it. I mean holy shit, if I thought things were bad now, what the hell would I do down a chef? But you could totally do it. Never tell Nina this or I'll, well, nothing but I'll be pissed, I actually think you might be exactly what we need. Like, Nina's great but she and I are both such messes. You're amazing but you're also organized and you know your shit. Yes! Things really are coming together! I really need to trust the signs right in front of me, huh?"

I chuckled and shook my head. "Baby, I have no idea what you're talking about." My arms circled around her, pulling her close. But she stiffened against me.

"Crap. Did I do my word-vomit-saying-every-wrong-thing again? I guess I also really need to learn to shut up sometimes. I didn't mean, like, you should feel pressured to work for your girlfriend. That all came out wrong. If you don't want to, I can figure it out."

This couldn't be real. No way would it be that easy for

me to get everything I wanted. To find this wild, gorgeous woman and for her to welcome me so easily into her bright and beautiful life. I crushed my mouth to hers and sifted my fingers up into her hair, hoping to free it fully, and pulled Beth down on top of me. Her breasts pressed against mine, her skin warm and welcome. Her mouth curved up in a smile. We kissed for a long time. Long enough, it seemed, that we both started to forget that we'd been in the middle of a serious conversation about the future of Beth's business. I pulled away gently and stared up into her face, loving the gold flecks in her toffee-colored eyes, the way the deep brown of her summer freckles had faded into a soft ochre, the ripe fullness of her lips after they'd met mine.

"I can't believe I'm suggesting more talking but if you're serious we need to hash this all out. I think those ideas sound great. We need a solid plan though. I mean, no offense, honey, but you've barely even thought this through."

Beth nodded and I relaxed. Then she said, "I get my best ideas suddenly like this. I came up with the whole concept for The Yellow House when I was driving back home from New Orleans and I'd already agreed to take it over from my mom. Learning by doing is kind of my jam." She tapped a kiss to the tip of my nose. "Besides, we'll figure this out together. And if you feel like you need a plan, a plan you shall have, okay?"

"Sweep me off my feet, why don't you?"

Then she did. Beth draped her body over mine and poured every last ounce of joy into me until I was so full up, I thought I might burst. We tangled together again, fingers and tongues and shared breath. Until a realization made me freeze up cold.

"Crap. What time is it?" I glanced around the room for an alarm clock. Judging by the long shadows and soft, golden light it was already mid-afternoon. When I'd walked out of Bella Vista this morning, one of the first things I'd done was text Vanessa that I would pick Pete up from school and that he wouldn't be going to his extended day program as usual. It had been an extra boost to know that, at least for a few days or weeks, I would be the one to walk my son home from school. That I would be the one there for him for the first time in a long time.

Beth didn't miss a beat, reaching quickly for her phone and letting me know that thankfully it was only quarter past two. I slipped out of the warm confines of Beth's soft sheets and heavy quilt and into the cool air. My skin pricked with goose bumps immediately as I searched the hardwood floors for my sports bra and briefs. Finally, I found them next to the nightstand and tugged them on. Now to find my dang socks.

"Hey, is everything alright?" Beth sounded worried enough that I froze with my jeans halfway up my thighs.

"Oh shoot. Sorry. Yeah, I forgot I said I'd pick Pete up today is all." I smoothed away the little worried wrinkle between her eyebrows. "You want to come with me? If you don't need to head back into work maybe we could make dinner together?"

Again, the knowledge that I could have everything I'd wanted dang near almost knocked me over. When I'd been back in Missouri, scared and sad and lying in bed trying to picture my future, it had been nothing more than a gray blank. Now it was all the colors at once, so bright I almost wanted to look away. But I didn't.

Beth slipped out of bed and twined her arms around my

neck, pulling my lips down to meet hers. "Do you and Pete want to come back over here for dinner? I have some lamb shanks in the freezer and a whole bunch of board games my mom gave me for some random reason. We could braise the lamb and serve them up over some mashed parsnips. Oh, and I have some really good purple carrots I bet Pete would love. It's freezing out so dinner and game night in front of the fire might be fun."

I was torn between joy at the sheer, easy domesticity of this conversation and wanting to argue that we should slow roast the lamb shanks in the oven with rosemary and lemon and pair them with a rice pilaf and a microgreen salad. The joy won out.

As the two of us stepped out into the sharp wind of the coming winter, I was sure for the first time that I'd found where I belonged.

Epilogue

Adah
6 months later

"Mom, the tape got all messed up again." Pete held up the dispenser to show me that the clear packing tape had indeed escaped from the two plastic prongs meant to keep it from sticking to itself.

"Here, hon, I got it," Vanessa shouted over the sound of Elvis crooning from the small portable speaker she'd brought up to make packing more pleasant and plucked the tape gun from his hand. Problem quickly solved, she got back to labeling boxes.

The apartment, our home for the last year, was all packed up and scrubbed within an inch of its life. I glanced at the door frame where I'd measured Pete's height. Over the past few months, he'd shot up like a weed in the springtime from a hair under four feet to almost four foot five. I was a little taller than average and Jeremy had been a downright beanpole. Beth liked to joke that Pete would probably be taller than her by the time he finished fourth grade. My eyes flicked to the painting, neatly wrapped in brown paper and moving blankets, propped against the opposite wall. I'd gotten home from work a few weeks ago to find it plopped on my porch with a note taped to the brown paper wrapping. In Beth's swooping cursive, it read simply, *Move in with me.*

If I'd thought I was choked up as I lifted the package to bring it inside, it was nothing compared to the ball of heat that lodged in my throat the moment I peeled away the paper. On the canvas Pete and I lay fast asleep in the meadow behind The Yellow House. We'd walked around the woods on the first warm spring day. Pete had chatted away about his new gym teacher and new friends and pointed out the plants Andrew had been teaching him to identify. We sat down to eat the sandwiches I'd packed up for us and must have both dozed off because when Beth found us, the shadows were long and she laughed as she showed us a picture she'd snapped of the two of us on her phone. I hadn't known, though, that she would turn the image into something so beautiful. Crocuses and snowdrops bloomed around us, painted in Beth's hazy, dreamy style. Pete's honey brown hair, a few shades darker than my own now since it seemed to darken as he got older, lay in a halo around his head. My arm was thrown over my eyes and my lips were parted. I looked free. Seeing myself through Beth's eyes, I saw the version of myself I'd always hoped I'd get to become.

"Sorry to see you two go. The new guy seems nice enough, but I sorta doubt he'll turn into the son I never had though." Vanessa sighed, putting a gentle hand on my shoulder. Her touch was a soothing anchor. I met her eye and had to press my lips together to keep from blubbering all over her. I'd already admitted she was like a mother to me and we'd spent a tearful night talking at my kitchen table. My sessions with Linda were helping me with the whole talking thing, but I still couldn't say I loved it.

"You'll see me tomorrow," I laughed and turned back to pulling black garbage bags over our winter coats on hangers.

"Can we go up to the beach next week?" Pete called from his bedroom, where he was no doubt avoiding taping up the boxes, a task he'd been gung ho about for all of two minutes.

"If you all aren't too busy. I thought I could barely keep up with your schedule before. Now it's soccer camp this, bank meetings that, and all the hullabaloo at the restaurant." Vanessa batted at the air and shook her head.

"We can go on Monday if the weather's good. Now for the love of all things holy, can y'all let me finish up. Beth's gonna be here in a few minutes."

A sharp rap on the kitchen door announced that a few minutes was, in fact, now. I flopped the coats down on the counter and jogged over to let Beth in. My heart still fluttered every time I saw her. Even after all this time I couldn't believe she was mine. She waved through the window, bouncing with excitement. Her hair was clipped back, the early morning sun catching the golden threads twisting through the copper. She wore a totally moving-day-impractical outfit of a flowy patchwork tank top and very tiny jean cutoff shorts. The sight of all that freckled skin made me wish I could pull her away for a few minutes and replay the mind-numbing sex we'd had out in the stone barn the night before after everyone else had gone home for the night. With the moonlight bathing her skin she'd glowed… *Nope. Focus. Moving.*

Beth brushed her lips against mine the moment I pulled open the door, the pastry box she was holding jabbing me in the ribs. But I didn't care. I didn't like anything better than the feel of her kiss.

"Oh I see how it is. It's all fine and good for your *girl-friend* to distract you. God forbid me and your son say anything though," Vanessa chided, her voice brimming with laughter.

"Well I come bearing gifts." Beth set the pastry box next to the sink. Whatever was inside smelled fantastic, all warm fruit and rich vanilla. She flipped the lid open to reveal a half dozen gorgeous muffins. "Strawberry rhubarb. My girl's favorite." Her fingers sifted through my hair, tugging just enough to send a hot twist of lust into my belly.

"Ew, you guys are being gross again." Pete rolled his eyes as he swiped a muffin out of the box. He'd given Beth and I a stern talking-to about being too "mushy," informing us that we were especially bad when we cooked together. Beth ruffled his hair and he only half-heartedly shrugged off her touch. She was great with him, surprisingly patient at talking through his steadily growing tweenage moodiness.

"Well I have Andrew's truck outside. I think we might

be able to get everything in two trips. How come you two have, like, no stuff?"

I'd gotten rid of a lot of my ragtag secondhand furniture once I'd agreed that Pete and I would move into Beth's cottage at the end of the month. Where pretty much everything I'd brought with me was meaningless junk rescued from other people's lives, every item in Beth's house had meaning. There was the rough-hewn farmhouse table her brother had made for her with the intricate wicker pendant light woven by a friend hanging over it. There were the tapestries collected from places I'd never even heard of. Plants lovingly propagated from cuttings from her mom's garden (a place so lush and colorful I could have sworn it came right out of a storybook). Even the quilt on her bed, a gift from an Amish family she'd worked a farm internship with, had a story. My bedding was all big-box store clearance stuff I'd accumulated over the years.

So when it came time to pack up, really all we had was some kitchen stuff, my tiny collection of clothes, and Pete's ever growing piles of sports gear, Legos, and comic books. It turned out, once we'd made a handful of trips up and down the sun-bleached wooden stairs to the sidewalk, we wouldn't even need to make two trips. Pete would have to ride with a canvas grocery bag of spices in his lap, but he didn't seem to mind. He was as eager to move into Beth's place as I was. One, because Hamlet was now officially Pete's best friend, and two, because he and his new friend Samina were convinced the woods outside Beth's cottage were teeming with real live fairies.

Vanessa hugged all three of us like we were headed off to war, when in reality she would see us the very next morning. She'd saved all of our hides when she'd agreed to start doing the bookkeeping for The Yellow House a few days a week.

My body felt lighter as Pete, Beth, and I piled into the truck and headed out of town. Downtown South Bay was a mess of slow-moving tourists, pedicabs, and street trolleys that stopped every block or so to highlight various historic landmarks. It took a solid ten minutes to move two blocks, but none of us seemed to mind. Beth turned up the volume on a playlist Pete loved and rolled down the windows. The air was warm, still not quite hot yet, with a nice salt breeze blowing in off the water. We drove past Bella Vista, now renamed Portside Grill and serving mostly wraps and overpriced salads. Pete and Beth both stuck their tongues out and booed. But I only shook my head and laughed. I was glad to be where I was. Leaving that place was the third best thing that had ever happened to me. The first and second were in the backseat howling along with an awful pop song and in the driver's seat conducting a drum solo against the steering wheel.

We pulled onto the coastal highway, headed north to Port Catherine. The traffic was light and I grinned to myself as we flew past glittering water, tiny islands dotting the shore, and sailboats bobbing with the waves. I wasn't really sure if I'd ever known what relaxation felt like until I let Beth fully into my life. But I felt it now.

"I'm so excited for you guys to move in!" Beth shouted over the wind and music. Her eyes flicked from me to the rearview mirror.

"Oh my gosh, you need to cool it." Pete sighed. "We

already stayed with you for like three weeks once school got out."

I turned around to pin my son with a raised eyebrow for his snarky tone. He sighed again and admitted that he was excited too.

The sign for Port Catherine's exit flashed by and I turned to look at Beth. "Honey, you missed it." Beth was a good driver but sometimes she got too caught up in dramatic singalongs or winding stories and forgot where she was going.

"I know. I'm getting off at 7A. I want to stop by the restaurant if that's cool with you? Apparently Eitan has some fancy-pants update to the reservation system he made and wants me to take a look at it. I tried to do it from home this morning but, honestly, I don't think I should ever be trusted with a computer again. And I figured you might want to check in with Andrew about the inspection."

The truck's tires crunched over the gravel of The Yellow House's newly expanded parking lot. We weren't set to fully open the new dining room until August and the inn wouldn't be dried-in until at least October, but the place still looked completely different than the first time I'd seen it a little over a year ago. The yellow cottage was exactly the same, down to the window boxes bursting with herbs and smoke pouring from the stone chimney. But now, where there had once been a few picnic tables haphazardly clustered under café lights, Andrew had built a beautiful stone patio surrounded by garden beds and dotted with tables. On one end he'd even installed a second fireplace and some benches where folks waiting for a table could enjoy drinks and snacks.

I almost wanted to pinch myself. It was so wild that this was my restaurant now, too. After I'd started as the head cook (it felt nice to shake off the stupid kitchen hierarchy labels I'd spent so much time caring about) I'd invested in The Yellow House's expansion with some of the money I'd saved. Beth had insisted on making us partners in the business. So now I was designing the menu and cooking at one of the best restaurants in the country, which I also happened to co-own.

A chicken pecking at the ground next to my boot startled me out of my thoughts and I looked up to find Andrew jogging over, wide grin on his face. Getting to know Beth's family had been an unexpected joy. I'd never met a family like theirs before. Robin, Beth's mom, was warm and loving and a little overbearing, but in a way that felt good. She did things like buy Pete new sneakers and show up on a random Tuesday night with enough frozen lasagna and chicken noodle soup to last us through two winters. And Beth's dad was so unlike the reverend I had a hard time even believing they belonged in the same category. Where the reverend had been hard and serious, John was goofy and soft. Pete adored going out in the boat with him and always came back from their outings with outlandish stories and tons of really bad jokes. But I had to admit Andrew was my favorite. The first few times I'd met him, I really hadn't liked him. He was big and traditionally handsome with the energy of an excited puppy. But his passion for growing had been an unexpected gift to the business. The expanded Yellow House farm CSA had helped us pull in money through the spring and he never stopped coming up with creative solutions to the litany of daily problems we ran into. Plus my son idolized him. The minute Andrew showed up, he and Pete were doing some kind of complicated handshake and talking a mile a minute about a baseball game they'd gone to a few nights earlier.

"Hey!" Grace shouted, poking her head out the kitchen window. Her glossy black hair was tied back with a white bandanna printed all over with smiling cartoon oranges. She was adorable and a total machine in the kitchen. "I was just gonna text you to see if you wanted me to bring anything over. I bet you're hungry from the move!" Grace was basically a human exclamation point, every word out of her mouth zinging with energy. She was a joy to work with, too, creative and easygoing. Her background cooking Korean food at home and making gourmet cupcakes at a fancy bakery in New York came together to create a pastry program I knew even Jay was jealous of. Not that they had much to complain about now that they were in the process of opening their own coffee shop and bakery in South Bay.

"We're good, thanks. Beth brought over some muffins and I know Robin probably put about four casseroles in the fridge at home," I called back. "But let's talk tomorrow about what we want to do for the Solstice Barbecue."

With a double thumbs-up and a big grin Grace popped back into the cottage.

I tipped my head back to let the warm summer sun sink into my skin. In the distance the sound of Ahmed navigating phone reservations twisted together with the low rumble of Eitan's voice. Pete and Andrew's conversation had shifted to a heated discussion of the best way to build a fairy house. Chickadees called to each other in the woods as the wind carried the scent of fresh earth and pine. Then Beth was next to me, her fingers lacing with mine. She pressed a quick kiss to the corner of my mouth, then grinned. I breathed in deep, rooted firmly in my place. The air smelled like home.

★ ★ ★ ★ ★

Reviews are an invaluable tool when it comes to spreading the word about great reads. Please consider leaving an honest review for this, or any of Carina Press's other titles that you've read, on your favorite retailer or review site.

Acknowledgements

Thank you to the wonderful team at Carina Press and to my amazing agent Claire Draper for taking a chance on me and on this story. Also a huge thank-you to Rebecca and M.A. for their thoughtful beta feedback. I am forever grateful to my readers! I hope you enjoyed Adah and Beth's story. Finally, I'm so thankful for my community: my wonderful friends in Maine and all over the country, my loving family, and to my encouraging and very patient partner.

*What happens when the search for the perfect date
goes perfectly wrong?
Don't miss* The Love Study, *a charming romantic comedy
from critically acclaimed author Kris Ripper,
out October 2020 from Carina Adores!*

Chapter One

Here's how my friends describe me to new people: "This is Declan. He left his last boyfriend at the altar, so watch out."

It's mostly a joke. Mostly. Not that I left my last boyfriend at the altar—that part's definitely true. But watch out is just a playful warning. Besides, I swore off romance after that. No one really has to watch out for me.

It was ages ago. The leaving-Mason-at-the-altar thing. The swearing-off-romance thing is ongoing. Though I guess "This is Declan. He swore off romance, so watch out" has less of a ring to it.

Leaving your boyfriend at the altar is the kind of meltdown no one gives you the chance to grow out of. Six years later my friends are still merrily using that line at parties. Case in point: Ronnie and Mia's Christmas recovery party, where the sparkling apple cider I was valiantly drinking in place of alcohol wasn't even close to taking the edge off my mood. And that was before Mia grabbed my arm and whispered, "There's someone I want you to meet, they're new."

I love Mia, but she is absolutely one of those I found true love and now everyone else should too types. I had just opened my mouth to protest when I caught sight of The Only Human I Didn't Already Know and shut it real fast.

Average height, shoulder-length dirty blond hair, angular chin with a few spare whiskers, and red-framed glasses. Who on earth wears red-framed glasses? Were they one of those people who had multiple pairs and matched them to their outfits? But no, no red anywhere else, all the way down to their plain black shoes.

Please don't let them be one of those people who wears fashion glasses. I adjusted my prescription lenses and prepared to judge. If those frames were the real deal, though, I was already intrigued. Because seriously: who wears red-framed glasses? Maybe I shouldn't be quite so quick to tell Mia off. She only had my best interests at heart, anyway. That and fulfilling her desire to play a romantic matching game with every human she knew.

She leaned in. (Goody; gossip.) "They've only been in town a few months and I think they might be perfect for Mason. Don't you? Not too tall, not too built. Smart, but not intimidating. They have a YouTube advice channel, so there's no way Mason will feel inferior, right?"

"Oh, burn." I secretly loved it when lesbians got catty, but one must maintain appearances.

"Hush, you know what I mean. He's so sensitive about relationships."

The thing about that whole unfortunate leaving-Mason-at-the-altar fiasco was that Mia had been in the limo when I'd opened the door on the way to my own wedding, seen all those faces staring at me, panicked, watched Mason's grin freeze (then wilt), and pulled back into the limo like a turtle into its shell. An effect I immediately ruined by crying dramatically, "Get me out of here!"

I've done a lot of guilt for that moment, but I think for her own penance, Mia plans to fix Mason up with everyone she knows until one sticks...to his crotch. Or I guess his heart. Whatever. She's gonna marry his ass off as soon as he falls in love with someone for longer than two hours.

He's weirdly commitment-averse for someone who desperately wants a partner. Can't imagine why. Cough, cough.

Now that we were close to The Only New Person in the Room, I could see that they were wearing prescription glasses. Damn. Mason arguably deserved first pick of the proverbial fish in the proverbial sea. It was an ethical principle. And I was an ethical man. I sighed and hoped this particular fish was... I didn't quite wish they were awful. I just hoped they were awful for me, to save me the pain of wanting them only to watch them drift off with one of my best friends. To the altar. Where they would undoubtedly not leave anyone standing, ever, with a grin wilting on his face.

"Sidney, this is Declan. He left his last boyfriend at the altar, so watch out." Mia beamed as if she hadn't said this dozens, if not hundreds, of times before.

I readied a perfect I am not an asshole expression and

shook their hand. "It was years ago and I haven't been anywhere near an altar since, I promise."

Sidney's hand was cold, but their smile was warrrrrrm. "I'm not interested in altars, so you're safe from the temptation. Good to meet you."

"Yeah, you too. You might be careful around Mia, here. She's in a bit of a 'fix everyone up' phase since she got engaged." So there, lady.

Unfortunately Mia didn't seem the least deterred. "It's not fixing people up, it's just introducing them. We have this friend Mason I think you'd really like."

"Why?"

She blinked. "Why what?"

"Why do you think I'd really like him?"

"I guess because…he watches a lot of YouTube?" Mia, cheeks pink, continued quickly, "And he's a lovely person, and you seem incredibly kind and well spoken, and—sorry, are you exclusively into women? Or nonbinary folks? Did I get that wrong?"

I bit down on my tongue trying not to laugh.

Sidney's expression landed somewhere in the *my, what a fascinating specimen you have here* zone, but they didn't look annoyed. Just detached. "I'm not exclusively into anyone, no. It's more a skepticism about the process by which people decide other people would fit well together." They shrugged. "I don't mean to be rude, but I'm not looking to be set up with anyone."

"Totally get it and I'm sorry I assumed. Do you want to meet some people, though? Aside from the ones at work?" She nudged me. "We get together for drinks once a week.

It'd be low pressure and more queers. If you're...into that sort of thing."

This time I did laugh, then plastered both hands over my mouth.

Sidney genuinely smiled. "I am into queer people, yes. Definitely. Drinks sound good. Thank you for inviting me."

"You're so welcome! Ronnie will be thrilled too!"

Ronnie and Mia were more or less joined at the hip. Not that I judged. Whatever makes people happy, right? Especially when they're your friends.

"Anyway, why don't you two do phone numbers and Twitter things or whatever, and Dec, if you want to give Sidney Mason's info too, that'd be great." She waved. "I need to go check on food, but I'll see you around."

They leveled a look at me. "She's not going to let go of this setting me up thing, is she?"

"Honestly, it's been a year and a half since she and Ronnie decided to get married and we keep thinking she's going to stop doing this, but so far she hasn't." My strong ethical principles forced me to add, "Anyway, everyone likes Mason. It's a pretty safe bet that you will too, even if you don't want to date him."

"I don't date people."

That simplified matters. I hid my ~~disappointment~~ relief by forcing a laugh. "Oh, me neither. Mostly. Well. Not for a long time. I mean, it didn't seem like I was mature enough after thinking I was going to get married and then freaking out? So I figured I'd stick to getting laid, since that was safer. Like..." I focused on the gentle sweep of their hair back from their face as if it would introduce a new topic of conversation. It didn't.

"See, that sentence seemed like it was going to be followed by another thought." Their eyebrows very slightly inclined. Which I noticed because I was already staring at their face.

"Um, sorry, I realized I was basically spilling my guts to a stranger. You are totally not obligated to listen to me ramble. Only my oldest friends are contractually bound to deal with me being a hot mess." Cue self-deprecating smile.

Sidney's hands twitched outward, as if expressing a shrug without actually shrugging. "You don't seem like a hot mess to me and I don't feel obligated. What were you going to say?"

What the hell. If Mia and Ronnie were folding them into The Friend Group (or at least having them audition), they'd probably end up seeing me pathetic eventually. "Just, for a long time my not-dating policy worked? But lately it's kind of getting…old. I'm about to turn twenty-nine. And I'm not wigging about thirty or anything. But I am thinking maybe I should…at least try again. With the dating thing." I wrinkled my nose. "Then I think that's a horrible idea because oh my god where do you even start? Apps? Bars? I have no idea where people meet to date instead of hook up."

Their eyes were light brown behind their red-framed glasses and I felt a bit exposed under their gaze, like maybe the glasses had a filter that could read my thoughts. Right when I was starting to shift uncomfortably, they cleared their throat. "I have an idea. It might be a bit obscene, though."

I batted my eyelashes at them. "I enjoy the obscene."

"Would you be interested in coming on my YouTube channel? It's an advice show. I do one livestream and one pre-taped show each week."

"Er..."

"An interview would be cool, but what if we did a series? You could come on once a week and talk about your recent dating adventures. I could find you the dates if you wanted, since you'd be supplying me with content." Now their hands sort of danced in explanation. "I get a huge volume of emails asking for advice, but the format gets old. This way we could combine direct dating experience with advice. And if you're trying to get back into the dating thing anyway, maybe it's two birds with one stone."

My brain flooded with words and images—everything from *danger, Will Robinson* to a vision of Sidney and I shaking hands for the camera at an awards show where we'd just won for "Spectacular Advances in Dating Advice"—but I couldn't seem to speak.

"Yeah, you're right, it's a terrible idea." Their eyebrows were now a straight line behind their red frames. "Excuse my shameless desire to exploit your emotional turmoil for views. I was approached by this company that's doing a thing I actually think...might be good? So I've been considering doing a sponsorship deal with them and this, um, slightly obscene idea might be perfect. If you...were interested. In retrospect, I think maybe ambition makes me a crummy human being."

"Oh, no, I didn't... I didn't think that at all. I mean, I guess yes on the exploiting thing, but that doesn't bother me. I was more...processing."

"If it makes it any less gross, if I dated, I would absolutely mine my dating experiences for views." They frowned. "Okay, no, that doesn't make it less gross. Sorry. This is a nonideal first impression."

"I like your glasses," I blurted. "Just, that was my first impression. Well, actually I thought, Those better not be fucking fashion glasses, and then when I saw they weren't I was impressed. They look really good on you. Not everyone can pull off red frames."

"Oh. Um." They straightened their shoulders. "Thank you. And I know, fashion glasses feel…slightly ableist somehow? I tend to overthink things, so maybe they're harmless, but it feels a little weird that something I need in order to see is someone else's sartorial accent."

"Exactly! Yes. That's exactly it. But also I'm never saying that to anyone, because I don't want to be an asshole cis white guy who makes shit about them."

"Agreed," they said solemnly. "Let us never mention this to anyone else."

I held out my hand.

They held out theirs.

We shook in one sharp downward motion as if sealing the deal. I couldn't help but note that their hand was no longer cold.

"Please forget I even brought up my show? I feel like an ass for mentioning it."

I didn't quite bat my eyelashes again, but I allowed a hint of flirtation into my voice. "That's a little awkward since I was just going to ask you to tell me more about it."

They offered a rueful smile. I couldn't tell if they'd picked up on my timid flirtation or not. "It's called Your

Spinster Uncle. I do a livestream each Monday and post a taped show on Fridays. People write or call in and I answer their questions."

"Like Dan Savage?"

"More like Iron Man meets Professor McGonagall, teasing and stern. I do answer a lot of dating questions, but also a lot of family and school and work questions. More and more I answer a lot of..." They paused long enough for me to start brainstorming ways to salvage the conversation. Then they kind of sighed. "I think we have a distinct failure to address legitimate mental health issues in this country. I'm seeing more and more stuff that makes me wish people had free access to real therapy instead of schmucks on the internet."

I swallowed hard, taken by surprise. In the months following my derailed attempt at a wedding I'd gone to therapy. And it had helped. (Apparently the bit in the limo when we were driving away and I couldn't breathe or speak and my heart was pounding so hard I thought it was going to break my rib cage was a panic attack. And I thought I'd just been wigging out like a baby.)

Right, focusing. "Me too. I mean the thing about therapy. I'm not endorsing your assessment of yourself as a schmuck. I don't know you that well yet." I would have gone for a cheeky smile, but I didn't quite have the levity to pull it off.

"In the interests of, um, absolving my current schmuckyness, that's why I'm interested in this sponsorship. The company does therapy online so people in rural areas who need specialties not offered where they live have access to those services. Or even maybe you're the only trans person your therapist has ever seen, so they probably won't be able to meet your needs as effectively as someone who works with queer and trans people as a regular part of their practice. Ditto kinksters or people in polyamorous relationships." They paused. "Um, I'm not trying to pressure you into it. Sorry. I just wanted to explain why you mentioned a very basic thing and I jumped on it and tried to seduce you into coming on my YouTube channel."

There was something so completely charming about their rambling speech. Also points for using the word "seduce." I wasn't not feeling seduced. What the hell. "I think we should do it. Your series idea. I mean, it can't possibly make dating worse, right? And maybe it will help someone?"

Sidney pushed their hair back with one hand and stared at me steadily, almost as if part of them was being cool and part of them was totally nervous. "Are you sure? It was a ludicrous idea."

"I kind of like it. Plus, you said you'd find the people for these dates, right?"

"I could," they said carefully. "If you gave me some idea who you were interested in. Only if you're sure this wouldn't be terrible for you. And ethically I should tell you that I would be making money off your, um…" They cast around for a word. "Off your romantic journey. If you will."

Across the room Mia kissed Ronnie's cheek and Ronnie beamed. I knew I didn't want the exact relationship they had, but some deep thing inside me wanted that spark of desire, that casual affection.

"I think we should try it. And I'm pretty easy. All genders, all ages." I considered it. "Okay, over twenty-one. Not that I'm a huge drinker but I think I'd feel self-conscious around someone who couldn't."

Sidney's lips twitched as if they weren't sure if they should smile or not. "Are you serious right now?"

"Dude."

There. They smiled. "Okay."

"Good. And it's okay I called you 'dude'?"

"Yes. Thank you for asking."

"All right, then. That's settled. We're doing a YouTube thing." I gulped. "Oh god, what did I just agree to?"

They patted my arm. "Leave it to your spinster uncle. I'll take care of everything."

I forced myself to ignore the tingling still alerting my brain to the presence of their hand on my skin. "But wait, isn't it better for ratings or something if the dates go really horribly? You have a conflict of interest!"

"Maybe, but it's better for my fans if you have good experiences you can share with them. Even if they're also awkward or strange at times. I'd love it if people came away from this series thinking that maybe things weren't so bad out there in the world of romance."

"Let's...aim low," I managed. Romance. Oh god. I had definitely not been mature enough for this sort of thing with Mason. But that was years ago. Decades in developmental time. The mid-twenties changed everything. Didn't they? "Um, what if I'm like really, really bad at this? What if I fail you? That's sort of my entire track record right now."

Sidney's hand tightened on my arm. "You can't fail. If our goal is to do some shows, get word about this company out there, and facilitate you going on a few dates, there's no metric for failure there. There's no pressure. Anyway, why don't you think about it for a few days? I'll propose it to the sponsor and we can talk more when we see each other at drinks with Mia. All right?"

I looked at them, beyond the red frames, into eyes that were darker suddenly than I'd thought they were. "I left my last boyfriend at the altar. Are you sure you want to commit to a YouTube series with me?"

"I told you, I'm not interested in altars. I think we're safe."

It was probably just a mark of how weird the night had been, but I found myself thinking *we're safe* in Sidney's voice for the rest of the party and feeling a phantom warmth on my arm where they'd touched me.

Chapter Two

Drinks with the Marginalized Motherfuckers almost always happened at The Hole.

Technically it was The Hole in the Wall, which the gays called—obviously—The Gloryhole. Most people just called it The Hole. To be honest, it kind of resembled the proverbial hole, all brown wood paneling and a vague sense that it was bigger than expected once you were poking around in it.

Marginalized Motherfuckers didn't have to poke around; we had a favorite table, a second favorite table, and a third choice, which Oscar had decreed could not be considered anyone's anything-favorite. Despite Mia's openness with Sidney, very few people ever stuck around long after we asked them for drinks. It had become an unfunny joke, The Drinks Curse. When you sensed a relationship was heading toward a dead end you might gently inquire, "When are they coming for drinks?" Shorthand for "When are you gonna give up already?"

Apparently heading that off at the pass, here Sidney was, at drinks before even meeting the man Mia wanted them to spend the rest of their life with. Alas, very tragic, the end before the beginning and so forth.

I realized I was about to launch into a round of verse about death and volunteered to buy the first round since no one else had shown up yet. "If a random stranger demands to know if you're you, it's probably Mason or Oscar," I assured them.

They stood up. "How about I get the drinks and you wait for your friends?"

Which I supposed was a reasonable plan. Though I'm always uncomfortable when someone new buys me a drink. I know that's a little backwards, but it ends up making me feel indebted to them in an endless-cycle-of-debt-repayment-debt-repayment way. No, but you bought last time. Yes, but you bought the time before that.

I realized Sidney had said something. "Um, sure, thanks."

One corner of their mouth crept up. "I asked what you wanted."

"Right. Shit. Sorry, I'm a little distracted." I didn't even know why. It was just drinks. And Sidney, while attractive and smart, didn't date people, which was handy since neither did I, historically speaking. "I'll have a Coke, thanks."

"I'll be right back."

I was still watching their retreat when Oscar popped in as if from the ether. "That the one Mia wants to set up Mase with?"

"Seriously, how the hell do you do that?"

He frowned in Sidney's direction, hovering over our second favorite table without taking a seat. "That's the new person, right?"

"Yeah."

"I don't think I want to talk to new people today."

I weighed a couple of replies—I didn't think Sidney would be a drag on Oscar's anxiety too badly, but drinks in general was a drag on his anxiety, so I also didn't want to dismiss the possibility—before shrugging. "Next week?"

This got me a kiss on the cheek. "Thanks, Dec. Make my apologies."

"Sure. Love ya, kid."

His hand flapped in a wave as he melted back into the crowd.

Sidney returned with what looked, to my trained eye, like two Cokes. Damn, I should have told them they didn't have to abstain just because I was. "We're going to be one person down tonight," I said, accepting the glass. "Oscar is sitting this one out."

"Make that three. I just got a text from Mia that said she and Ronnie have some urgent responsibility having to do with Ronnie's sister."

"Ooooh. Such intrigue."

They cocked an eyebrow at me from behind their glasses. "Is it?"

"Kind of? Like, it's a big deal her sister agreed to be maid of honor, especially because half of her family still dead-names her to her face."

They grimaced. "That's awful."

"Yeah, it's super shitty. So the wedding is a big thing to

start and—" My eyes caught on Mason. My sweet, gorgeous, slightly melancholic ex.

We'd called ourselves the Marginalized Motherfuckers as a joke because for a while in college every conversation we had revolved around...marginalization. Which doesn't sound like fun, and we wouldn't do that again, but I think it was probably a developmental stage we all had to go through. And it brought us together as a family in a way that talking about, I don't know, Kant or chemistry or something probably wouldn't have.

Mia was the Korean one (also a lesbian!), Ronnie was white (but trans!), I was white (but queer!), Oscar was half-white, half-Mexican (and gay!), and Mason was the self-appointed token black guy (and pansexual!) approaching the table with a guarded smile.

"Hey, Dec."

I sprang up to give him a hug. "Mase! We've been abandoned by the other Motherfuckers. But look, Sidney's here!" I made an extravagant Vanna White arm motion in Sidney's general direction because apparently I couldn't stop being a jackass.

"I'm Sidney Worrell. Nice to meet you."

"Mason Ertz-Scott."

They shook hands, both of them looking like models for different things. Mase would be Suave Young Businessman on His Way to an Important Meeting, and Sidney would be Nerdy Person at Cafe Table Staring Contemplatively into Their Coffee. Not that I spend a lot of time coming up with stock photo descriptions for real people or anything like that.

Suave Young Businessman and Nerdy Person at Cafe

Table both sat down again, which meant I did too. Except now Mase didn't have a drink. This would be the perfect opportunity to give them a chance to chat, right? I sprang back up. "Beer, babe?" Horror at the slip almost stopped my heart. "Oh my god I haven't called you that in years, what is wrong with me? Sorry. Do you want a beer?"

"You're buying me a drink and calling me 'babe'? I sure hope you're planning to text me in the morning, Casanova."

"Oh shove it—" I broke off. Because Sidney. "Just for that I'm getting you a light beer!" I—okay—flounced off in the direction of the bar, ignoring his laughter behind me.

I'd at least stopped blushing by the time I returned to the table, though the reprieve was short lived. They were talking about Sidney's video series idea.

"Wait." I set a beer (not light) in front of Mason. "You're calling it The Love Study? That sounds terrible."

Mase punched my arm.

"What? It does! I mean…doesn't it?"

Sidney nodded, not quite in agreement, more like they knew what I meant and were acknowledging it. "I think it gets across the crudest sense of what we're trying to do in the fewest number of words. It abbreviates decently, though I did try to think of a name that could be spoken, like AWOL. The Love Study is short, to the point, and easy for people to remember. Which makes it perfect for YouTube."

"Yeah, but…" I took a disconsolate sip of my Coke. "Doesn't it sorta make me sound like a tool? I'm the subject of—" I made my voice into Dramatic Movie Announcer Voice, "—The Love Study."

Mason giggled, momentarily pressing the back of his

hand against his lips to stifle it before giving in and flat-out giggling, the monster. "Honey, you've been the subject of plenty of love studies before. Maybe Sidney will get somewhere when the rest of us couldn't."

"Hey! Uncool!" Blushing again. "So uncool."

"Well, look," Sidney said, ignoring our childish byplay. "The name isn't set in stone, though I'd probably have to run a new one by the sponsor, and—"

"Oh, you got the sponsorship?" I interrupted.

"Yes. But I'm sure I can find someone else if you're not into it. I don't want to force you into anything you're not comfortable with."

"No one's comfortable with dating," Mase mumbled.

Sidney turned on him. "You could do it too! You could both be part of The Love Study. We could compare and contrast your experiences, and the fact that you have a history with each other only adds—"

"Not gonna happen."

"Er, sorry, I…lost control for a second there. Forget I asked."

He waved. "You seem like a perfectly nice person and everything, but I'm not going to date for the benefit of your audience. I have a hard enough time dating for my own benefit." Mason, the man I'd once almost pledged to spend my whole life with, slumped and sipped his beer.

I reached for his hand. "I'm really sorry. Again."

"I know. And it wouldn't have been good. I know that too. I want, like, romance and flowers and shit. You aren't even a little interested in that stuff, which I thought was a compromise I could make, but in reality it would have hurt me too much. It's just endless trying to meet new people."

His eyes narrowed on mine. "Plus, you didn't tell me you were dating again."

"I'm not. In practice. It's more sort of…theoretical. At this point. Until Sidney puts me in front of their audience, or whatever." Also, right, Sidney. I looked over to find them watching us, something I couldn't quite make out in their expression. Not quite sadness, not quite longing? Yearning, maybe, but only at the edges.

A second later it was gone. "Okay, not talking about your experiences I get," they said to Mase. "But do you think you could come on the show to speak to Declan's past experiences? What made him the man he is today, something like that?"

"Oh sure. If we're just roasting Declan, count me in."

I stuck my tongue out at him.

"Maybe not roasting. I find the…cultural context of having left someone at the altar fascinating. What it means to so publicly commit, especially for queer people, and then to so publicly break up."

"Ha, yeah, I can totally star as the poor loser who got dumped on his wedding day and never recovered." He gestured to himself. "I'm basically Ms. Havisham right now."

I hit him. "He's lying, don't listen to him."

He leaned forward to say, confidentially, to Sidney, "I sleep in my wedding gown every night. It's tragic."

"Oh my god." I did stop it eyes at him. "Seriously, he's just messing around."

Sidney looked from one of us to the other, eyebrows slightly raised. "I've always wondered if more people wish they hadn't gone through with a marriage when they did. Or wish they had when they didn't."

Mason and I traded glances. "Not us," I said.

"Nope. I could have seriously throttled this asshole six years ago, and I'm pretty sure our friends would have helped me hide the body, but in a way, he saved us a world of pain. Or at least made it come all at once instead of unraveling for years as we grew to hate each other."

"You don't seem to hate each other now." They pushed their glasses up and I had to stifle the urge to mirror the gesture.

"Nah, I love the bastard." Mase leaned over to kiss my cheek. "I am so watching The Love Study. I can't wait. I'm gonna make popcorn. Oh! I'll have everyone over to watch at my place. It's going to be dee-lightful to see you going on a bunch of stupid dates and then being forced to talk about them."

"I'm not forcing him—" Sidney was saying, right as I said, "They might not be stupid—" We stopped, both of us looking away.

"Oh yes," Mason murmured. "Yes, yes, yes, I foresee a whole lot of popcorn. We're gonna make a drinking game up for this thing. Maybe we'll make up a drink too. I can't wait."

I pouted. "You're the worst."

"You left me at the altar, sunshine."

For a second I tried to think about a comeback that would somehow make gathering our friends to eat popcorn and watch me embarrass myself on YouTube a bigger crime than leaving him at the altar, but...it wasn't. "Yeah, okay, you win. Forever."

"You're damn right I do." As if he felt accomplished now that he'd scored that point, Mason turned to Sidney.

"What else do you do, when you're not giving out advice? You work with Mia, right?"

"Yep, though in a different department. I stock groceries. What do you do?"

"I'm a loan officer at a bank. It's exactly as glamorous as it sounds. I'd like to work my way up to financial manager, but it's slow going."

I cleared my throat. "Plus, you don't really want to be a financial manager."

He rolled his eyes. "It's a career. I really do want a career."

"A boring one."

"Not everyone can live the glamorous life of an office temp forever, Dec." He took a pull on his beer and since we had company I resolved to leave him alone. "Sidney, you gotta tell me how you moved up here. I hyperventilate if I even think about moving, it's so fucking expensive."

"It really is. I'd been working as a server in a restaurant, and making decent money I guess? But I was skipping sleep to get videos out, and I rented a room in a house mostly because moving is awful, but I had no control over background noise."

"So you were making money but hated your life?"

Sidney laughed low, like the laugh itself acknowledged it was being kind of dark. "It was time for a change, let's say."

"What's your, like, long-term plan? Keep stocking groceries and doling out advice on YouTube until you make enough to do it full-time?"

Which was a super good question and I was a little chagrined I hadn't asked it myself, though I had been sorta distracted by the whole going on YouTube so Sidney could advise me thing.

"I'm not sure I have a concrete plan right now. I didn't start out thinking I was actually going to make any money on YouTube. But in the last year I've received more interest from advertisers than before, so at this point it's looking like that might be a semi-reasonable goal."

Mase nodded. "It's hard for me to imagine being comfortable being on video that much. Like, I could come on to poke Dec, but I think if I had a channel of my own it'd be overwhelming."

"It can be, for sure. But I think it helps in a way that I…" They paused. "I guess I've always been really awkward face-to-face? So being on video is easier for me. It's a way of connecting to people that doesn't rely on in-person human interaction. Um. That sounds terrible." Their nose crinkled up. Adorably. In a vaguely intriguing way.

"Yeah, I can sort of see that. Would YouTube be your primary job if you had that option?" Mase gestured with his beer. "In a perfect world, would you do it full-time?"

"I'm not sure…in a perfect world? I think I would be able to quit the store, keep doing videos, and go back to school. Maybe become a therapist, or a psychologist."

Oooooh, I could totally picture that. "Wow, that would be amazing." I poked Mason meaningfully. He'd been thinking about grad school basically since we graduated from college.

"It's so expensive, though," he said. "At least when I've looked into it, it was."

"Exactly. I still have student loans from undergrad, how can I sign up for more?"

They lapsed into a conversation about the ins and outs of financial aid for graduate school and I listened with only half of my brain reporting for duty. I was pretty sure the "humans only use 10 percent of their brain" thing was a myth, but whatever the percent, I was using quite a bit less than that on tracking my companions' conversation.

Mostly I was thinking about how great it would be to have more queer therapists in the world. Or more specifically, how great it would have been for me to have seen a queer therapist after the whole attempted-wedding-freakout thing. Not that my straight AF therapist had been bad! She'd been nice! But I didn't think she'd totally understood the, like…cultural phenomenon that was suddenly being allowed to get married. It was 2015, it was legal, everyone was doing it, so it seemed like we might as well. It wasn't that I didn't love Mason. I loved him a lot. I loved him so much that I failed to realize until it was too late that I didn't really want to get married at all.

Then I was there, and he was there, and everyone we knew and loved was there, and I couldn't breathe. The rest of my life was a blur of impossibility because I didn't know if I was going to get through the next thirty seconds. I didn't calm down until the limo was miles away. The therapist eventually told me that thinking you're going to die right where you're sitting is some kind of classic panic attack thing, but I didn't know that then.

What I knew was that not getting married felt better than getting married. So I'd decided to save myself and everyone else the hassle of ever going through that again.

No more romance. Full stop. The end.

If that wasn't the end, if I was going to try doing this again, how could I ever ask anyone to put their faith in me? Most days I could only commit to getting out of bed if I had to go to work. I regularly skipped breakfast because I hit snooze too many times.

I'd left my last boyfriend at the altar. How do you ever prove you're trustworthy if you've done something like that?

Sidney laughed, bringing me back to our second favorite table at The Hole, back to this moment, in which I was nursing a Coke and ruminating over the past. Not the best idea.

I leaned forward and said confidentially to Sidney, "Do you want to hear about the time Mase moaned so loudly we thought the gay history professor was going to bust in on us while we were having sex in the empty office next to his?"

They grinned. "Hell yes."

Mason pulled out all the dignity he could manage while slumped into a bar booth. "I still maintain that he would have joined in, which means technically I should have been louder. He was super hot."

Sidney and I laughed. After a second Mase gave up the stoic act and grinned. Weirdly, I thought old Sidney might make it back to drinks again. Maybe the trick was not banging any of the Motherfuckers. Good plan, I thought at them, and started another story.

Don't miss The Love Study *by Kris Ripper,*
out from Carina Adores!
www.CarinaPress.com

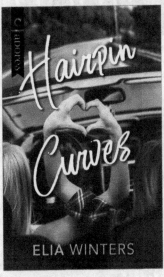
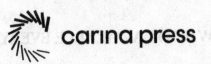